THE BLIND BARBER

The Blind Barber

JOHN DICKSON CARR

With an Introduction by
Anthony Boucher

COLLIER BOOKS
Macmillan Publishing Company
New York

Macmillan Publishing Company
866 Third Avenue, New York, N.Y. 10022
Collier Macmillan Canada, Inc.

Library of Congress Cataloging in Publication Data

Carr, John Dickson, 1906–1977.
  The blind barber.
  I. Title.
PS3505.A763B55   1984   813'.52   83–23975
ISBN 0–02–018300–3 (pbk.)

This edition is published by arrangement
with Harper & Row Publishers, Inc.

10 9 8 7 6 5 4 3 2

Printed in the United States of America

Introduction

THIS BOOK is a farce about murder.

I feel I should give you fair warning, because this sort of thing hasn't been common lately. But if your instant reaction is shocked withdrawal, please pause a moment and hear me out.

If I have one major complaint about the 300-odd mysteries that I read each year as a reviewer, it is that none of them are funny. Oh, I admit Richard S. Prather or Carter Brown can be amusing, but only in the trimmings: it's the writing that's funny, rather than the story.

And I long for the days of Craig Rice and Alice Tilton and Richard Shattuck and Jonathan Latimer when there was a wild cockeyed preposterousness in the events surrounding murder and even in murder itself—and not just in the style of the narrator.

I suppose this longing dates me. It's a 1930ish attitude. There was a fine film late in the Depression, starring Carole Lombard and written by Ben Hecht, called *Nothing Sacred*. It was a rowdy comedy about a (supposed) cancer victim. The "nothing-sacred" approach seems out of place today; now we take things more seriously, especially death.

But death and laughter are old friends. The medieval *Totentanz* is comic; and the macabre poet Thomas Lovell Beddoes christened his major tragedy *Death's Jest Book*. As Duncan sinks in his gore, the drunken porter rises with merry and improper quips. And the murders of real life seldom lack their element of comedy. One of the most terrible days in the annals of American murder opened on a scorching morning with a man named John Vinnicum Morse eating warmed-over mutton soup for breakfast.

I suspect that many readers—particularly the new young readers of mysteries—may relish a more generous ration of comedy-in-murder than publishers have been giving them; this series hopes to bring you, from time to time, Alan Green, Richard Shattuck and other prime practitioners of the criminally absurd,* starting now with John Dickson Carr.

There's a strong comic element in many of Carr's books. It's most prevalent in the cases of Sir Henry Merivale, by "Carter Dickson" (and I realize with a sudden shock that it's almost ten years since H. M. has appeared in a new book); but it turns up frequently in Dr. Gideon Fell's cases, too—as in the noble drinking sequences in *The Case of the Constant Suicides*.

But these are intrusions, like the porter. Just once did Carr set himself to write an all-out farce (with murder as the intrusion). And, being the incomparable technician that he is, he produced something unique.

Wisely, he kept Dr. Fell out of the merry maelstrom and made him act, for once, as a pure armchair detective, in the manner of the Baroness Orczy's Old Man in the Corner. Then he threaded through his fantastic plot a careful set of clues for a faultless formal problem in detection.

Unlike almost all other comedies of terrors, *The Blind Barber* is a detective story, in the strictest sense. But never was a reader more bedeviled with distractions from detection. Who observes clues while he's wiping his laughter-streaming eyes?

I hope you enjoy the challenge . . . and the fun.

ANTHONY BOUCHER

* And meanwhile let me call your attention to two earlier Collier Books reprints: Elliot Paul's *Mysterious Mickey Finn* (AS244X) and *Mayhem in B-Flat* (AS245X).

Contents

The Blind Barber

PART ONE

Chapter 1

Strange Cargo

WHEN THE LINER *Queen Victoria* left New York bound for Southampton and Cherbourg, it was said that two fairly well-known people were aboard, and it was whispered that a highly notorious third person was aboard also. Moreover, there was a fourth—but inconspicuous—person who will take rather a large part in this rowdy and topsy-turvy chronicle. Although he did not know it, this young man had in his luggage something more valuable than the marionettes of M. Fortinbras or the emerald elephant of Lord Sturton, which partly explains why there were puzzles and high carnival in the sedate bosom of the *Queen Victoria,* and monkey business not altogether according to the customary pattern.

No more dignified ship than the *Queen Victoria* flies the house-flag of any British line. She is what is sometimes described as a "family" boat: which means that no hilarity is permitted in her state-room after 11 p.m., and all the cross-ocean changes in time are punctiliously observed— so that the bar always closes three-quarters of an hour before you expect it, and makes you swear. Melancholy passengers sit in her glazed writing-room and seem to be composing letters to the relatives of the deceased. In the heavily-ornamented lounge there is soft conversation, not so loud as the creaking of woodwork when the green swell lifts and glitters past the portholes; and knitting is in progress before some electric lights arranged to represent a fire. There is a semblance of gaiety when a serious-minded orchestra plays in the gallery of the dining-saloon at lunch and dinner. But there was one east-bound crossing, in the spring of last year, which Commander Sir Hector Whistler will never forget. Under his professional bluff *camaraderie* Captain Whistler possesses the most pyrotechnic temper of

11

any skipper who has forsaken sail for steam, and the richness of his language is the admiration of junior officers. When, therefore—

The *Queen Victoria* was to dock at Southampton on the afternoon of May 18th, after the weirdest voyage she had ever made. On the morning of the next day Mr. Henry Morgan was ringing the bell of Dr. Fell's new house at No. 1 Adelphi Terrace. Henry Morgan, it may be remembered, was that eminent writer of detective-stories who took his own profession with unbecoming levity, and who had made Dr. Fell's acquaintance during the case of the Eight of Swords. On this particular morning—when there was a smoky sun on the river and the quiet gardens below Adelphi Terrace—Morgan's long, bespectacled, deceptively-melancholy face wore an expression which might have been anger or amusement. But he certainly looked like a man who had been through much; as he had.

Dr. Fell boomed a welcome, greeted him warmly, and pressed upon him a tankard of beer. The doctor, his guest saw, was stouter and more red-faced than ever. He bulged out over a deep chair in the embrasure of one of the tall windows overlooking the river. The high room, with its Adam fireplace, had been set to rights since Morgan had seen it some months before, when Dr. and Mrs. Fell moved in. It was still untidy, for that was the doctor's way; but the five-thousand-odd books had been crammed somehow into their oak shelves, and the litter of junk had found place in corners and nooks. Dr. Fell has an old-fashioned weakness for junk, especially for bright pictures of the hunting-print or Dickens variety, and scenes showing people getting out of stage-coaches and holding up mugs of beer before country inns. He also likes carved porcelain tankards with pewter lids, curious book-ends, ash-trays filched from pubs, statuettes of monk or devil, and other childish things which, nevertheless—in the sombre room with the oak bookshelves, with the frayed carpet on the floor—formed a fitting background for his Gargantuan presence. He sat in his chair in the window embrasure, before a broad study table littered with books and papers; there was a grin under his bandit's moustache, and a twinkle in his eye as he blinked at his visitor over eyeglasses on a broad black ribbon. And when the cigars had been lighted Dr. Fell said:

"I may be mistaken, my boy, but I seem to detect a professional gleam in your eye." He wheezed and folded his big hands on the table. "Is there anything on your mind, hey?"

"There is," said Morgan grimly. "I have to unfold just about the rummiest story you've ever listened to, if you've got time to hear it. It's rather a long one, but I don't think it'll bore you. And—if you want any corroboration—I've taken the liberty of asking Curt Warren to come round here. . . ."

"Heh!" said Dr. Fell, rubbing his hands delightedly. "Heh-heh-hehe! This is like old times. Of course I've got time. And bring round anybody you like. Replenish that glass again and let's have the details."

Morgan took a deep drink and a deep breath.

"First," he said, in the manner of one commencing lecture, "I would direct your attention to a group of people sitting at the captain's table on the good ship *Queen Victoria*. Among whom, fortunately or unfortunately, I was one.

"From the beginning I thought it would be a dull crossing; everybody seemed to be injected with virtue like embalming fluid, and half an hour after the bar had opened there were only two people in it, not counting myself. That was how I made the acquaintance of Valvick and Warren.

"Captain Thomassen Valvick was a Norwegian exskipper who used to command cargo and passenger boats on the North Atlantic route; now retired, and living in a cottage in Baltimore with a wife, a Ford, and nine children. He was as big as a prize-fighter, with a sandy moustache, a lot of massive gestures, and a habit of snorting through his nose before he laughed. And he was the most genial soul who ever sat up all night telling incredible yarns, which were all the funnier in his strong squarehead accent, and he never minded if you called him a liar. He had twinkling, pale-blue eyes half-shut up in a lot of wrinkles and a sandy, wrinkled face, and absolutely no sense of dignity. I could see it was going to be an uncomfortable voyage for Captain Sir Hector Whistler.

"Because, you see, Captain Valvick had known the skipper of the *Queen Victoria* in the old days before Whistler became the stuffed and stern professional gentleman at the head of the table. There was Whistler—growing stout, with his jaw drawn in like his shoulders, strung with gold braid like a Christmas tree—there was Whistler, his eye always on Valvick. He watched Valvick exactly as you'd watch a plate of soup at a ship's table in heavy weather; but it never kept the old squarehead quiet or muzzled his stories.

"At first it didn't matter greatly. We ran into heavy weather immediately and unexpectedly; rain-squalls, and a dizzying combination of pitch-and-roll that drove almost all the passengers to their state-rooms. Those polished lounges and saloons were deserted to the point of ghostliness; the passages creaked like wickerwork being ripped apart, the sea went past with a dip and roar that slung against the bulkhead or pitched you forward on the rise, and navigating a staircase was an adventure. Personally, I like bad weather. I like the wind tearing in when you open a door; I like the smell of white paint and polished brass, which they say is what brings the sea-sickness, when a corridor is writhing and dropping like a lift. But some people don't care for it. As a result, there were only six of us at the captain's table: Whistler, Valvick, Margaret Glenn, Warren, Dr. Kyle, and myself. The two nearcelebrities we wanted to see were both represented by vacant chairs. . . . They were old Fortinbras, who runs what has become a very swank marionette-theatre, and the Viscount Sturton. Know either one of them?"

Dr. Fell rumpled his big mop of grey-streaked hair.

"Fortinbras!" he rumbled. "Haven't I seen something about it recently in the highbrow magazines? It's a theatre somewhere in London where the marionettes are nearly life-size and as heavy as real people; he stages classic French drama or something—?"

"Right," said Morgan, nodding, "He's been doing that to amuse himself, or out of a mystic sense of preserving the Higher Arts, for the past ten or twelve years; he's got a little box of a theatre with bare benches, seating about fifty people, somewhere in Soho. Nobody ever used to go there but all the kids in the foreign colony, who were wild about it. Old Fortinbras's *pièce de résistance* was his dramatisation of "The Song of Roland," in French blank verse. I got all this from Peggy Glenn. She says he took most of the parts himself, thundering out the noble lines from back-stage, while he and an assistant worked the figures. The marionettes' weight—nearly eight stone, each of 'em stuffed with sawdust and with all the armour, swords and trappings—was supported by a trolley on which the figures were run along, and a complicated set of wires worked their arms and legs. That was very necessary, because what they did mostly was fight; and the kids in the audience would hop up and down and cheer themselves hoarse.

"The kids, you see, never paid any attention to the lofty sentiments. They probably didn't even hear them or understand what it was all about. All they knew was that out would stagger the Emperor Charlemagne on the stage, in gold armour and a scarlet cloak, with a sword in one hand and a battle-axe in the other. After him would come bumping and reeling all the nobles of his court, with equally bright clothes and equally lethal weapons. From the other side would come in the Emperor of the Moors and *his* gang, armed to the eyebrows. Then all the puppets would lean against the air in various overbalanced positions while Charlemagne, with a voice of thunder said, "Pry, thee, friend, gadzooks, gramercy, what ho, sirrah!", and made a blank-verse speech lasting nearly twenty minutes. It was to the effect that the Moors had no business in France, and had better get to hell out of there—or else. The Emperor of the Moors lifted his sword and replied with a fifteen-minute address whose purport was, "Says you!" And Charlemagne, whooping out his war-cry, up and dots him one with the battle-axe.

"That was the real beginning, you see. The puppets rose from the stage and sailed at each other like fowls across a cockpit, thrashing their swords and kicking up a battle that nearly brought down the roof. Every so often one of them would be released from the trolley as dead, and would crash down on the stage and raise a fog of dust. In the fog the battle kept on whirling and clashing, and old Fortinbras rushed behind the scenes screaming himself hoarse with noble speeches, until the kids were delirious with excitement. Then down would tumble the curtain; and out would come old Fortinbras, bowing and puffing and wiping the sweat off his face, supremely happy at the cheers of the audience; and he would make a speech about the glory of France which they applauded just as loudly without knowing what he was talking about. . . . He was a happy artist; an appreciated artist.

"Well, the thing was inevitable. Sooner or later the highbrows would 'discover' him, and his art; and somebody did. He became famous overnight, a misunderstood genius whom the British public had shamefully neglected. No kids could get into the place now; it was all top-hats and people who wanted to discuss Corneille and Racine. I gather that the old boy was rather puzzled. Anyhow, he got a thumping offer to exhibit his various classic dramas in America, and it was one long triumphal tour. . . ."

Morgan drew a deep breath.

"All this, as I say, I got from Miss Glenn, who is—and has been long before the thing grew popular—a sort of secretary and general manager for the foggy old boy. She's some sort of relation of his on her mother's side. Her father was a country parson or schoolmaster or something; and when he died, she came to London and nearly starved until old Jules took her in. She's devilish good-looking, and seems prim and stiffish until you realise how much devilment there is in her, or until she's had a few drinks; then she's a glittering holy terror.

"Peggy Glenn, then, made the next member of our group, and was closely followed by my friend, Curtis Warren.

"You'll like Curt. He's a harum-scarum sort, the favourite nephew of a certain Great Personage in the present American Government. . . ."

"What personage?" inquired Dr. Fell. "I don't know of any Warren who is—"

Morgan coughed.

"It's on his mother's side," he replied. "That has a good deal to do with my story; so we'll say for the moment only a Great Personage, not far from F.D. himself. This Great Personage, by the way, is the most dignified and pompous figure in politics; the glossiest Top-Hat, the neatest Trouser-Press, the prince of unsplit infinitives and undamaged etiquette. . . . Anyhow, he pulled some wires (you're not supposed to be able to do this) and landed Curt a berth in the Consular Service. It isn't a very good berth: some God-forsaken hole out in Palestine or somewhere, but Curt was coming over for a holiday round Europe before he took over the heavy labour of stamping invoices or what-not. His hobby, by the way, is the making of amateur moving-pictures. He's wealthy, and I gather he's got not only a full-sized camera, but also a sound apparatus of the sort the news-reel men carry.

"But, speaking of Great Personages, we now come to the other celebrity aboard the *Queen Victoria,* also paralysed with sea-sickness. This was none other than Lord Sturton—you know—the one they call the Hermit of Jermyn Street. He'll see nobody; he has no friends; all he does is collect bits of rare jewellery. . . ."

Dr. Fell took the pipe out of his mouth and blinked.

"Look here," he said suspiciously, "there's something I want to know before you go on. Is this by any chance the familiar chestnut about the fabulous diamond known as the Lake of Light, or some such term, which was pinched out of the left eye of an idol at Burma, and is being stalked by a sinister stranger in a turban? Because, if it is, I'll be damned if I listen to you. . . ."

Morgan wrinkled his forehead sardonically.

"No," he said. "I told you it was a rummy thing; it's much queerer than that. But I'm bound to confess that a jewel *does* figure in the story—it was what tangled us up and raised all the hell when the wires got crossed—but nobody ever intended it to figure at all."

"H'm!" said Dr. Fell, peering at him.

"And also I am bound to admit that the jewel got stolen—"

"By whom?"

"By *me*," said Morgan unexpectedly. He shifted. "Or by several of us, to be exact. I tell you it was a nightmare. The thing was an emerald elephant, a big pendant thing of no historical interest but of enormous intrinsic value. It was a curiosity, a rarity; that's why Sturton went after it. It was an open secret that he had been negotiating to buy it from one of the busted millionaires in New York. Well, he'd got it right enough; I had that from Curt Warren. The Great Personage, Curt's uncle, is a friend of Sturton's, and Curt's uncle told him all about it just before Curt sailed. Probably half the people on the boat heard the rumour. I know we were all waiting to catch a glimpse of him when he came aboard—queer, sandy old chap with ancient side-whiskers and a hanging jaw; only attendant a secretary. He popped up the gangway all swathed round in checked comforters, and cursed everybody in reach.

"Now it's a very odd thing, for a variety of reasons, that you should have mentioned the old familiar story about the fabulous jewel. Because, on the afternoon when all the trouble started—it was the late afternoon of the fourth day out, and we were to dock three days later—Peggy Glenn and Skipper Valvick and I had been discussing this emerald elephant, in the way you do when you're lying back in a deck-chair with a robe across your knees, and nothing much to think about except when the bugle will blow for tea. We discussed whether it was in Lord Sturton's possession or locked in the captain's safe, and, in either case, how you could steal it. Peggy, I know, had evolved a very complicated and ingenious plan; but I wasn't listening closely. We had all got to know one another pretty well in those four days, and we stood on very little ceremony.

"As a matter of fact," said Morgan, "I was more than half-asleep. Then—"

Chapter 2

Indiscretions of Uncle Warpus

LOW ALONG THE SKY there was a liquid yellow brightness, but twilight had begun to come down, and the grey sea wore changing lights on its white-caps when the *Queen Victoria* shouldered down against a heavy swell. The sky-line tilted and rose above a boiling hiss; there was a stiff breeze along the almost deserted promenade-deck. Lying back drowsily in a deck-chair, well wrapped against the cold, Morgan was in that lethargic frame of mind when the booming sea-noises are as comfortable as a fire. He reflected that shortly lights would go on along the ship; tea would be set out in the lounge while the orchestra played. Both his companions were momentarily silent, and he glanced at them.

Margaret Glenn had dropped her book in her lap; she was lying back in the deck-chair with eyes half-closed. Her rather thin, pretty, impish face—which ordinarily wore such a deceptive look of schoolmistress primness—now seemed puzzled and disturbed. She swung shell-rimmed reading-glasses by one ear-piece, and there was a wrinkle above her hazel eyes. She was muffled in a fur coat, with a wildly-blowing batik scarf; and from under her little brown hat a tendril of black hair danced above the windy deck.

She observed: "I say, what can be keeping Curt? It's nearly tea-time, and he promised to be here long ago; then we were going to round you two up for cocktails. . . ." She shifted, and her earnest eyes peered round at the port-hole behind as though she expected to see Warren there.

"*I* know," said Morgan lazily. "It's that bouncing little blonde from Nashville; you know, the one who's going to Paris for the first time and says she wants to gain experiences for her soul."

Turning a wind-flushed face, the girl was about to rise

to the remark when she saw his expression, and stuck out her tongue at him instead.

"Bah!" she said, without heat. "That little faker; I know her type. Dresses like a trollop and won't let a man get within a yard of her. You take my advice," said Miss Glenn, nodding and winking wisely. "You stay clear of women who want to gain deep experience for the soul. All that means is that they don't want to employ the body in doing it." She frowned. "But I say, what *can* have happened to Curt? I mean, even with the notorious unpunctuality of American men——"

"Ha-ha-ha!" said Captain Thomassen Valvick, with an air of inspiration. "I tell you, maybe. Maybe it is like de horse."

"What horse?" asked Morgan.

Captain Valvick uttered one of his amiable snorts and bent his big shoulders. Even though the deck was rolling and pitching in a way that made the deck-chairs slide into each other, he stood upright without difficulty. His long sandy-reddish face was etched out in wrinkles of enjoyment, and behind very small gilt-rimmed spectacles his pale-blue eyes had an almost unholy twinkle. He wrinkled them up; he snorted again, hoarsely, through his sandy moustache, pulled down his large tweed cap over one ear, and made a massive gesture that would have been as heavy as a smaller man's blow.

"Ha-ha-HA!" thundered Captain Valvick. "Ay tell you. In my country, in Norway, we haff a custom. When *you* wont to make a horse stop, you say, 'Whoa!' But we don't. We say, *"Brubublubluoooo-bl-oooo!"* "

Shaking his jowls and lifting his head like Tarzan over a fresh kill, Captain Valvick here uttered the most extraordinary noise Morgan had ever heard. It cannot be reproduced into phonetic sounds, and so loses its beauty and poignancy. It was something like the noise of water running out of a bath-tub, but rising on a triumphant note like a battle-cry, and trembling on in shadings of defective drains and broken water-pipes; as though Mr. Paul Whiteman (say) had built a symphony round it, and come out strongly with his horns and strings.

"Bru-bloo-bulooooluloo-buloooooo!" crowed Captain Valvick, starting low with his shakings of head and jowl, and then rearing up his head at the climax.

"Isn't that a lot of trouble?" inquired Morgan.

"Oh, no! Ay do it easy," scoffed the other, nodding complacently. "But ay was going to tell you, de first time I try it on a English-speaking 'orse, de 'orse didn't understand me. Ay tell you how it was. At dat time, when I was young, I was courting a girl who lived in Vermont, where it always snow like Norway. So ay t'ink ay take her out for a sleigh-ride, all nice and fine. I hire de best horse and sleigh dey got, I tell de girl to be ready at two o'clock in de afternoon, and I come for her. So of course I want to make a good impression on my girl, and I come dashing up de road to her house, and I see her standing on de porch, waiting for me. So ay t'ink it be fine t'ing to make de grand entrance, and ay say, *'Brubu-bluooo-bloo!'* fine and strong to de 'orse so ay can turn in de gates. But he don't stop. And ay t'ink, 'Coroosh! What is wrong wit' de goddam 'orse?'" Here Captain Valvick made a dramatic gesture, "So I shout, *'Brubu-bloooo-bloooo!'* and lean over de footboard and say it again. And dis time de 'orse turn its head round to look at me. But it don't stop, you bet. It keep right on going, straight past de house where de girl is standing, and it only gallop faster when I keep saying, *'Brubu-blubluoooo-bl-oooo!'* And my girl open her eyes at me and look fonny, but de 'orse fly straight on up de road; and all I can do is stand up in de sleigh and keep taking off my hat and bowing to her w'ile all de time ay go farder and farder away from her; and still ay am doing dat we'en we go round a bend and ay can't see her no more. . . ."

All this was recited with much pantomime and urging the reins of an imaginary horse. With an expiring sigh Captain Valvick shook his head in a melancholy fashion, and then twinkled benevolently.

"Ay could never get dat girl to go out again. Ha-ha-ha!"

"But I don't see the point," protested Peggy Glenn, who was regarding him in some perplexity. "How is that like Curt Warren?"

"Ay don't know," admitted the other, scratching his head. "Ay yust wanted to tell de story, ay guess. . . . Maybe he is sea-sick, eh? Ha-ha-ha! Ah! Dat remind me. Haff ay ever told you de story about de mutiny ay 'ave when de cook always eat all de peas out of de soup and—"

"Sea-sick?" the girl exclaimed indignantly. "Bosh! At least—poor old fellow, I hope not. My uncle is having a terrible time of it, and he's suffering worse because he's promised to give a performance of his marionettes at the ship's concert. . . . Do you think we'd better go and see what's wrong with Curt?"

She paused as a white-coated steward struggled out of a door near by and peered round in the darkening light. Morgan recognised him as his own cabin steward—a cheerful-faced young man with flat black hair and a long jaw. He had, now, a rather conspiratorial manner. Sliding down the gusty deck, he beckoned towards Morgan and raised his voice above the crash and hiss of water.

"Sir," he said, "it's Mr. Warren, sir. 'Is compliments, and 'e'd like to see you. And 'is friends too. . . ."

Peggy Glenn sat up. "There's nothing wrong, is there? Where is he? What's the matter?"

The steward looked dubious, and then reassuring, "Oh no, miss! Nothing wrong. Only I think somebody's 'it him."

"What?"

"Hin the eye, miss. And on the back of th 'ead. But 'e's not a bit upset, miss, not 'im. I left 'im sitting on the floor in the cabin," said the steward, rather admiringly, "with a towel to 'is 'ead and a piece of movie film in 'is 'and, swearing something 'andsome. And 'e'd taken a nasty knock, miss; that's a fact."

They stared at each other, and then they all hurried after the steward. Captain Valvick, puffing and snorting through his moustache, threatened dire things. Tearing open one of the doors, they were kicked by its recoil in the wind into the warm, paint-and-rubbery odour of the corridor. Warren's cabin, a large double which he occupied alone, was an outside one on C deck, starboard side. They

descended heaving stairs, struck off past the gloomy staircase to the dining-room, and knocked at the door of C 91.

Mr. Curtis G. Warren's ordinarily lazy and good-
humoured face was now malevolent. The odour of recent
profanity hung about him like garlic. Round his head a wet
towel had been wound like a turban; there was a slight cut
of somebody's knuckles. Mr. Warren's greenish eyes regarded them bitterly out of a lean, newly-scrubbed face;
his hair, over the bandage, stuck up like a goblin's; and
in his hand he had a strip of what resembled motion-
picture film with perforations for sound, torn at one end.
He sat on the edge of his berth, faintly visible in the yel-
lowish twilight through the porthole, and the whole cabin
was wildly disarranged.

"Come in," said Mr. Warren. Then he exploded. "When
I catch," he announced, drawing a deep breath like one
who begins an oration, and spacing his words carefully—
"when I catch the white-livered, greenly empurpled so-
and-so who tried to get away with this—when I get one
look at the ugly mug of the lascivious-habited son of a
bachelor who runs around beaning people with a blackjack—"

Peggy Glenn wailed, "Curt!" and rushed over to examine his head, which she turned to one side and the other
as though she were looking behind his ears. Warren broke
off and said, "Ow!"

"But, my dear, what happened?" the girl demanded.
"Oh, why do you *let* things like this happen? Are you
hurt?"

"Baby," said Warren in a tone of dignity, "I can tell you
that it is not alone my dignity which has suffered. By the
time they have finished stitching up my head, I shall probably resemble a baseball. As to my deliberately encouraging all this to happen. . . . Boys," he said, appealing
moodily to Morgan and the captain, "I need help. I'm in
a jam, and that's no lie."

"Ha!" growled Valvick, rubbing a large hand down
across his moustache. "You yust tell me who smack you,
eh? Ha! Den ay take him and—"

"I don't know who did it. That's the point."

"But why . . . ?" asked Morgan, who was surveying the litter in the cabin; and the other grinned sourly.

"This, old son," Warren told him, "is right in your line. Do you know if there are any international crooks on board? The Prince or Princess Somebody kind, who always hang out at Monte Carlo? Because an important State document has been pinched. . . . No, I'm not kidding. I didn't know I had the damned thing; never occurred to me; I thought it had been destroyed. . . . I tell you I'm in bad trouble, and it's not funny. Sit down somewhere and I'll tell you about it."

"You go straight to the doctor!" Peggy Glenn said, warmly. "If you think I'm going to have you laid up with amnesia or something—"

"Baby, listen," the other begged, with a sort of wild patience; "you don't seem to get it yet. This is dynamite. It's—well, it's like one of Hank's spy stories, only it's something new along that line, now that I come to think of it. . . . Look here. You see this film?"

He handed it to Morgan, who held it up for examination against the fading light through the porthole. The pictures were all of a portly, white-haired gentleman in evening clothes, who had one fist lifted as though making a speech and whose mouth was split wide as though it were a very explosive speech. There was, moreover, a very curious, bleary look about the dignified person; his tie was skewered under one ear, and over his head and shoulders had been sprinkled what Morgan at first presumed to be snow. It was, in fact, confetti.

And the face was vaguely familiar. Morgan stared at it for some time before he realised that it was none other than a certain Great Personage, the most pompous starched-shirt of the Administration, the potent rain-maker and high priest of quackdoodle. His cheerful, soothing voice over the radio had inspired millions of Americans with dreams of a fresh, effulgent era of national prosperity in which there should be instalment plans without ever any payments demanded, and similar American conceptions of the millennium. His dignity, his scholarship, his courtly manners—

"Yes, you're right," Warren said wryly. "It's my uncle. Now I'll tell you about it . . . and don't laugh, because it's absolutely serious.

"He's a very good fellow, Uncle Warpus is; you've got to understand that. He got into this position through the ordinary, human behaviour that might happen to anybody, but others mightn't think so. All politicians ought to have a chance every once in a while to blow off steam. Otherwise they're apt to go mad and chew off an ambassador's ear, or something. With the whole country in a mix-up, and everything going wrong, and wooden-heads trying to block every reasonable measure, there are times when they explode. Especially if they're in congenial company and have a social highball or two.

"Well—my hobby is the taking of amateur moving-pictures, with, Lord help me, sound. So about a week before I was to sail I was due to visit Uncle Warpus in Washington for a good-by call." Warren put his chin in his hands and looked sardonically on the others, who had moved backwards to find seats. "I couldn't take my movie apparatus abroad with me; it was much too elaborate. Uncle Warpus suggested that I should leave it with him. He was interested in such things; he thought he might get some pleasure in tinkering with it, and I should show him how to work everything. . . .

"On the first night I got there," pursued Warren, taking a deep breath, "there was a very large, very dignified party at Uncle Warpus's. But he and a few of his Cabinet and senatorial cronies had sneaked away from the dancing; they were upstairs in the library, playing poker and drinking whisky. When I arrived they thought it would be an excellent idea if I arranged my apparatus, and we took a few friendly talking-pictures there in the library. It took me some time, with the assistance of the butler, to get it all arranged. Meanwhile, they were having a few friendly drinks. Some of 'em were a good deal the strong, silent, rough-diamond administrators from the prairies; and even Uncle Warpus was relaxing considerably."

Warren blinked with reminiscent pleasure at the ceiling.

"It all began with much seriousness and formality. The butler was camera man, and I recorded the sound. First the Honourable William T. Pinkis recited Lincoln's Gettysburg Address. *That* was all right. Then the Honourable Secretary of Interstate Agriculture did the dagger scene from *Macbeth,* a very powerful piece of acting, with a bottle of gin as the dagger. One thing led to another. Senator Borax sang 'Annie Laurie,' and then they got up a quartet to render 'Where is my Wandering Boy Tonight?' and 'Put on Your Old Grey Bonnet.' . . ."

Sitting back in the berth with her back against the wall, Peggy Glenn was regarding him with a shocked expression. Her pink lips were open, her eyebrows raised.

"Oh, I say!" she protested. "Curt, you're pulling our legs. I mean to say, just fancy our House of Commons. . . ."

Warren raised his hand fervently. "Baby, as Heaven is my witness, that is precisely—" He broke off to scowl as Morgan began laughing. "I tell you, Hank, this is serious!"

"I know it," agreed Morgan, growing thoughtful. "I think I begin to see what's coming. Go on."

"Ay t'ank dey did right," said Captain Valvick, nodding vigorously and approvingly. "Ay haff always wanted to try one of dem t'ings too. Den ay giff my imitation of de two cargo-boats in de fog. It is very good, dat one. I show you. Ha-ha-ha!"

Warren brooded.

"Well, as I say, one little thing led to another. The signal for the fireworks was when one Cabinet member, who had been chuckling to himself for some time, recounted a spirited story about the travelling saleman and the farmer's daughter. And then came the highlight of the whole evening. My uncle Warpus had been sitting by himself—you could almost see his mind going round *click-click—click-click*—and he was weighed down by a sense of injustice. He said he was going to make a speech. He did. He got in front of the microphone, cleared his throat, squared his shoulders, and then the cataract came down at Lodore.

"In some ways," said Warren, rather admiringly, "it was

the funniest thing I ever heard. Uncle Warpus had had to repress his sense of humour for some time. But I happened to know of his talent for making burlesque political speeches. . . . Wow! What he did was to give his free, ornamental, and uncensored opinion of the ways of government, the people in the government, and everything connected with it. Then he went on to discuss foreign policy and armaments. He addressed the heads of Germany, Italy, and France, explaining exactly what he thought of their parentage and alleged social pastimes, and indicating where they could thrust their battleships with the greatest possible effect. . . ." Warren wiped his forehead rather dazedly. "You see, it was all done in the form of a burlesque flag-waving speech, with plenty of weird references to Washington and Jefferson and the faith of the fathers. . . . Well, the other eminent soaks caught on and were cheering and applauding. Senator Borax got hold of a little American flag, and every time Uncle Warpus made a particularly telling point, Senator Borax would stick his head out in front of the camera, and wave the flag for a second, and say, 'Hooray!' . . . Boys, it was hair-raising. As an oratorical effort I have never heard it surpassed. But I know two or three newspapers in New York that would give a cool million dollars for sixty feet of that film.

Peggy Glenn, struggling between laughter and incredulity, sat forward, with her bright hazel eyes fixed on him; she seemed annoyed. "But I tell you," she protested again, "it's absurd! It—it isn't *nice,* you know. . . ."

"You're telling me," said Warren, grimly.

". . . and all those awfully nice high-minded people; it's disgusting! You can't really tell me! . . . Oh, it's absurd! I don't believe it."

"Baby," said Warren gently, "that's because you're British. You don't understand American character. It's not in the least unreasonable; it's simply one of those scandals that sometimes happen and have to be hushed up somehow. Only this one is a scandal of such enormous, dizzying proportions that—Look here. We'll say nothing of the explosion it would cause at home. It would ruin Uncle Warpus, and a lot of others with him. But can you imagine the effect of those pronouncements on, say, certain dignitaries in Italy and Germany? They wouldn't see anything funny about it in the least. If they didn't jump up and down, tearing out handfuls of hair, and rush out and declare war immediately, it would be because somebody had the forethought to sit on their heads. . . . Whoosh! T.N.T.? T.N.T.'s as mild as a firecracker compared with it."

It was growing dark in the cabin. Heavy clouds had massed up; there was a tremble through the ship above the dull beat of her screws, and a deeper thunder and swish of water as she pitched. Glasses and water-bottle were rattling in the rack above the washstand. Morgan reached up to switch on the light. He said:

"And someone stole it from you?"

"Half of it, yes. . . . Let me tell you what happened.

"The morning after that little carnival, Uncle Warpus woke up with a realisation of what he'd done. He came rushing into my room, and it appears he'd been bombarded with phone-calls from other offenders since seven o'clock. Fortunately, I was able to reassure him—as I thought, anyhow. What with other difficulties, I'd taken in all only two reels. Each reel was packed into a container like this. . . ."

Reaching down under his berth, Warren pulled out a large oblong box, bound in steel, with a handle like a suitcase. It was unlocked, and he opened the snap-catch. Packed inside were a number of flat circular tins measuring about ten inches in diameter painted black, and scrawled with cryptic markings in white chalk. One of these had its lid off. Inside had been jammed a tangled and disarranged spool of film from which a good length seemed to have been torn off.

Warren tapped the tin. "I was taking some of my better efforts with me," he explained. "I've got a little projector, and I thought they might amuse people on the other side. . . .

"On the night of Uncle Warpus's eloquence, I was a little tight myself. The packing up I left to the butler, and I showed him how to do the marking. What must have happened—I can see it now—was that he got the notations mixed. I carefully destroyed two reels that I thought were the right ones. But, like an imbecile"—Warren got out a pack of cigarettes and stuck one askew into his mouth—"like an imbecile, I only examined one of the reels with any care. So I destroyed the Gettysburg Address, the Dagger Scene, and the singing of 'Annie Laurie.' But the rest of it . . . well, I can figure it now. What I got rid of were some swell shots of the Bronx Park Zoo.'

"And the rest of it?"

Warren pointed to the floor.

"In my luggage, without my knowing it. Never a suspicion, you see, until this afternoon. Gaa! what a situation. Well, you see, I had an urgent radiogram I had to send off to somebody at home—"

"Oh?" said Miss Glenn, sitting up and eyeing him suspiciously.

"Yes. To my old man. So I went up to the wireless-room. The operator said he'd just received a message for me. He also said, 'This looks like code. Will you check it over and make sure it's all right?' Code. Ho-ho! I glanced over it, and it seemed so queer that I read it aloud. You must remember, what with the excitement of going away and things on board here and all, I'd forgotten that little performance entirely. Besides, the radiogram was unsigned; I suppose Uncle Warpus didn't dare. . . ." Warren shook his head sadly, a weird turbaned figure with the cigarette hanging from one corner of his mouth and his face scrubbed like a schoolboy's. Then he took the cable from his pocket. "It said, *'found traces in sweeping out. Hiller*—' that's his butler; old family retainer; wouldn't squeal if Uncle Warpus pinched the silver out of the White House—*'Hiller nervous. They look like bears. Is this real reel. Urgent no hitch in sarcasm effaced. Advise about bears.'* "

"Eh?" demanded Captain Valvick, who was puffing slowly.

"That's the closest he could take a chance on coming to it," Warren explained. "Bears in the zoo. But it's not the sort of thing that makes much sense when it's sprung on you unexpectedly. I argued it out with the wireless operator, and it wasn't until ten minutes later that it struck me—how the devil was I to know Uncle Warpus had sent it? So I couldn't connect up the words; then suddenly it hit me.

"Well, I rushed down here to my cabin. It was getting dark, and besides, the curtain was drawn over the porthole . . . but there was somebody in here."

"And of course," said Morgan, "you didn't see who it was?"

"When I get that low-down"—snarled Warren, going off at a tangent and glaring murderously at the waterbottle— "when I find—no, damn it! All I knew was that it was a man. He had my film-box over in the corner, half the tins with their lids off (I found this later) and had the right roll in his hands. I dived for him, and he let go a hard one at my face. When I grabbed him I grabbed a piece of the film. He cracked out again—there isn't much space in here, and the boat was pitching pretty heavily—then we staggered over against the washstand while I tried to slam him against the wall. I didn't dare let go of the film. The next thing I knew the whole cabin went up like a flashlight powder; that was his blackjack on the back of my head. I didn't quite lose consciousness, but the place was going round in sparks; I slugged him again, and I was bent over the part of the film I had. Then he yanked the door open and got out somehow. I must have been knocked out for a few minutes then. When I came to, I rang for the steward, sloshed some water on my head, and discovered—" With his foot Warren raised the tangle of film on the floor.

"But didn't you *see* him?" asked the girl, in her fluttering concern, again taking hold of his head and causing an agonised "Ow!" She jumped. "I mean, old boy, that, after all, you were fighting with him. . . ."

"No, I didn't see him, I tell you! It might have been anybody. . . . But the question is, what's to be done? I'm appealing to you for help. We've got to get that piece of film back. He got—maybe fifty feet of it. And that's as dangerous as though he'd got all of it."

Chapter 3

Trap for a Film Thief

"WELL," Morgan observed thoughtfully, "I admit this is the rummiest kind of secret-service mission that a self-respecting hero was ever called on to undertake. It rouses my professional instincts."

He felt a glow of pleasurable excitement. Here was he, an eminent writer of detective stories, involved in one of those complicated spy plots to recover a stolen document and preserve the honour of a great Personage. It was the sort of thing that would have been nuts to Mr. Oppenheim; and, Morgan reflected, he himself had often used the background of a luxurious ocean liner, sweeping its lighted decks through waters floored with stars—full of monocled crooks sipping champagne; of pale, long-necked Ladies with a Purpose who are not interested in love-making; and of dirty work in general. (The women in a secret-service story seldom *are* interested in love-making; that is the trouble with it.) Although the *Queen Victoria* was scarcely the boat for such goings-on, Morgan considered the idea and found it good. Outside, it had begun to rain. The liner was bumping like a tub against the crash of the swell, and Morgan lurched a little as he stalked up and down the narrow cabin, revolving plans, pushing his glasses up and down his nose, becoming each second more excited with the prospect.

"Well?" demanded Peggy Glenn. "Say something, Hank! Of course we help him, don't we?"

She still seemed hurt by the behaviour of the eminent soaks; but her protective instincts had been roused and her small jaw was very square. She had even put on her shell-rimmed reading-glasses, which lent a look of unwonted sombreness (or flippant make-believe, if you like) to the thin face. And she had removed her hat, to show a mop of

31

bobbed hair. Sitting with one leg curled under her, regarded Morgan almost fiercely. He said:

"My girl, I wouldn't miss it for—well, for a good deal. Ha! It is obvious,' he continued, with relish, and hoped it was true, "that there is aboard a wily and clever international crook who is determined to secure that film for purposes of his own. Very good. We therefore form a Defensive Alliance. . . ."

"Thanks," said Warren, in some relief. "God knows I need help and—you see, you were the only people I could trust. Well, then?"

"Right. You and I, Curt, will be the Brains. Peggy will be the Siren, if we need one. Captain Valvick will be the Brawn—"

"Hah!" snorted the captain, nodding vigorously and lifting his shoulders with approval. He twinkled down on them, and raised his arm with terrific gusto. " 'For God! For de cause! For de Church! For de laws,' " he thundered unexpectedly. " 'For Charles, King of England, and Rupert off de Rhine!' Ha-ha-ha."

"What the devil's that?" demanded Morgan.

"Ay dunno yust what it mean," admitted the captain, blinking on them rather sheepishly. "Ay read it in a book once, and ay t'ink it iss fine. If ay ever get stirred up in de heart—hoooo-o!—Ay say it." He shook his head. "But ay got to be careful wit' de books. When ay finish reading one, ay got to be careful to write its name down so I don't forget and go back and read it all over again."

He looked on them with great amiability, rubbing his nose, and inquired, "But what iss dere you want me to do?"

"First," said Morgan, "it's agreed that you don't want official steps taken, Curt? I mean, you could tell Captain Whistler—?"

"Lord, no!" the other said violently. "I can't do that, don't you see? If we get this back at all, it's got to be under the strictest cover. And that's where it's going to be difficult. Out of the whole passenger-list of this boat, how are we going to pick out the person who might want to steal the thing? Besides, how did the fellow know I had that film, if I didn't know it myself?"

Morgan reflected. "That wireless message—" he said, and stopped. "Look here, you said you read it aloud, And it was only a very short time afterwards that the chap tried to burgle this cabin. It seems too much to be a coincidence. . . . Was there anybody who might have overheard you?"

The other made scoffing noises. In the pure absorption of the debate he had absent-mindedly fished out a bottle of whisky from one of his suit-cases. "Bunk!" said Warren. "Suppose there were a crook of some description aboard. What would that cock-eyed message mean to him? It took some time for *me* to figure it out."

"All right. All right, then! It's got to mean this. The thief was somebody who already knew about the film; that is, that there had been one made. . . . That's possible, isn't it?"

Warren hesitated, knocking his knuckles against his turbaned forehead.

"Ye-es, I suppose it is," he admitted. "There were all sorts of rumours afloat next day; you know how it is. But we were in the library with the door locked, and naturally it can't be any of the people who were in the game. . . . I told you there was a reception downstairs, but how anybody down there could have known—"

"Well, evidently somebody *did* know," Morgan argued. "And it's at a crush of a reception like that, at the home of some big pot, where you'd expect to find a specimen of the gentry we're looking for. . . . Put it this way, just for a starter." He meditated, pulling at his ear-lobe. "The thief —we'll call him, say, Film-Flam—gets wind of your important document. But he thinks it's been destroyed and abandons any idea of pinching it. Still, he is travelling abroad on the *Queen Victoria*—"

"Why?" inquired Miss Glenn practically.

"How should I know?" Morgan demanded, with some asperity. His imagination had been working on opulent ballrooms full of tiaras and red shirt-ribbons; and sinister whiskery strangers smoking cigarettes round the corners of pillars. "Maybe it was accident, maybe Film-Flam is a professional diplomatic crook who dashes about from capital to capital and hopes for the best. Anyway, you've got to admit it was somebody who'd been in Washington and heard all about the indiscretion. . . . Righto, then. He's abandoned the idea, but all the same he happens to be travelling aboard the same boat as Curt. If you looked at the passenger-list, Curt, would you recognise the name of anybody who'd been at your uncle's house that night?"

Warren shook his head.

"There were millions of 'em and I didn't know anybody. No, that won't work. . . . But you mean this. You mean that this bird (after abandoning the idea) overhears that cable in the wireless-room, tumbles to it before I do, and takes a long chance on stealing it before I've got time to realise what I'm carrying?"

"He'd have to work fast, man. Otherwise, as soon as you knew you'd chuck it overboard. And here's another thing," crowed Morgan, stabbing his finger into his palm as the idea grew on him. "The field of search isn't as wide as you'd think at first. Again this is only a theory, but look here!—isn't this chap pretty sure to be somebody who has scraped an acquaintance with you already? I mean, if I were an international crook, even though I didn't think you were carrying that roll of film, I'm jolly certain I'd try to get into your good graces. As Uncle Warpus's favourite nephew, you'd be a valuable person to make friends with. . . . Doesn't that sound reasonable?"

By this time they were all eagerly engrossed in the business, floundering as they tried to stand or sit in the creaking cabin, and each playing with theories. Warren, who had produced paper cups and was pouring out drinks, stopped. He handed a cup carefully to Peggy Glenn before he spoke. Then he said:

"It's a funny thing you should say that. . . ."

"Well?"

"Aside from yourselves, I know very few people aboard this tub. The weather's been too bad, for one thing. But it's funny." He blew into a folding paper cup savagely to open it; then he looked up. "There were—let's see—there were five people in the wireless-room at the time my cable came through, aside from the operator and myself. There was

Captain Whistler, who was having some kind of whispered row with the operator; he walked out in a turkey-cock rage. There was a girl I hadn't seen before. Wash out the captain and that girl, and there were three men. One of 'em I didn't know; didn't notice him at all. . . . But the last two are the only other people I *do* know. One was that fellow Woodcock, the travelling salesman for the bug-powder firm; and the other was Dr. Kyle, who sits at our table."

There was a hoot of derision from Peggy Glenn at the mention of the latter name. Even Morgan, whose profession of necessity made him doubly suspicious of any respectable person, inclined to agree with her. They had both heard of Dr. Kyle. He was one of the more resounding names in Harley Street—a noted brain specialist who had figured as alienist in several murder trials. Morgan remembered him at the table—a tall, lean, rather sardonic Scot, slovenly except for his well-brushed hair, with shrewd eyes under ragged brows whisking upwards at the outer corner, and two deep furrows running down his cheeks. To imagine this distinguished loony-doctor in the role of Film-Flam strained even Morgan's credulity. If he were given a choice in crooks, he would have preferred to fasten on the bouncing Mr. Charles Woodcock, commercial traveller for "Swat," the instant eradicator of insects. But, distinctly, Dr. Kyle must be counted out.

However, when he pointed out this difficulty to Warren, it seemed to make the American all the more certain Dr. Kyle was the culprit.

"Absolutely!" said Warren excitedly. "It's always people like that. Besides—suppose somebody's impersonating him? There's an idea for you! What better disguise would there be for an international crook than as the respectable head of a bughouse? Say, if we were to tax him with it—jump on him suddenly, you see—"

"You want to be shoved in the psychopathic ward?" demanded Morgan. "No, we can't do that; not with Kyle. Besides, it's nonsense! We've got to rule out Kyle, and get a good working plan. . . ."

Captain Valvick shifted from one foot to the other.

"Excuse me," he suggested, with a sort of thunderous timidity, and beamed on them. "Ay got a idea, ay haff."

"H'm!" said Morgan dubiously.

"Ay tell you," pursued the captain, peering round to be sure they were not overheard, "dis feller dat bat you one, he hass got only half de film, eh? Well, den, ay tell you what. He got only half de film; den maybe he iss going to come back, eh? So we stand watch and when he come back we say, 'Hey—!' "

"Yes, I know," interrupted Warren, with a gloomy air. "I'd thought of that, too, but it won't work. That's what always happens in the stories; but you can bet your last shirt this bird is too cagy for that. He knows I'm wise to him, he knows I'll take good care of that film; *if* I don't pitch the rest of it overboard right away. No, no. He won't take any risk like that."

For some time Peggy Glenn had been sitting silent, her chin cupped in her hands, studying the matter. Her glossy hair was tousled across her forehead, and now she suddenly looked up with such an expression of diabolical brightness and practicality that she almost crowed.

"You men," she said, rather scornfully—"you men—just messing about, that's all! Now you let *me* tell you what to do, and you'll have your film back to-night. Yes, I mean it. I fancy I've got an idea"—she struggled to conceal the pleasure that was making her tilt up her chin and grow as excited as Warren—"and it's a *ripping* idea! Whee! Listen. In a way, Captain Valvick is right. We've got to trap this chap into coming back for the rest of the film. . . ."

Warren made a weary gesture, but she frowned him down.

"Will you listen to me? I tell you we can do it. Because why? Because *we* are the only people on the whole boat—we four—who know Curt was attacked and why he was attacked. Very well. We give it out publicly that we came in here and found Curt lying on the floor unconscious, dead to the world with a bad scalp wound. We have no suspicions that there was an attack or theft. We don't know how it happened; we suppose that he must have come in here drunk or something, and staggered about and finally fell and bashed himself over the head—"

Warren raised his eyebrows.

"Baby," he said with dignity, "it is not that I myself have any objection to the charming picture you have just described. But I only want to remind you that I am a member of the American Diplomatic Service. The DIPLOMATIC Service, Baby. The rules laid down for the strictness of my behaviour would cause annoyance among the seraphim and start a riot in a waxworks. I dislike offering suggestions, but why don't you say that in the course of my customary morning opium debauch I went cuckoo and batted my head against the wall? My chief would like that fine."

"Oh, all right," she conceded primly, "if you must keep to your nasty old rules. Then—say you were ill or sea-sick; anyway, that it was an accident. Well, that you haven't recovered consciousness. . . ."

Morgan whistled. "I begin to see this. Curt, I believe the wench has got something!"

"Yes," said Warren, "and in another minute I'm going to tell you what it is. Go on, Baby. Here, have another drink. After I am picked up insensible, what then?"

"Then," the girl continued, beaming excitedly, "we tell everybody you were taken to the infirmary, where you are still in a stupor. You see, if we tell it at the table it will go all about the boat. It's supposed to be an accident, so there'll be no investigation. In the meantime here will be the cabin, open and unguarded. Don't you think this crook will see his opportunity? Of course he will. He'll come back straightaway—and there you are."

She tossed up her head, her hazel eyes shining and her lower lip folded over the upper in defiant triumph. There was a silence.

"By God! it's good!" exploded Morgan, driving his fist into his palm. Even Warren was impressed; he sat like a thoughtful Indian prophet, staring at the paper cup, while Captain Valvick chuckled and Peggy said: "Hoo!" in a pleased tone. "But wait a bit," Morgan added, "what about the steward, the one you sent to tell us? *He* knows."

"Stewards never talk," the girl said wisely; "they know too much as it is. Make it certain with a good tip. Then you can go ahead. . . . By the way, Curt, is the cabin next to this one vacant? That's where you want to hide and wait for him, if it is."

"Why not in here?"

"He'd see you straightaway, you silly! And you've got to catch him with the goods. It's no good saying, 'Cough up, you villain!' unless you can catch him dead to rights. He'd only say he'd got into the wrong cabin by mistake, and then where are you? He must have the film on his person—then," she added judicially, "I dare say you may land him one, dear, if you like."

"Ah-hh!" Warren breathed, and dreamily fingered a large fist. "Yes, Baby, the next cabin is unoccupied, as it happens. Tell you what. I'll install myself in there, and get the steward to bring me some dinner. Captain Valvick can keep watch with me. You two go down to dinner and spread the glad news. Then you can join us afterwards. We'll probably have a long wait. The ingredients for cocktails might not be out of place. . . ."

"But we mustn't get drunk," said Miss Glenn, as though she were uttering a careful definition of terms.

"Oh, no!" said Warren vigorously. "Not at all. Of course not. Ha-ha! The idea is absurd. But look here, I wish we had more dope on our mysterious crook. If we could only find out something about him. . . ." He frowned. "Wait a minute. I've got an idea. Captain, you know Captain Whistler pretty well, don't you?"

"Dat old barnacle?" inquired the other. "Coroo! Ay know him when he wass not so stuck up, you bet. He got a hawful temper, I tell you. De first time ay know him wass in Naples, when he come in wid de cargo-boat where de chief mate hass de religious mania and go crazy and t'ink he is Yesus." The breath whistled through Valvick's large moustache; his sandy eyebrows rose and he illustrated the drama. "De chief mate walk up on de bridge and fold his arms and say, 'Ay am Yesus.' De captain say, 'You are not Yesus.' De chief mate say, 'Ay am Yesus and you are Pontius Pilate,' and *smack*—he haul off and bust

Captain Whistler in de yaw, and dey got to put 'im in irons. Iss a fact. Ay t'ank of it w'en you say Dr. Kyle iss a mad doctor, because Captain Whistler don' like de people which go nutty. Anudder time—'

"Listen, old man," begged Warren. "Spare the Odyssey for a minute. If there were any big international crook aboard, or there were a rumour of it, Captain Whistler would be the one to know about it, wouldn't he? They'd wireless him, wouldn't they, even if he kept it under cover?"

Valvick massively lifted his head sideways and scratched his cheek.

"Ay dunno. It depend on wedder dey know it at de port. Maybe. You want me to hask him?"

"Well—not exactly. Sort of sound him out, you see? Don't let on you know anything. You might do it before dinner; and then we'd be all ready to keep watch."

The other nodded vigorously, and Warren looked at his watch. "Nearly time for the bugle to dress for dinner. We're all set, then?"

There was an enthusiastic chorus in the affirmative. For all these people had within them the true, glorious hare-brained spirit of adventure; and Warren poured them a quick one as a toast to the new gamble as lights came on through the vibrating sleekness of white decks, and rain-squalls spattered the portholes, and the voice of a bugle began to brattle past state-room doors, and the stately *Queen Victoria* shouldered on towards the wild business that was to be.

Chapter 4

A Matter of Skulls

"BUT didn't you know it?" inquired Peggy Glenn, in her sweetest and most surprised tone.

Her voice was clear in the almost deserted dining-saloon, its lights winking against polished rosewood and its vast height wrenched with ghostly cracklings. The roof writhed in the fashion of tottering blocks; Morgan was not at all sure about that glass dome. To eat (or do nearly anything else) was a sporting performance in which you must look sharp for sudden rushes of the crockery from any corner of the table, from the snake-like dart of the water-glass to the majestic ground-swell of the gravy. Morgan felt like a nervous juggler. The dining-saloon would slowly surge up with an incredible balloon swell, climb higher, tilt, and plunge down from its height with a long-drawn roar of water that dislodged stewards from their pillars and made diners—clutching their chairs—feel a sudden dizziness in the pit of the stomach.

There were possibly a dozen people to stem a clattering avalanche of dishes and silver. In general, they were eating away grimly but cautiously, while a gallant orchestra attempted to play "The Student Prince." But none of this bothered Peggy Glenn. Suave in black velvet, with her black bobbed hair done into some sort of trick wave that lent a hoydenish air to her thin face, she sat at Captain Whistler's elbow and regarded him with naïve surprise.

"But didn't you know it?" she repeated. "Of course Curtis can't help it, poor boy. It runs in the family, sort of. I mean, I shouldn't exactly call it insanity, of course. . . ."

Morgan choked on a bit of fish and peered sideways at her. She appealed to him.

"I say, Hank, what was the name of that uncle of his Curt was telling us about? I mean the one who had the fits-and-gibbers or something in his sleep, or maybe it was claustrophobia, and used to give a terrific spring out of bed because he thought he was being strangled?"

Captain Whistler laid down his knife and fork. He had obviously been in an ill temper when he came to the table; but he had concealed it under gruff amiability and absent-minded smiles. Wheeling round his chair he had announced that he must return to the bridge and could stay only for one course or two. Captain Whistler was stout and short of breath. He had protruding eyes of a pale brown colour, something like the hue of pickled onions, a ruddy face, and a large loose mouth which was always booming a professional and paternal "Ha-ha" to nervous old ladies. His gold braid blazed, and his short white hair stood up like the foam on a beer-glass.

Now he addressed Peggy with coy heartiness. "Come, come," he said in his best nursery manner, "and what is the little lady telling us now? Eh, my dear? Something about an accident to a friend of yours?"

"A *dreadful* accident," she assured him, looking round to make sure the dining-room would overhear. The only people at their own table were the captain, Dr. Kyle, Morgan, and herself; so she wanted to make sure. She described Warren's being picked up unconscious, with a wealth of graphic detail. "But, of course, poor boy, he isn't responsible for his actions when he gets into those fits. . . ."

Captain Whistler looked concerned, and then rather alarmed. His fleshy face grew redder.

"Ah, hurrumph!" he said, clearing his throat. "Dear me! Dear me!"—it speaks much for the captain's social polish that he could sometimes force himself to say "Dear me!"— "Bad, bad, Miss Glenn! But there's nothing—ah—seriously wrong with him, is there?" He peered at her in gruff anxiety. "Is it maybe something in Dr. Kyle's line now?"

"Well, of course, I shouldn't like to say—"

"Have you known cases of the kind, Doctor?"

Kyle was not a man of many words. He was methodically disposing of grilled sole—a lean, long-faced figure with a bulging shirt-front, and traces of a thin smile had pulled down the furrows in his cheeks. He glanced at Peggy from under grizzled eyebrows, and then at Morgan. Morgan received the impression that he believed in Warren's lurid ailment about as much as he believed in the Loch Ness monster.

"Oh, yes," he replied in his heavy, meditative voice. "Not unknown. I've met it before." He looked hard at Peggy. "A mild case of *legensis-pullibus,* I should think. Patient'll recover."

In a harassed way Captain Whistler wiped his mouth with his napkin.

"But—ah—why wasn't I told of this?" he demanded. "I'm master here, and it's my right to be told of things like this. . . ."

"I did tell you, Captain!" Peggy protested indignantly. "I've been sitting here the whole time telling you; I told you three times over before you understood. I say, what *is* worrying you?"

"Eh?" said the captain, jumping a little. "Worrying me? Rubbish, my dear! Rubbish! Ha-ha!"

"I mean, I hope we're not going to hit an iceberg or anything. That would be dreadful!" She regarded him with wide hazel eyes. "And, you know, they *do* say the captain of the *Gigantic* was drunk the night they hit the whale, and—"

"I am not drunk, madam," said Captain Whistler, his voice taking on a slight roar. "And I am not worried either. Rubbish!"

She seemed to have an inspiration. "Then I know what it is, poor dear! Of course. You're worried about poor Lord Sturton and all those valuable emeralds he's got with him. . . ." Commiseratingly she looked at the chair which a very sea-sick peer had not yet occupied on the voyage. "And I don't blame you. I say, Hank, just fancy. Suppose there were a notorious criminal aboard—just suppose it, I mean—and this criminal had decided to pinch Lord Sturton's jewels. Wouldn't it be thrilling? Only not for poor Captain Whistler, of course; because he'd be responsible, wouldn't he?"

Under the table Morgan administered an unmannerly kick towards the shins of his beaming partner. His lips framed "Easy on!" But undoubtedly a number of diners had pricked up their ears.

"My dear young lady," said the captain, in an agitated voice, "for Go—ah—please kindly get that nonsense out of your pretty little head. Ha-ha! You'll alarm my passengers, you know; and I can't have that, can I? (*Lower your voice, will you?*) The idea's fantastic. Come, now!"

She was appealing. "Oh dear, have I said anything I shouldn't? I mean, I was only supposing, to sort of relieve the monotony; because it *has* been rather dull, you know, and there hasn't been anything really funny, dear Captain Whistler, since I saw you playing handball on the boat-deck. But if there were a notorious criminal on board, it would be exciting. And it might be anybody. It might be Hank. Or it might be Dr. Kyle—mightn't it?"

"Verra likely," agreed Dr. Kyle composedly, and went on dissecting fish.

"But if I did have anything on my mind," declared the captain, in heavy joviality, "it would be about your uncle, Miss Glenn. He's promised to give us a full-dress performance of his marionettes at the ship's concert. And that's to-morrow night, my dear. He mustn't be ill for that, you know. He and his assistant—ah—well, they're—they're improving, aren't they?" said the captain, his voice rising to a desperate bellow as he tried to divert her. "I have looked forward, I have hoped, I have waited for the—ah —pleasure, the supreme honour," yelled Captain Whistler, "of being present at a performance. And now you really must excuse me. I mustn't forget my duties, even at the expense of your charming company. I must—er—go. Good night, my dear. Good night, gentlemen."

He rolled away. There was a silence. Of the diners left at roundabout tables, Morgan noticed swiftly, only three people glanced after him. There was the sharp-edged, bony, shock-haired face of Mr. Charles Woodcock, the commercial traveller, who peered out motionless with his soup-spoon poised above his mouth as though he were going to pose for a figure on a fountain. At another table some distance away Morgan saw a man and a woman— both thin and well-dressed, their pale faces looking curiously alike except that the woman wore a monocle and the man a floating blond moustache like a feather waving from his lip. They stared after the captain. Morgan did not know who they were, but he saw them every morning. They made endless circuits of the promenade-deck, in absolute silence walking rapidly, with their eyes fixed straight ahead. One morning, in dull fascination, Morgan had watched them make one hundred and sixty-four circuits without a word. At the hundred and sixty-fifth they had stopped; the man said, "Eh?" and the woman said, "Ah!" and then they both nodded and went inside. It had occurred to Morgan to speculate how their marital relations were conducted. . . . Anyhow, they seemed to be interested in the movements of Captain Whistler.

"The captain," said Morgan, frowning, "seems to have something on his mind. . . ."   ;

"Verra likely," agreed Dr. Kyle composedly. "I'll have the tripe and onions, steward."

Peggy Glenn smiled at him. "But I say, Doctor, do you think there might be a mysterious master criminal aboard?"

"Why, I'll tell you," said the doctor, bending his head. His shrewd eyes were amused; under the ragged brows whisking upwards at the corners, and with the furrows deepening round his mouth, Morgan thought uncomfortably that he looked a little too much like Sherlock Holmes. "And I'll put in a word of warning gratis. You're a clever young lady, Miss Glenn. But don't pull Captain Whistler's leg too hard. He'd be a bad man to have on the wrong side of anybody. Please pass the salt."

The dining-saloon soared up on another swell, and tilted amid sour notes from the orchestra. "But, really," said Peggy, "I mean, it's perfectly true about poor old Curt. . . ."

"Oh, ah!" said Dr. Kyle. "Was he sober?"

"Doctor," she told him, lowering her voice confidentially, "I hate to tell it, but he was terribly, *terribly* drunk, poor boy. I mean, it's all right to speak of these things to a medical man, isn't it? But I pitied him from the bottom of my heart, poor boy, when I saw. . . ."

Morgan got her away from the table after a brief and

telegraphic exchange of kicks. They navigated the big staircase and stood in a breezy, lurching hall upstairs while Morgan said things. But Peggy, her prim little face beaming, only chortled with pleasure. She said she must go to her cabin and get a wrap, if they were going to watch with the others; also that she ought to look in on her Uncle Jules.

"By the way," she said, doubtfully, "I don't suppose you'd care to be a Moorish warrior, would you?"

"Not particularly," said Morgan, with conviction. "Is this relevant to the issue?"

"All you'd have to do, you know, would be blacken your face and put on some gilt armour and shawls and things; and stand at one side of the stage with a spear while Uncle Jules speaks the prologue. . . . I wonder if you're tall enough, though? I say, Captain Valvick would make a *ripping* Moorish warrior, wouldn't he?"

"Oh, unquestionably."

"You see, there have to be two extras, a French warrior and a Moor, who stand on either side of the stage for effect. The stage isn't high enough for them to be on it; they're outside, on a little platform. . . . When the play begins they go backstage, and sometimes they help move the figures—the unimportant ones that have nothing to do. Only my uncle and Abdul (that's his assistant) move the chief figures; they're the only ones with speaking parts. . . . I say, it would be simply awful if Uncle Jules can't play. There's a professor or somebody aboard who's written all kinds of articles about his art. Abdul's all right and he could take the main part in place of uncle. But I'm the only other one, and I couldn't very well say the men's lines, could I?"

They had gone down into a tangle of passages on D deck, and Peggy knocked at a door. In response to a spectral groan, she pushed the door open. The cabin was dark except for a faint light over the washstand. That scene— with the cabin twisting sideways, and rain slashing the porthole—gave Morgan a slight shiver. Two or three witless-looking dummies were sprawled against the bulkhead in a seated position, and swayed with the motion as though they were moving their heads in a horrible chorus. The straps and hooks for their wires rattled eerily; they were solid lumps about four and a half feet tall; they glittered with gilt armour, red cloaks, and gaudy jewelled accoutrements. Their faces, bearded formidably in dark wool, smirked from under spiked helmets. While they swayed, a powerful-looking man with a flattish dark face sat on the couch with another dummy across his knee. In the dim light he was mending the figures cloak with a long needle and blue thread. Occasionally he glanced towards the dark berth where something heavy was burrowing and groaning.

"*Je meurs!*" whispered a voice from the berth, dramatically. "*Ah, mon Dieu, je meurs! Ooooo! Abdul, je t'implore. . . .*"

Abdul shrugged, squinted at his needle, shrugged again, and spat on the floor. Peggy closed the door.

"He's no better," she said, unnecessarily, and they started back to the cabin where Warren was waiting. Morgan, in fact, was not eager for more than a glimpse into that cabin. Whether it was merely night and the rain in the middle of a shouting Atlantic, or merely that dull after-dinner feeling which is not dispelled on shipboard without bibulous hilarity, still he did not like the look of those smirking dummies. Moreover, such an irrelevant impression as that had given him another impression—of trouble ahead. There was no Q.E.D. about it, or even a rational subtlety. But he glanced round rather sharply when they reached the side passage that led to Warren's cabin.

It opened off a main corridor, and its short length contained two cabins on either side. Warren's was an end one on the left, beside a door opening out on C deck. It was dark, and the white-painted door was hooked open. Morgan knocked in the manner agreed on at the door beside it, and they slipped inside.

Only the light inside the lower berth was on. Warren sat gingerly on the edge of the berth. And he looked worried.

Morgan said sharply, but in a low voice, "Anything wrong?"

"Plenty," said the other. "Sit down and keep as quiet as you can. I think we've got a long time to wait, but you never can tell what *this* joker will be up to. Valvick's gone for some soda-water. And we're set now." He nodded towards the ventilator high in the wall, communicating with the next cabin. "If anybody goes in there, we can hear him in a second. Then we nab him. Moreover, I've got the hook on the door wedged so that, no matter how quiet he tries to be, he'll make a racket as loud as an alarm clock."

Warren paused, rubbing his jaw rather nervously and peering about the dim-lit state-room. He had discarded the towel round his head, but absorbent gauze and sticking-plaster along the back of the skull still made his dark hair stand up in a goblin-like way. The glow in the berth illumined one side of his face, and they could see a vein beating in his temple.

"Curt," said the girl, "what *is* wrong?"

"All hell, I'm afraid. Old Valvick went to see Captain Whistler before dinner. . . ."

"Yes?"

"Well, I don't know how much in earnest you people were when we were sitting in there piling up theories about fancy crooks. But the impossible happened. We were right. There's a very badly wanted little joker aboard, and no joke about it. He's after old Sturton's emerald. And—he's a killer."

Morgan felt in the pit of his stomach an uneasy sensation which was partly the motion of the ship. He said:

"Are you serious, or is this—?"

"You bet I'm serious. So is Whistler. Valvick got the information from him, because Whistler badly needs advice. Old Valvick's story is pretty muddled; but that much is clear. Whistler wonders whether to keep it dark or broadcast the news to the ship. Valvick advised the latter: it's customary. But Whistler says this is a respectable boat, a family boat, and the rest of that stuff. . . ."

Morgan whistled. Peggy went over and sat down beside Warren. She protested stoutly that it was nonsense and she didn't believe it.

"Who is he, Curt? What do they know about him?" she demanded.

"That's just it. Nobody seems to know, except that he's travelling under an alias. You remember, I told you this afternoon that when I was in the radio-room old Whistler seemed to be having a row with the wireless operator? . . . Well, that was it. He'd got a radiogram. Fortunately, Valvik had the sense to persuade Whistler to let him take a copy of it. Have a look."

From his inside pocket he took an envelope, on the back of which was sprawled in crooked handwriting:

Commander S.S. *Queen Victoria,* at sea. Suspect Man responsible for Stelly job in Washington and Macgee killing here sailed under alias your ship. Federal officer arriving to-night from Washington and will send fuller information. Look out for smooth customers and advise if any suspects.

ARNOLD, COMMISSIONER N.Y.P.D.

"I don't know anything about this MacGee killing, whatever it is, in New York," Warren went on, "but I know a little about the Stelly business because it raised such a row and looked like magic. It was tied up with the British Embassy. Stelly seems to have been a pretty well-known English jewel-cutter and appraiser. . . ."

"Hold on!" said Morgan. "D'you mean that Bond Street fellow, the one who's always designing the necklaces for royalty and having pictures of his work in the newspapers?"

Warren grunted. "Probably. Because it seems he was staying in Washington, and the wife of the British ambassador asked him to reset or redesign a necklace for her. I don't know the details of it—nobody knows much about it. But he left the British Embassy with the necklace one night, as safe as you please, and about four hours later they found him somewhere out Connecticut Avenue way. He was sitting on the kerbstone with his back propped up against a street lamp, and the back of his head smashed in. He didn't die, but he'll be a paralysed moron for the rest of his life, and never speak a word. That seems to be a quaint habit of this joker. He doesn't exactly kill; but he has a knack of softening their heads so that they're worse than dead. , . .

"By the Lord!" said Warren, clenching and unclenching his hands, "I'm wondering whether that's what *I* nearly got in the other cabin, only the fellow missed his aim when the ship rolled."

There was a silence, made portentous by creaking bulkheads and the blustering roar outside.

"I say, Peggy," Morgan observed, thoughtfully, "you'd better get out of this, old girl. It isn't funny. Go up to the bar and entice some gullibles into a bridge game. If this basher comes along and tries to pinch the rest of the film, we'll let you know. Meantime—"

The girl said, with vehemence, "Bah! You can't scare me. You *are* a cheerful lot, though. Why don't you start telling ghost stories? If you start off by being afraid of this chap—"

"Who's afraid of him?" shouted Warren. "Listen, Baby. I've got something to settle, I have. When I get *at* him—" Satirically he watched her jump a little when there was a knock at the door. Captain Valvick bearing two large siphons of soda-water, bent his head under the door and closed it behind him with a mysterious air.

Morgan always remembered the ensuing two hours (or possibly three) on account of the interminable game of Geography that was played to pass away the time. Captain Valvick—cheerfully twinkling, in no whit disturbed—insisted that they should turn out the light, hook the door partly open, and get enough light from the dim bulb in the passage. First he administered to each a hair-raising peg of whisky, which made them feel anew the excellence of the adventure; then he placed them in a weird circle on the floor, with the bottle in the middle like a camp fire; finally, he filled up the glasses again.

"Skoal!" said the captain, raising his glass in the dim light. "Ay tell you, diss iss de life. Coroosh! But ay got to feel bad about Captain Whistler. Ho-ho! Dat poor old barnacle iss near crazy. you bet, on account of de crook

which like to steal de jewellery. He iss afraid diss crook
going to rob de English duke, and he try to persuade de
duke to let him lock up de hemereld helephant in de
captain's safe. But dat duke only give him de bird. He
say, 'It be safer wit' me dan in your safe, or wit' de purser
or anybody.' De captain say no. De duke say yes. De
captain say no. De duke say yes. . . .''

"Look here, you can omit the element of suspense,"
said Morgan, taking another drink. "What did they decide?"

"Ay dunno yust what dey decide. But ay got to feel
bad about dat poor old barnacle. Come on, now; we play
Geography."

This game was trying, but in many senses lively. As
the whisky diminished, it led to long and bitter arguments
between Warren and the captain. The latter, when stumped
for a place-name, would always introduce some such place
as Ymorgenickenburg or the River Skoof, in Norway.
Warren would heatedly cast slurs on his veracity. Then
the captain would say he had an aunt living there. As this
was not considered *prima facie* evidence, he would embark on a long and complicated anecdote about the rela-
tive in question, with accounts of such other members of
his family as happened to occur to him. Morgan's watch
ticked on, and the stir about the boat gradually died away
into a roaring night, as they heard about the captain's
brother, August, his Cousin Ole, his niece Gretta, and his
grandfather who was a beadle. Footsteps went by in the
main corridor, but none of them turned into the side
passage. It was growing stuffy in the cabin. . . .

"I—I think he probably won't come," Peggy whispered,
reverting to the subject for the first time. There was an
uneasy hopefulness in the way she said it.

"It's hotter than hell in here," muttered Warren. Glassware rattled faintly. "I'm tired of the game, anyhow. I
think—"

"Listen!" said Morgan.

He had scrambled up and was holding to the side of the
berth. They all felt it—a terrific draught blowing through
the passage outside, rattling the hooks of the doors, and

they heard the deeper tumult of the sea boiling more loudly. The door to D deck had been pushed open.

But it did not close. They were all standing up now, waiting to hear the swish and slam of that door as it closed against the compressed-air valve. Those doors were heavy; and in a wind you dodged inside quickly. But for an interminable time something seemed to be holding it partly open, while the draught whistled. The *Queen Victoria* rose, pitched, and went over in a long roll to starboard, but still the door stayed open. It was impossible to distinguish smaller noises above the crazy wickerwork creaking, but yet Morgan had an eerie sense that the door did not close because it could not; that there was something caught there, trapped in a snare and in pain, between the black sea and warm security inside.

They heard a moan. A faint voice seemed to be muttering something, muttering and repeating thinly in the passage. "Warren!" they thought it said. And again, *"Warren. . . ."* until it died off in pain.

Chapter 5

Enter the Emerald Elephant

MORGAN almost pitched head foremost into the wardrobe as his clumsy fingers fumbled at the hook on the door. He righted himself. squeezed outside, and called to Valvick to follow.

There was something caught there. It was small and broken-looking, snapped between the jamb and the heavy door—a woman fallen forward across a sill six inches high. She wore no hat, and her dishevelled brown hair, which had tumbled down along one side, blew wildly in the draught. They could not see her face. Her hands, flung forward out of the sleeves of a green, fur-edged coat, were groping in weak movements—horribly, as though she were tapping at the keys of a piano. The head and body rolled with the ship. As they did, a splashing of blood ran thinly along the rubber matting of the floor.

With his shoulder, Morgan forced the door wide while Captain Valvick picked the woman up. Then the door boomed shut once more with a cessation of draught that made them shiver.

"Dat blood," said Valvick, suddenly, in a low voice. "Look! It iss from her nose. She been hit on de back off de head. . . ."

Her head lay limply in the crook of the captain's arm; and he moved his arm as though with a notion he must not touch her there. She was a sturdy, wiry girl with thick eyebrows and long lashes—not unattractive under a pallor that made her rouge stand out, but with one of those straight Greek-coin faces which have a look of heaviness rather than beauty. Her throat quivered as the head lolled over. Breathing raspingly, with eyes squeezed shut, she seemed to be trying to move her lips.

"In here," Warren's voice said in a whisper from the door of the dark cabin. They carried her in, a trembling

Peggy making way for them, laid her down on the berth, and switched on the dim lamp inside. Morgan closed the door.

Peggy was very pale, but with some sudden mechanical impulse she seized a towel off the rack and wiped the blood from the nose and mouth of the inert girl.

"Who—who is she? What—?"

"Get some whisky," said the captain, curtly. Blinking his pale blue eyes, he puffed slowly through his moustache; there was a scowl on his face as he ran one finger along the base of the woman's skull. "Ay dunno, but she may be hurt bad. Ha! Turn her on de side, and you wet de cloths. Ay haff to know somet'ing of what de doctor know because dere is no doctor on de cargo-boat. . . . Ha! Maybe—"

"I've seen her before," said Warren. He steadily poured out whisky and put it to the girl's lips as the captain eased up her head. "Hold it. . . . I'll see if I can force her teeth apart. Damn it! she's jerking like a mule. . . . She was the girl in the wireless-room this afternoon, the one who was there when I got my cable. You think her skull's fractured?"

"She might—" Peggy observed, in a small voice—"she might have fallen—"

"Haaaah!" growled the captain, jerking his neck. "She fall like Mr. Warren fall in de next cabin, you bet." His fingers were still exploring; his face looked heavy and puzzled. "Ho! Ay dunn, but ay don't *t'ink* she got de skull fractured; don't feel like it. See, it pain her when ay feel, eh? And dat iss not de way dey act if dey are bad 'urt. . . ." He drew a wheezing breath. "Try de whisky again. So."

"I'll swear I heard her saying my name," Warren whispered," "Got those wet towels, Hank? Put 'em on. Come on—er—ma'am" he said, with a kind of wild, coaxing note, "take some of this liquor. . . . Up you go! . . . Come on!"

His face wore a rather weird encouraging smile as he clicked the glass against her locked teeth. A shudder went over the white face. The *Queen Victoria* pitched down in a long foam of water, diving with such a deeper cyclone plunge that it flung them all against the forward bulkhead, and they could feel the thick shaking as the propellers beat out of water. But they could hear something else also. It had been done softly. with little draught and no slam whatever, but the door to D deck had again been opened and closed.

They were silent amid the rattling of the cabin. Warren, who had been cursing in a whisper when the contents of the glass splashed wide, turned round sharply. His face, under the wild goblin hair, wore a look of triumphant malevolence. Clinging to furniture, they waited. . . .

Somebody was trying the latch-hook of the cabin next door.

There was an elaborate pantomime of communication. Morgan's lips elaborately writhed to frame, "Let him get inside," as he jerked his thumb at the next cabin. Valvick and Warren nodded; they were all making fierce gestures, and nodding to one another, and trying to reach the passage-door without sprawling full-length. Warren glared at Peggy, and his lips formed, "You stay *here*," as he pointed at the girl in the berth and then savagely stabbed his finger at the floor. Giving him an answering glare, she folded over her under-lip mutinously and shook her head until the hair obscured her eyes. He repeated his order, first pleadingly and then with a graphic pantomime of somebody being strangled. Rearing out of the trough, the ship was climbing again on a steep upward slant. . . .

The light in the next room was switched on. . . .

Here on the floor, the whisky-bottle was rolling and bumping wildly. Captain Valvick made a dart for it, as a man chases his hat in a gale. The pantomime still went on, grotesque against the dim light in the berth, where that pale-faced figure was twisting. . . .

The door of the next cabin slammed.

Whether or not it was the wind, they could not tell. Warren tore open the door of his state-room, the sticking-plaster on his head going before like a banner, and lurched into the passage. Plunging out after Valvick's big figure, Morgan seized the handrail in the passage just in time to steady himself as the ship plunged once more. *The door opening out on C deck was closing again.*

Either he had been too quick for them or he had been frightened away. With a rather satiric wink, the rubber edging of the door caught and contracted; the gilt piston closed softly. Over the tortured wrenching and bone-cracking of the woodwork, when the whole ship seemed to be heeling over down a colossal chute, Warren let out a howl and charged for the door. The inrush of wind smashed over them as he got it open; they were whirled sideways in the trough of the wave, and the wind carried away something Captain Valvick was crying, about "be careful," and "hold de rail," and "close to water line."

The spray took Morgan in the face as he clambered out into darkness. Between spray and bellowing wind, he was momentarily blind. The wind cut through him with paralysing chill, and his foot slipped on the wet iron plates. A whistle and drumming went by in the halloo of the blast. A few lights from high up in the ship gleamed out across a darkness shot with ghostly white. The lights shone on creaming white flickers; on a curl of grey-black swell that shone like grained wood, and then a mist of spray as the wet deck tilted sickeningly and the crash of water rose high in a spectral mane. Morgan seized at the bulhead rail, steadied himself, and shaded his eyes.

They were on the windward side. D deck was long, rather narrow, and very dimly lighted. He saw it go up before them on the rise—and he saw their man. A little way ahead, not holding to the rail, but, head down, a figure was hurring towards the bows. Even in the dull yellow flicker in the roof they could see that this figure carried something under its arm. And this was a circular black box, flattish, and about ten inches in diameter. . . .

"Steady, boys!" said Warren, exultantly, and flapped against the rail. "Steady, boys! Here we go down again. Hang on!" He stabbed his finger ahead. "And *there's* the son-of-a—"

The rest of the sentence was lost, although he seemed to keep on speaking. They were after him. Far ahead,

Morgan could see the lamp on the tall foremast swing up, rear, and swerve like a diver. He thought (and thinks to this day) that they did not so much run down that deck as hook their elbows to the rail and sail down it like a stupendous water-chute. They were going so fast, in fact, that he wondered whether they could stop in time, or whether they would go straight at the big enclosure of glass that protected the fore part of the deck from the wind's full violence. Their quarry heard them now. He had reached the turn of the deck by the glass enclosure when he heard the clatter of pursuit; he was almost in darkness, and he whirled round towards them. Juggled on flying water, the liner crested another rise. . . .

"HAAA!" screamed Warren, and charged.

To say that Warren hit the man would be a powerful understatement. Morgan afterwards wondered why that crack did not jar the other's head loose from his spine. Warren landed on his quarry's jaw, with the weight of his own thirteen stone and the catapult-start of the Atlantic Ocean behind. It was the most terrific, reverberating smack since Mr. William Henry Harrison Dempsey pasted Mr. Luis Angel Firpo clean over the ropes into the newspapermen's laps; and it is to be recorded that, when the other hit the glass enclosure, he bounced. Warren did not afterwards even give him time to fall. "You'll go around smacking people with a blackjack, will you?" he demanded —a purely rhetorical question. "You'll come into a guy's cabin, hey! and crack him one with a lead pipe? Oh, you will, will you?" inquired Mr. Warren, and waded in.

Both Captain Vavick and Morgan, who had been ready to lend assistance, clutched the rail and stared. The circular tin box slid from the victim's arms, clattered on the deck, and rolled. Valvick caught it as the deck was carrying it overboard.

"Yumping Yudas!" said the captain, his eyeballs bulging. "Ho! Hey! Go easy! Ay t'ank you going to kill him if you keep on. . . ."

"Whee!" said a voice behind them. "Darling! Sock him again!"

Reeling, Morgan turned round to see Peggy Glenn,

without hat or coat, capering in the middle of the spray-drenched deck. Her hair was blowing wildly, and she beamed as she spun to keep her footing. She had the whisky-bottle in one hand ("in case somebody needed it," as she afterwards explained), and she was waving it encouragingly.

"You blasted little fool," yelled Morgan, "go back!" He seized her arm and dragged her to the inside rail, but she broke loose and stuck out her tongue at him. "Go back, I tell you! Here, take this—" he got the tin box from Valvick, and thrust it into her hands—"take this and go back. We'll be there. It's all over. . . ."

It was, and had been for some seconds. By the time she was persuaded to work her way back some distance. Warren had arranged his tie, smoothed the hair over his sticking-plaster, and come up to them with the deprecating air of a person who regrets having caused a fuss.

"Well, boys," he said, "I feel a little better. Now we can examine this blackjacker-user and see if he's carrying the first part of the film on him. If not, we can easily find out his cabin." He drew a deep breath. A high wave careered, swung and broke close to the deck, drenching him; but he only adjusted his tie and wiped the water from his eyes in a negligent fashion. He was beaming. "This isn't a bad night's work. As a member of the Diplomatic Service, I feel that I have earned considerable thanks from Uncle Warpus, and—What the devil's the matter with—!"

The girl had screamed. Even with the sea noises, it went up shrill and thin above them, paralysing on the darkened liner.

Morgan whirled round. She had taken the lid off the tin box, and Morgan noted in fascinated horror that the lid had a hasp and a hinge, which he did not remember having seen. . . . Holding tight to the rail, he wove his way to where the girl, under a sickly electric bulb, was holding the box out and staring into it.

"Coroosh!" said Captain Valvick.

The box was not tin; it was thin steel. Inside, it was padded and lined with gleaming white satin. Bedded into a depression in the middle was a glow of green brilliancy which shifted and burned under the moving light. There were two rubies for eyes in the exquisitely carven thing; a piece of subtle Persian workmanship somewhat larger than a Vesta matchbox, and wound with gold links into a pendant.

"*Hold it!*" shouted Morgan, as a jerk of the deck nearly carried the box overboard. He clutched it in. Wet splashes flashed out on the satin. . . . "Thought," he yelled, "gone overboard. . . ."

He swallowed hard, and a nauseating suspicion struck him as he peered over his shoulder.

"By the Lord! had he pinched the emerald elephant?" demanded Warren. "Look here; we did better than we knew. Getting this back—ha! Why old Sturton'll—What's the matter with you all? What are you thinking about?" His eyes suddenly widened. They all stared at one another under the wild screaming of the night. "Look!" muttered Warren, swallowing hard. "That is, you don't think— *hurrum?*"

Captain Valvick groped his way down to where a stout mass in a waterproof, dead to the world, was wedged into an angle of the glass enclosure. Bending down, and sheltered by the enclosure, they saw the spurt of a match.

"Oh, Yesus!" said the captain, in an awed voice. He got up. He pushed back his cap and scratched his head. When he came back to them his leathery face had a queer, wrinkled, wryly amused expression, and his voice was matter-of-fact.

"Ay t'ank," he observed, scratching his head again— "ay t'ank we haf made a mistake. Ay t'ank we are in one most hawful yam. Ay t'ank de man you haff busted in de yaw is Captain Whistler."

Chapter 6

The Missing Body

MORGAN reeled, in a more than merely literal sense. Then he recovered himself, after a long silence in which everybody stared at everybody else. He hooked his arms in the rail and took a meditative survey of the deck. He cleared his throat.

"Well, well!" he said.

Captain Valvick suddenly chuckled, and then let out thunderous guffaws. He doubled up his shoulders, shook, writhed in unholy fashion, and there were tears in those honest old eyes as he leaned against the rail. Warren joined him; Warren could not help it. They chortled, they yowled, they slapped one another on the back and roared. Morgan eyed them in some disapproval.

"Not for the world," he observed, in a thoughtful yell, "would I care to be a spirit of Stygian gloom upon the innocent mirth and jollity of this occasion. Go on and gather rosebuds, you fatheads. But certain facts remain for our consideration. I am not thoroughly familiar with maritime law. Beyond the obvious fact that we have compounded and executed a felony, I am therefore not fully aware of the exact extent of our offence. But I have my suspicions, gentlemen. It would strike me that any seagoing passenger who wilfully up and busts the captain in the eye, or is found guilty of conniving at the same, will probably spend the rest of his life in clink. . . . Peggy, my dear, hand me that bottle. I need a drink."

The girl's lips were twitching with unholy mirth, but she put the steel box under her arm and obediently handed over the whisky. Morgan sampled it. He sampled it again. He had sampled it a third time before Warren got his face straight.

"It's aaal-ri-whooooosh!" roared Warren, doubling up again. "It's all riii-whi-choosh! I mean, wha-keeeee! It's all right, old man. You people go on back to the cabin and sit down and make yourselves comfortable. I'll throw some water over the old walrus and confess to him. Huh-huh-huh!" His shoulders heaved; he swallowed and straightened up. "I pasted him. So I'll have to tell him. . . ."

"Don't be a howling ass," said Morgan. "You'll tell him what?"

"Why, that—" said the other, and stopped.

"Exactly," said Morgan. "I defy anybody's ingenuity to invent a reasonable lie as to why you came roaring out of your cabin, slid down sixty yards of deck, and bounced the captain of the *Queen Victoria* all over his own deck. And, when that walrus comes to, my boy, he's going to be WILD. If you tell him the truth, then the fat's in the fire and you've got to explain about Uncle Warpus—not that he'd probably believe you, anyway. . . ."

"Um," said Warren, uneasily. "But, say what do you suppose *did* happen, anyway? Hell! I thought I was hitting the fellow who tried to break into my cabin. . . ."

Morgan handed him the bottle. "It was his captainly solicitude, my lad. Peggy told him all about your accident at dinner. Now that I come to think of it, what she neglected to tell him was that you were supposedly taken to the infirmary. So he came to call on the wreck. . . ."

"After—" shouted Captain Valvick excitedly—"after he hass persuaded de English duke to give him dat hemerald helephant, and he take it wit' him to put in de safe. . . .'"

"Exactly. He glanced in your cabin, saw you weren't there, went out, and—*bang*," Morgan reflected. "Besides, my lad, there's another good reason why you can't confess. The one thing we'll be forced to report to him is that girl—the one in the cabin now—with a crack over the back of the head. You'll certainly be for it if you admit slugging the captain. To our friend Whistler's forthright intelligence, the explanation would be simple. If one of your simple pleasures is to go about assaulting the skippers of ocean liners, then you would consider beaning his lady-passengers with a blackjack as only a kind of warm-ing-up exercise. Especially as—Holy Mike!" Morgan stopped, stared, and then seized the rail again as the ship roared down. "Now that I remember it, our good Peggy informed the captain at dinner that she was afraid you suffered from bats in the belfry. . . ."

"Oooo, I never did!" cried the girl, and undoubtedly believed it. "All I said was—"

"Never mind, Baby," said Warren, soothingly. "The point is, what's to be done? We can't stand here arguing, and we're soaked to the skin. I'm pretty sure the old what-not didn't recognise me, or any of us. . . ."

"You're positive of that?"

"Absolutely."

"Well, then," said Morgan, with a breath of relief, "the only thing to do is to shove the box inside his coat and leave him where he is. Every second we stay here we're in danger of being spotted, and then—whaa! I—er—don't suppose there's any danger of his rolling overboard, is there?" he added, doubtfully.

"Noooo, not a chance!" Captain Valvick assured him, with cheerful scorn. "He be all right where he iss. Ay fold him up against de bulkhead, Ha-ha-ha! Giff me de box, Miss Glenn. Ah, you shiver! You should not haf come out wi'out de coat. Now you giff me de box and go back where it iss warm. Dere iss not'ing to be afraid of now, because we haf—"

"*Captain Whistler,* sir!" cried a voice, almost directly above their heads.

Morgan's heart executed a somersault over a couple of rowdy lungs. He stared at the others, who were stricken silent, and stayed motionless without daring to look up. The voice seemed to have come from the top of the companionway to B deck, near which Warren and Valvick were standing. They were in shadow, but Morgan feared the worst. He glanced at Peggy, who was petrified, and who held the steel box like a bomb. He saw what was passing in her mind. She looked at the rail, as though she had a wild impulse to toss the box overboard, and he gestured a savage negative. Morgan felt something knocking at his ribs. . . .

"Captain Whistler, sir!" repeated the voice, more loudly. The sea battered back in answer. "I could've sworn," the voice continued, in tones which Morgan recognised as belonging to the second officer, "I heard something down there. What's happened to the old man, anyway? He said he'd be up. . . ." The rest of it was lost in the gale, until a second voice—it sounded like the ship's doctor—said:

"It sounded like a woman. I say, you don't suppose the old man's up to any funny business with the ladies, do you? Shall we go down?"

Feet scuffled on the iron companion-ladder, but the second officer said: "Never mind. It might've been imagination. We'll—"

And then, to the horror of the little group by the glass enclosure, the captain's corpse sat up.

"!!!!¾ ½ & £ !?!??°???" roared Captain Whistler—weakly it is true, and huskily, but with gathering volume as his sticky wits ceased to whirl. "!&£&/£/!" He gasped, he blinked, and then, as the full realisation smote him, he lifted shaking arms to heaven and set sòaring his soul in one hoarse blast: "!!!!&/£—!!?????&—&£/!!/?⅔¾⅓!? THIEVES! MURDERERS! HELP!"

"That's torn it," breathed Morgan, in a fierce whisper. "Quick! There's only one. . . . What are you doing?" he demanded, and stared at Peggy Glenn.

After saying, "Eiee!" the girl did not hesitate. Just behind her there was the porthole to somebody's cabin, open and fastened back. As the obliging boat rolled over to assist her aim, she flung the steel box inside. It was a dark cabin, and they heard the box bump down. Without looking at the others, who were staring aghast, she had turned to run, when Morgan caught her arm. . . .

"Gawd lummy!" said the ghostly voice from the top of the companionway, as though it were coming out of a trance, "that's the old man! Come on!"

Morgan was shooing his charges before him like chickens. He spoke so fast, under cover of the crashing swell, that he wondered if they heard him: "Don't try to run, you fatheads, or Whistler'll see you! He's still groggy. . . . Stick in the shadow, make a lot of noise with your feet as though you'd heard him and were running to help! Say something! Talk! Run about in circles. . . ."

It was an old detective-story trick, and he hoped it would work. Certainly their response was magnificent. To Captain Whistler, opening gummy eyes as he sat on the deck, it must have seemed that he was being rescued by a regiment of cavalry. The din was staggering especially Captain Valvick's realistic impersonation of a horse starting from far away and growing louder and more thunderous as it galloped near. Morgan's stout-hearted trio also cut the gale with such cries as, "What is it?" "What's wrong?" "Who's hurt?" They had timed themselves to spin round the forward bulkhead just as the second officer and the doctor came pelting up, their waterproofs swishing and the gilt ensigns on their caps gleaming out of the murk. There was silence while everybody clung to what was convenient, and several moments of hard breathing. The second officer, bending down, snapped on his flashlight. One good eye—undamaged, although the pickled-onion blaze of its pupil was distended horribly—one good eye smouldered and glared back at them out of a face which resembled a powerful piece of futurist painting. Captain Whistler was breathing hard. Morgan thought of the Cyclops, and also of incipient apoplexy. Captain Whistler sat on the wet deck, supporting himself with his hands behind him, and his cap was pushed back over his short white hair. He did not say anything. He was incapable, at that moment, of saying anything. He only breathed.

"Gor!" whispered the second officer.

There was another silence. Without removing his gaze from that terrifying face, the second officer beckoned behind him to the doctor. "I—er—" he faltered; "that is, what happened, sir?"

A certain terrible spasm and shiver twitched over the captain's face and chest, as though a volcano were trembling at its crust. But he still said nothing, and continued to wheeze noisily. His Cyclopean eye remained fixed.

"Come on, sir!" urged the second officer. "Let me help you up. You'll—er—catch cold. What happened?" he demanded, bewilderedly, turning to Morgan. "We heard—"

"So did we," agreed Morgan, "and came running when you did. I don't know what happened to him. He must have fallen off the bridge or something."

Among the dusky figures Peggy pressed forward. "It *is* Captain Whistler!" she wailed. "Oh, the poor dear! This is awful! Whatever can have happened to him? I say—" She seemed to have a shocking presentiment. Although she lowered her voice, there was only a hissing recoil of waters on the rise, and her shocked whisper to Warren carried clearly. "I say, I hope the poor man hasn't been drinking, has he?"

"What's that rattling on the deck?" demanded Warren, who was peering about him in the gloom. Following his glance, the uneasy second officer directed the beam of the flashlight down on the deck. . . .

"I—I do believe it's a whisky-bottle," said Peggy, earnestly contemplating the object that rolled there. "And —er—it seems to be empty. Oh, poor man!"

Morgan looked at her over his misted spectacles. A fair-minded person, he was bound to consider that this was laying it on a bit thick. Besides, he was momentarily afraid that Captain Whistler might have an apoplectic stroke. There were even richer hues blooming in the Cyclopean-eyed face; there were gurglings and rattlings and mysterious internal combustions which apparently defied nature. The second officer coughed.

"Come along, sir," he urged, soothingly. "Let me help you up, now. Then the doctor can—"

Captain Whistler found his voice.

"I WILL NOT GET UP!" he roared, gasping. "I AM PER-FECTLY SOBER!" But so violent was the steam pressure that it even blocked the escape-valve; he could only gurgle insanely, and the pain of his swollen jaw made him grimace and stop, clapping a hand to it. Yet one thought remained burning. "That bottle—that bottle. That's what they hit me with. I AM PERFECTLY SOBER, I TELL YOU. That's what they hit me with. There were three of 'em. Giants. They all jumped on me at once. And—my ele-phant. O, my God! what's happened to my elephant?" he demanded, galvanised suddenly. "They stole my elephant!

Don't stand there like a dummy, damn you! Do something. Look for it. Find that elephant or, strike me blind? I'll have the ticket of every crimson immoral landlubber on this. . . ."

There is no discipline like that of the British merchant service. The second officer stiffened and saluted. His not to reason why.

"Very good, sir. A search shall be instituted immediately, sir. It cannot have got far. In the meantime," he continued crisply, and turned to the others with a jealous safeguarding of the captain's reputation, "while the hunt for the commander's elephant is in progress, it is his instructions that all of you go below. Captain Whistler feels that it will be unnecessary for any of his guests to mention what has occurred to-night. . . . Let me help you up, sir."

"Sure thing," said Warren affably. "You can trust us. We'll keep quiet. If there's anything we can do—"

"But do you really think it's safe?" Peggy asked the second officer in some anxiety. "I mean, poor man, suppose he sees the elephant sitting up on top of the smokestack or something, making faces at him, and orders one of you to go and coax it down. . . ."

"Smell my breath!" cried the captain passionately. "Smell my breath, blast you; that's all I ask. I tell you I have not taken one single scarlet drink since five o'clock this evening."

"Look here," said the ship's doctor, who had been kneeling beside the anguished commander, "you people be sensible. He's not—upset. He's quite all right, Baldwin. There's something very queer going on here. Steady on, sir; we'll have you feeling top-notch in a moment. . . . We can get you up to your room without anybody seeing you, you know. . . . No?" Evidently Captain Whistler's soul shrank from encountering passengers or crew at that instant. "Well, then, there's a recess forward here on the leeward side, with some tables and chairs. If Mr. Baldwin will hold the flashlight I've got my bag. . . ."

This, Morgan felt, was the psychological moment for a retreat. The real object in remaining so long had been to ascertain definitely whether Captain Whistler had recognised his assailant. And it seemed they were safe. But he felt that suspicion was growing in the air. The doctor's sharp words had roused the first officer, who now seemed uneasy, and glanced several times at them. Doctor and officer were hoisting up their commander. . . .

"Wait a minute!" shouted Whistler, as there began to be a general melting-away of spectators. The good eye glared. "Hold on, there, you, whoever you are! You thought I was drunk, did you? Well, I'll show you! I want to ask you a lot of questions in a very few minutes. Stop where you are. I'll show you how drunk—"

"But look here, Captain," protested Warren, "we're wet through! *We'll* stay, if you like, but let this young lady go back to her cabin—to get a coat, anyway. She hasn't got a coat! There's no reason why she should stay, is there? None of us can run away and—"

"YOU'LL TELL ME WHAT TO DO, WILL YOU?" said the captain, his chest swelling. "YOU'LL GIVE ORDERS ABOARD MY SHIP, WILL YOU? Haa! Strike me blind! There! Now just for that, my lad, you'll all stop exactly where you are; you won't move as much as a fraction of an inch from where you are, or sink me! I'll put the whole crew of you under arrest! Sink me! I'll put *everybody* under arrest, that's what I'll do. And when I find the so-and-so who hit me with a bottle and stole that emerald—"

"Don't!" Morgan said to Warren in a fierce whisper, as he saw the other lowering his head curiously and shutting up one eye as he regarded Captain Whistler, "for the love of God don't say anything, Curt! In another minute he'll be making us walk the plank. Steady."

"You won't move," pursued Captain Whistler wildly, lifting up his hands, squinting at them, and holding them a fraction of an inch apart before his face, "you won't move so much as *that* distance from where you are. You won't even move that far. You won't stir. You won't— Who was that who spoke?" he broke off to demand. "Who's there anyway? Who are you? What was that about a coat? Who had the nerve to ask me something about a blasted coat, eh?"

"My name's Warren, Captain. Curtis Warren. You know me. I hope you don't think *I'm* the crook you're after?"

Whistler stopped, stared, and seemed tumultuously to reflect.

"Ah!" he said in a curious tone. "Warren, hey? Warren. Well, well! And who is with you?" When three voices spoke up simultaneously he took on a grim but rather nervous tone. "Stay where you are now! Don't move. . . . Mr. Baldwin, you watch them. I mean, watch *him*. You've been wandering round the boat, have you, Mr. Warren? And what's that on your head? Come into the light. Sticking plaster. Oh, yes. You hurt your head. . . ."

Warren made a gesture. "Yes, I did. And that's what I want to tell you. If you won't let us go, at least send somebody back to my cabin. Send the doctor, you old fool! You're all right. Send the doctor, I tell you. There's a young girl back there—unconscious—maybe dead—I don't know. Have some sense, can't you? She's been hit over the head and knocked unconscious. . . ."

"What?"

"Yes. Somebody cracked her over the head and then—"

Between them, the doctor and the second officer got the captain away to a sheltered recess, where he did not stop talking. He would hear of nothing, not a step or a movement. He insisted that the four conspirators should remain within reach of the eye of Mr. Baldwin, who was holding up the flashlight for the repair-work. So they huddled against a glass front that was stung with whips of rain; Warren took off his coat and wrapped it round the girl, and they took whispered communion.

"Listen," said Morgan, peering over his shoulder to make sure they were out of earshot. "We're going to be jolly lucky if we don't get shoved in the brig. Scuttle my hatches, the old man's raving. He's insane, and you don't want to cross him. What fathead dropped that whisky-bottle beside him, anyway?"

"Ay did," replied Captain Valvick, thumping his chest. He beamed proudly. "Ay t'ank dat was a touch of yenius, eh? What iss wrong? Dere wass no more whisky in it, honest. Eh, eh; you t'ink dere be fingerprints on it, maybe?"

Warren frowned and ran a hand through his goblin hair. "Say, Hank," he muttered uneasily, "that's an idea. If it occurs to the old boy. . . . And there's another thing. Baby, what possessed you to fire that box through the porthole of somebody's cabin?"

She was indignant. "Well, I like that! With those officers coming down on us—you didn't want me to chuck it overboard, did you? Besides, I think it was a splendid idea. It can't be blamed on us, and it won't be blamed on anybody else. I don't know whose cabin that was. But there'll be a hunt for the box. And then whoever has the cabin will wake up to-morrow morning and find it on the floor; then he'll take it to the captain and explain it was thrown through the porthole, and there you are."

"Well," said Warren, drawing a deep breath, "all I can say is that we had a piece of luck. I tell you, I damn near died when you did that. I had visions of somebody sticking his head out the porthole just as those officers were coming up, and saying, 'Hey, what's the idea of throwing things through my window?' "

He brooded, staring out through the glass at the murky night ahead, dimly luminous from the glow above on the bridge; at the sharp bows shouldering up in mist; at the white torrent that poured, swirled, and fell away round stubborn winches. From far above smote the clang of the liner's bell—*one-two, one-two, one-two*—that is the drowsiest of sea noises by night. The wind had a flat whine now; it was dying, and rain had ceased to tick on the glass. Stately as a galleon, the tall foremast rose, swung, and tilted as the bows smashed down again into a fan of spray. . . .

Warren glared straight ahead.

"I've let you people in for all this," he said in a low voice. "I'm—I'm damned sorry."

"Dat iss de bunk, son," said Captain Valvick. "Ay ain't had so much fun in a long time. De only t'ing, we got to agree on a story dat we are all going to tell. . . ."

"I got you into this," continued Warren doggedly, "and I'm going to get you out. Don't worry about that. You let me do the talking, and I'll convince him. There's nothing wrong with my diplomatic talents. I very, very seldom go off half-cocked"—Morgan coughed but the other obviously believed what he was saying, so nobody spoke—"and I'll fix it. All that burns me up—" declared Warren, lifting a heavy fist high and bringing it down on the rail—"all that makes me burn and sizzle with bright murderous flames is that there really is a lousy, low-down, black-jack-using crook aboard this tub, and he's giving us the merry horse laugh right now. Goroo! This was made to order for him. And I'm mad now. I'm good and mad. I'll catch him. I'll get him, if it's the last thing I ever do, and if I have to sit up every night and wait for him to come after that fi—"

He stopped, stiffening, as an idea struck him. Slowly he turned round a lean, hollow-eyed, startled face.

"Film!" he said, clutching at the ends of his spiked hair. "Film! In my cabin. The rest of it. Unguarded! The rest of poor old Uncle Warpus's speech, and he's probably pinching it right now. . . ."

Before anybody could stop him, he had whirled round and was stumbling back towards his cabin along the slippery deck.

"Curt!" said Morgan, with a groan which ended deep in his stomach. "Listen! Hey! Come back! The captain—"

Over his shoulder Warren called out a suggested course of action for the captain. Whistler was out of his alcove at a bound and trumpeting. He shouted to the second officer to follow; then he stood and gibbered while Baldwin pursued the flying shirt-sleeved figure down the deck. Warren got inside the door, and Baldwin after him. In vain stout Valvick attempted to pacify his fellow skipper. Captain Whistler, *imprimis,* objected to being addressed as "barnacle," and described horrible surgical tortures he would like to perform. He was in no better mood when presently Warren, with Second-Officer Baldwin keeping a firm grip on his arm, emerged from the door. Warren seemed to be expostulating as they skidded back down the deck.

"But haven't you got any heart?" he demanded. "All I ask you to do, one little thing, is go into that next cabin and see whether that poor girl is alive—whether she needs help—whether—Or let *me* go. But no. I've got a good mind," said Warren, closing one fist with a meditative air, "to—"

"What was he up to?" Whistler demanded eagerly, as the culprit was led up. "Why did he bolt?"

A very harassed-looking Baldwin regarded Warren in some uneasiness.

"I don't know, sir. He rushed in 'is own cabin, and when I got there he was kneeling on the floor throwing motion-picture films over his shoulder and saying, 'Gone! Gone!'"

"Yes," agreed Warren. Wryly he shook his head as he glanced from Peggy to Morgan. "The little joker's been there in the meantime. He's swiped it all right."

"What is gone, young man?" inquired Captain Whistler.

A little of the first shock of rage had gone from him. He was still in a thrice-dangerous mood, but the insult of the attack had been partly put aside in favour of appalling reflections as to its consequences. Evidently what bulked large in the captain's rather small brain, larger than whisky-bottles or upper-cuts, was the fact that an emerald trinket worth fifty thousand pounds had been stolen while in his possession. And Lord Sturton had a crusty reputation. Captain Whistler savagely waved aside the doctor, who had not yet completed his ministrations. A few strips of sticking-plaster lent an even subtler Cézanne touch to his purple countenance; he narrowed his good right eye, squared his shoulders, and repeated with hoarse control of his temper: "What is gone, young man?"

"I can't tell you," returned Warren. "And anyway it's not important. To you, anyway. It doesn't concern whatever he stole from you. All I would beg and plead of you, if you have any heart, is don't let that poor girl lie there, maybe dying. . . !"

"Mr. Warren," said the skipper, with a tense and sinister calmness, "I *will* have some sense out of this. . . . I will start at the beginning, and I will tell you that there is known to be aboard this ship a dangerous criminal who has stolen from me an object of enormous value. . . ."

"Ay told you, Barnacle," interposed Valvick, shaking his head gloomily—"ay told you it be better to post a notice and warn all de people. Now look at what iss done."

"NEVER YOU MIND WHAT YOU TOLD ME, SIR. You keep out of this, Sharkmeat. You stow your t'g'lant-royals and come off the high and mighty when you talk to me, Sharkmeat. I remember the time—" He caught himself up. "Hurrum! No matter, I will continue, Mr. Warren. You are the nephew of a very distinguished gentleman and were confided especially to my care. I have read Mr. Morgan's stories; he has travelled with me before, and I know him. Captain Valvick, God knows, I am familiar with. I am not drunk or mad, sir. I do not believe that any of you is this notorious criminal. Kindly understand that. But I do believe, Mr. Warren, that from the time Miss Glenn told me about you at dinner to-night, you have been guilty of very odd behaviour. Now, when you tell me about a young lady who has received an injury to the back of her head, I insist on hearing your full story."

"Right!" said Warren, with the air of one coming to an agreement. "That's fair enough, Skipper, and here you are. We don't know anything about the attack on you. It happened this way. We were all together, you see, when this unknown girl staggered in, badly hurt. We knew somebody had hit her, so we rushed out to see whether we could find the assailant. While we were on deck we heard your yell—"

("Not bad for a start," thought Morgan uneasily. "Steady now.")

"I see," said the captain. "And where were you then?"

"Eh?"

"I said," repeated the captain, looking so curiously like the headmaster at old St. Just's that Morgan shivered a little, "where were you when this alleged unknown woman came in? You weren't in your cabin. I looked in there and I know."

"Oh! Oh! I see! No, of course not," Warren answered, with some heat. "Naturally not. We were in the empty cabin next door."

"Why?"

"Why? Well—er—well, it was just an idea, you see. A kind of idea I had. I mean," said Warren, his wits clicking out words desperately in the hope of finding the right ones, "I mean, I thought it would be a good idea. Anyway, we *were* there, damn it! You can ask any of them. They were sort of taking care of me. . . ."

"Taking care of you," repeated Captain Whistler heavily. "And what were you doing there?"

"Well, we were sitting on the floor playing Geography. And then we heard the door to C deck open, and this girl who was attacked started calling my name. I don't know who she is; I only saw her once before," pursued Warren, acquiring greater assurance and fluency as he hurried on, "and that was in the wireless-room, when I got the cablegram about—euh!—I mean, when I got the cablegram—about the bears, you see."

"What bears?"

Warren's jaws moved. He glanced wildly at Morgan for assistance.

"Its quite all right, Captain," the latter explained as smoothly as he could. He had a lump in his throat and a feeling that if Warren kept on explaining he would go insane himself. "Naturally Curt's a bit upset, and I suppose he tells things in rather an odd way. But it's quite simple, after all. It's about some stocks—you understand. The bears were raiding the market, you see, and his stocks had depreciated."

"Oh! He's been worried about financial matters has he? Yes, yes," said the captain heavily. "But let's come down to terms, Mr. Morgan? Do *you* vouch for the truth of this crazy story?"

"Go and see, why don't you?" shouted the exasperated Warren. "That's what I've been asking you to do from the first, if you'd had any sense. Here you're keeping Miss Glenn shivering in my coat, and all of us standing out here on a zero deck when that poor girl may be dying. Aren't you coming, Doctor?"

"We are all coming," said the captain, with sudden decision. He beckoned his two subordinates, and the weird little procession went down to the door. Warren tugged it open, while they all piled through; a pale-faced Peggy, trembling and breathing deeply in the warm air. For a moment they blinked against the light.

"All right, there you are," said Warren, himself shivering as he stood against the wall of the white passage. "There's where she got caught in the door. You see the blood on the rubber matting. . . ."

The captain looked at him.

"Blood? What blood? I don't see any blood."

There was none, although Morgan knew it had been there. He took off his spectacles, wiped them, and looked again without result. And again he felt in the pit of his stomach that uneasy sensation that behind this foolery there was moving something monstrous and deadly.

"But—!" said Warren desperately. He stared at the captain, and then threw open the door of the state-room beside his.

The light in the roof was burning. The berth on which they had laid the injured girl was empty; the pillow was not disarranged, or the tucked-back sheets wrinkled. There was not even the smeared towel with which Peggy had wiped blood from the girl's face. A fresh towel, white and undisturbed, swung from the rack of the washstand.

"Yes?" said Captain Whistler stormily. "I'm waiting."

Chapter 7

Into Which Cabin?

IN its own way that was the beginning. It was the mere prospect of an empty bed and a clean towel, not in themselves especially alarming things, which sent through Morgan a sense of fear such as he had not known even in the past during the case of the Eight of Swords, or was to know in the future during the case of the Two Hangmen. He tried to tell himself that this was absurd and was a part of the crack-brain comedy on C deck.

It wasn't. Afterwards he realised that what had struck him first was something about the position of those sheets. . . .

During the brief moment of silence while they all looked into the white state-room, he thought of many things. That girl—he saw again her straight, heavy, classic face, with its strong eyebrows, twitching and blood-smeared against the pillow—that girl *had* been here. There was no question about that. Ergo, there were three explanations of why she was not here now.

She might have recovered consciousness, found herself alone in a strange cabin, and left it for her own. This sounded thin, especially as her injury had been severe and as a normal person on recovering consciousness would have called for help, kicked up a row, rung for the steward, at least shown sign of weakness or curiosity. But there was an even stronger reason. Before leaving the cabin, she would not have remade the bed. She would not carefully have put on *fresh sheets and a pillow-case,* in addition to disposing of a soiled towel and hanging another exactly in its place. Yet this had been done. Morgan remembered that, as they put her down, there had been spots of blood flicked on the sheet. He remembered that a lurch of the ship had caused the contents of a whisky-glass to soak the pillow and a part of the top sheet. The bed had been remade! but why and by whom?

The second explanation was a piece of fantasy which even Morgan doubted. Suppose the girl had been acting? Suppose she was in league with their friend the joker; that she had only pretended being hurt to distract their attention while somebody rifled Warren's cabin? Ridiculous or not, that film had very dangerous potentialities in countries where it is not considered humorous to direct raspberries at the Chancellor. The world wags, and Progress brings back the solemn nonsense of autocracy. In England or the United States the thing would be regarded with levity, as the sort of diplomatic howler often perpetrated by a Tophat; but elsewhere—? Still, Morgan did not believe in any such abstruse plot. Aside from the fact that the joker could gain very little freedom of movement merely because he had got a woman to sham injuries in the next cabin, there was the question of the girl's condition. The dangerous contusion along the skull, the blood of a real cerebral hæmorrhage, the white eyeballs uprolled in unconsciousness, were not feigned. She had been hurt, and badly hurt.

The third explanation he did not like to think of. But he was afraid of it. It was five miles, they said, to the bottom of the sea. As he saw weird images in the stuffy little cabin, he felt a jerk of relief—yes, in a way—that Peggy Glenn had disregarded orders and had not stayed at the bedside. *Somebody* would have come in and found her there.

These thoughts were so rapid that Captain Whistler had spoken no more than one sinister sentence before Morgan turned round. The captain, his fat figure hunched into a waterproof, had lowered his head nearly into the collar. Under the full electric light the colours of his swollen face were even more of the paint-palette variety, especially the left eye that had closed up behind a purpling hatch. He knew that they were looking at this, and it made him madder still.

"Well?" he said. "What kind of a joke is this? Where's the woman you said was dying? Where's the woman you begged me to help? Blast my compass with lightning! What's your idea in wasting my time when there's fifty thousand pounds' worth of emeralds stolen somewhere on this ship? There's nobody in that bunk. There's *been* nobody in that bunk." A ghoulish thought seemed to strike him. "You don't tell me there's anybody there now, do you? Come on, young man; you don't seriously think you see anybody there now, do you?"

He backed away a little, his eyes on Warren.

"Barnacle," said Captain Valvick violently, "dere iss no yoke. Ay tell you he iss right! Ay saw her—ay have my fingers on her head. Ay carry her in here. She wass—" Words failed him. He strode over, seized the pillow out of the berth and shook it. He peered under the berth, and then into the one above. "Coroosh! You don't t'ink we are in de wrong place, do you?"

Peggy, who had been stretching her arms out of Warren's loose blue coat to push the hair from her eyes, seized the captain's arm.

"It's true, Captain. Oh, can't you see it's true? Do you think we could have been mistaken about a thing like that? There's my compact, see? I left it on the couch. She was here. I saw her. I touched her. Maybe she just woke up and left. She had on a yellow crêpe de chine frock, a dark green coat with—"

Captain Whistler inspected each one of them with his good eye and then shut it up. Then he passed the back of his hand across his forehead.

"I don't know what to make of you," he said. "So help me Harry! I don't. Forty years I've been at sea, thirteen in sail and seventeen in steam, and I never saw the beat of it. Mr. Baldwin!"

"Sir!" answered the second officer, who had been standing outside the door with a blank expression on his face. "Yes, sir?"

"Mr. Baldwin, what do *you* make of all this?"

"Well, sir," replied Mr. Baldwin doubtfully, "it's all these elephants and bears that bothers me, sir. Not knowing, can't say; but I'd got a bit of a notion we were trying to round up a bleeding Zoo."

"I don't want to hear anything about elephants and bears, Mr. Baldwin. WILL YOU SHUT UP ABOUT ELEPHANTS AND BEARS? I asked you a plain question and I want a plain answer. What do you think of this story about the woman?"

Mr. Baldwin hesitated. "Well, sir, they can't *all* be loonies, now, can they?"

"I don't know," said the captain, inspecting them. "My God! I think I must be going mad, if they're not. I know all of them—I don't think they're crooks—I know they wouldn't steal fifty thousand pounds' worth of emeralds. And yet look here." He reached over and touched the berth. "Nobody's lain on that, I'll swear, if there was the blood they say. Where's the towel they say they used, hey? Where's the blood they say was outside the door? The woman didn't change the linen on that bed and walk off with the towel, did she?"

"No," said Morgan, looking straight at him. "But somebody else might have. I'm not joking, Captain. Somebody else might have."

"You, too, eh?" said Whistler, with the air of one whom nothing surprises now. "You, too?"

"The whole bed was changed, Captain, that's all. And I'm just wondering why. Look here—it won't take a second. Lift off that bedding and look underneath at the mattress."

This, allied with Morgan's absent expression as he blinked at the bed, was too much for the captain's grim-faced attempt to listen to everybody's side of the case. He picked up the pillow and slammed it down on the berth.

"I'll do no such damn fool thing, sir!" he said in what started to be a bellow but trailed off as he remembered where he was. "I've had about enough of this. You may be right or you may not. I won't argue, but I've got more important things to attend to. To-night I'm going to call a conference and start one of the finest-toothed-comb searches that you ever heard of on sea or land. That elephant's aboard, and, strike me blind, I'll find it if I have to take this tub apart one plate from another. That's what *I'm* going to do. And to-morrow morning every passenger will come under my personal observation. I'm master here, and I can search the cabin of anybody I like. That's what *I'm* going to do. Now, if you'll kindly get out of my way—"

"Look here, Skipper," said Morgan, "I admit we wouldn't be much help, but why don't we join forces?"

"Join forces?"

"Like this. I admit appearances are against us. We've told you a story you don't believe, and nearly given you apoplexy. But in all seriousness, there's a very sound reason behind everything. It's a big thing—bigger than you know. And why don't you believe us?"

"I believe," said the captain grimly, "what I see and hear, that's all."

"Yes, I know. That's what I'm kicking about," the other nodded. He got out his pipe and absently knocked the bowl against his palm. "But we don't. If we did, what do you suppose we should have thought when we walked up and found you sitting bunged-up and gibbering on a wet deck, with an empty whisky-bottle beside you and babbling wildly about your lost elephant?"

"I WAS PERFECTLY SOBER," said the captain. "If any illegitimate lubber," said the captain, lifting a shaking arm . . . "if any illigitimate lubber refers again to what was pure misfortune—"

"I know it was, sir. Of course it was. But it's six of one and half a dozen of the other, don't you see? The misfortunes are precisely alike. Symbolically speaking, as Mr. Baldwin says, they are elephants and bears. And if you insist on having your elephants, why shouldn't you allow Curt his bears?"

"I don't understand this," said the captain dazedly. "I'm a plain man, sir, and I like plain speaking. What are you getting at? What do you want?"

"Only this. If I were to sit down at the breakfast table to-morrow morning and tell only what I had *seen* to-night —Oh, I don't say I *would,* of course," said Morgan, assuming a shocked expression and also closing one eye significantly. "I only use the illustration as an example, you understand—"

This was the sort of plain speaking the captain clearly comprehended. For a moment his head rose in appalling wrath out of the collar of the waterproof.

"Are you," he said thickly, "trying to blackmail—"

It took all Morgan could do, with a swift tactical change, to smooth him down. But it was like a shrewd lawyer's inadmissable question to the witness at a trial which the judge orders the jury to disregard: the suggestion had been put forth, and the effect made. An effect had been made, unquestionably, on the captain.

"I didn't mean anything," Morgan insisted. "Lord knows, we won't be much help. But all I wish you'd do is this. We're as interested as you are in catching this crook. If you'd keep us posted as to any developments—"

"I don't see any reason why I shouldn't," growled the other after a pause, during which he cleared his throat several times. Whistler's eye and jaw were paining him considerably, as Morgan observed; it was much to his credit that he could keep his temper down to a simmering point. Still, ramifications were beginning to suggest themselves to him, and it was apparent that he did not like them. "I don't see any reason why I shouldn't. I tell you straight, right here and now, to-morrow morning I'm going to haul all of you up to Lord Sturton and make you tell him the story you told me. If it weren't so late, I'd take you all up now. Oh, you'll be in it, right enough. . . .

"I'll tell you frankly, Mr. Warren," he added, in a rather different tone, and swung round on him, "that if it weren't for your uncle, you certainly wouldn't get the consideration you are getting. And I'll be fair. I'll give this cock-and-bull story of yours a chance."

"Thanks," said Warren dryly. "And I can take my oath Uncle Warpus will appreciate it if you do. And how?"

"Mr. Baldwin!"

"Sir?"

"Make a note of this. To-morrow morning you will institute an inquiry, with whatever reason or pretext you like, to find out whether any passenger on this boat got an injury along the lines you've heard described. Be discreet, burn you! or I'll have your stripes. Then report to Mr. Morgan. Now I've done all I can for you," he snapped, turning round, "and I'll bid you good night. But, mind I expect co-operation. CO-OPERATION. I've done a good deal already, and if so much as one word of all this is breathed, God help you! . . . And you want to know the truth, Mr. Warren," said Captain Whistler, his Cyclops eye suddenly bulging past all control, "I think you're mad, sir. I THINK YOU'RE STARK, RAVING MAD, and these people are shielding you. One more questionable action, sir, just one more questionable action, and into a strait-waistcoat you go. That's all !!!'&—£&&'''£&£⅔¼⅔¾⅛!!!???! . . . Good night."

The door closed with a dignified slam, and they were alone.

Brooding, Morgan stared at the floor and chewed at the stem of his empty pipe. Besides, his eyes would keep wandering to the berth; and he did not like to think of that. The *Queen Victoria* was pitching less heavily now, so that you could feel the monotonous vibration of the screw. Morgan felt cold and unutterably tired. He jumped as voices began to sing and glanced up dully. Peggy Glenn and Curtis Warren, with seraphic expressions on their faces (at two o'clock in the morning) had their heads together and their arms round each other's shoulders; they were swaying slowly as they uplifted throats in harmony:

> *"Oh, a life on the ocean wave* [sang these worthies]
> *A ho-ome on the ro-olling deep . . . !*
> *A life on the ocean wave . . ."*

"Shut it, will you?" said Morgan, as Captain Valvick uttered a hoot of approval and joined his unmusical bass to the chorus. "Aside from the fact that there are people hereabouts trying to sleep, you'll have the captain back in here."

This threat quieted them in the middle of a bar. But they shook hands all around, gleefully, and Warren insisted on shaking Morgan's hand in a shoulder-cracking grip. The Englishman studied them: Valvick draping himself affably over the washstand, and Peggy and Warren chortling on the berth. He wondered if they had any idea what had really happened. He also wondered if it would be wise to tell them.

"Boy," said Warren in admiration, "I don't mind telling you it was a swell piece of work. It was great. It was *the nuts*." He waggled his hand high in the air and brought it down on his knee. "That crack about elephants and bears, and the horrible threat to spill the beans on that incorrigible souse, Captain Whistler . . . yee! Great! You are hereby elected Brains of this concern. Henceforth anything you say goes. As for me, I'm going to be good, and how. You heard what the old sea-terrier said."

"Au, sure," agreed Valvick, with a ponderous gesture. "But it iss going to be all right in de morning. He find de emerald. Whoever hass de cabin where Miss Peggy t'row it in iss going to wake up in de morning and see it. And dere you be."

Warren sat up, impressed by this new thought. "By the way, Baby, whose cabin *did* you throw it in, anyway?"

"How should I know?" she asked, rather defensively. "I don't know who has every cabin on the deck. It was just a convenient porthole, and I sort of obeyed the impulse. What difference does it make?"

"Well, I was only wondering. . . ." He peered at the light, at a corner of the roof, at the wardrobe door. "I—that is, I don't suppose by any chance you heaved it on somebody to whom it would—er—prove a temptation?"

"Caroosh!" said Captain Valvick.

By one accord they looked at Morgan. The latter would have immensely enjoyed the throne to which this trio of genial idiots had elected him, that of Brains in the combine to catch the joker, if it were not for that disturbing, nagging doubt which was apparently shared by none of his lieutenants. He did not want to examine that berth, and yet he knew he must. Meanwhile his lieutenants—ready to go off at any new tangent, and obsessed now with a thought which had nothing to do with the main problem —were regarding him in expectancy.

"Well," he said rather wearily, "if you really want to know whose cabin it is, that ought to be easy. Pick out the cabin that's attached to the porthole in which you threw that box (am I making myself clear?) and spot its number. Then look up the number in the passenger-list, and there you are. . . . What porthole did you throw it through, Peggy?"

The girl opened her mouth eagerly and shut it again. Her brows contracted. She wriggled, as though to assist thought.

"Dash it!" she said in a small voice. "I think—well, honestly, I don't remember."

Chapter 8

Blood Under a Blanket

WARREN hopped up.

"But, Baby," he protested, "you've *got* to remember. Why shouldn't you remember? It's a cinch: there's a row of portholes, and they're all near the companionway on the starboard side. All right. You were standing near one, and all you've got to do is remember which one. Besides —" A new aspect of the matter struck him. "Say, I never thought of it before, but this is terrible! Suppose by some chance you slung that box into the *criminal's* cabin? By Jiminy!" said Warren, now almost convinced that this was the case, "he's got away with a lot, but I won't stand for this! I've got a score to settle with that guy. . . ."

"Son," said Morgan, "permit me to suggest that we have enough difficulties on our hands without your imagining fresh ones. That's foolish! You're only getting the wind up about nothing."

"Yes, I know, but it bothers me," returned Warren, moving his neck uncomfortably. "The thought of that fellow getting away with a thing like that would make me wild. After he's walked in as easy as pie, and stolen my film, to have us deliberately hand him the emerald elephant as well! . . . Baby, you've got to remember which porthole it was! Then, if we went down to that cabin and sort of busted down the door, you see, and said, 'Hey, you! . . .'"

Morgan lowered his head to cool it, and swallowed hard in a dry throat. Never before had he seen the true extent of American energy.

"So now," he said, "so now you want to go around breaking down doors, do you? Kindly reflect a moment, Curt. Consider what you have already done to Captain Whistler's blood pressure. You fathead, why don't you go up and smash down the captain's door and get put into a strait-waistcoat and have done with it? You said I was to give the orders, and I'm giving some now. You're to stop absolutely quiet. Do you understand?"

"Ay haf an idea," volunteered Captain Valvick, who was scratching his short sandy hair. "Coroosh! Ay yust t'ink of it. Suppose de port where you t'row dat elephant wass in de cabin of dat English duke which own de elephant in de first place? Corrrsh! But he iss going to be surprised if he wake up in de morning and find it dere. Maybe he t'ink Captain Whistler hass got mad at him for somet'ing and come down in de night and t'row dat elephant back at him t'rough de port."

"No, that won't work," said Warren. "Old Sturton's got a suite on B deck. But we've got to find out who does sleep in that cabin. Think. Baby! Get your brain working."

Peggy's face was screwed up with intense concentration. She made slow gestures to bring the scene back.

"I've got it now," she said. "Yes, I'm sure. It was either the second or third porthole from the end of the wall where we were standing. They look so much alike and *you* ought to remember it yourself. But it was either the second or third porthole."

"You're absolutely sure of that, are you?"

"Yes, I am. I won't say which one, but I'll swear it was one of those two."

"Den dass all right," rumbled Valvick, nodding. "Ay go out right now and find de numbers on dem cabins, and we look it up in de passenger-list. Also ay got anudder bottle of Old Rob Roy in my locker, and ay get it and we out of it a nightcap haff, hey? Yumping Yudas, but ay am t'irsty! Hold on. Ay won't be a minute."

Morgan protested in vain. The captain insisted that he would only be a minute, and went out foraging, with the approval of the other two lieutenants.

". . . Also," Morgan continued, turning to them when Valvick had gone, "what the devil's the use of bothering about that emerald now? Has it occurred to you what happened in this place to-night? What about that woman? What happened to *her*?"

Warren made a savage gesture. "I've got it all figured

out," he snapped. "I knew it the minute we came back in here, but I didn't very well see how I could tell old Popeye. We've been outsmarted, that's what. They got us to fall for that as neat as you please, and it's another thing that makes me mad. . . . Why, that girl was our crook's accomplice, don't you see? They arranged it between them for her to pull a fake faint, calling my name, mind you—which wasn't natural to begin with. . . ."

"And you don't think the injury was real?"

"Of course it wasn't real. I read a story once about a bird who could suddenly make funny noises and go into a cataleptic fit, and while the doctor was poking him his gang came in and robbed the doctor's house. I thought it was a low-down dirty trick at the time; but that's what they've done. Yes, and don't you remember in your own books, in *Aconite in the Admiralty?* where that detective what's-his-name gets into the master criminal's luxurious den in Downing Street, and they think they've stabbed him with the poisoned needle?"

"The literary formula," agreed Morgan, "is excellent. Still, I doubt it in this case. Granted that the crook was watching us, knew where we were, and all that, I don't see how it would help him much. He knew we'd certainly take the girl into one of these two cabins, so it wouldn't be much easier. It was only chance in old Whistler's coming in when he did, so that we were dragged away and the crook had a clear field."

Peggy also refused to listen to this line of argument. Warren had got out a damp package of cigarettes, and he and Peggy lit one while Morgan filled his pipe. The girl said, between short puffs, as though she were rather angrily trying to get rid of the smoke:

"But, I say, it's going to be *easy* now, isn't it? It was rather a dreadful bloomer on their part, wasn't it? Because we shall know that girl when we see her again, and then we've got 'em. She wasn't disguised, you know. She hardly had any make-up on, even. That reminds me—my compact. Give it me, Curt. I say I must look a sight! Anyway, we can't miss her. She's still aboard the boat."

"Is she?" said Morgan. "I wonder."

Warren, who was about to make some impatient comment, glanced up and saw the other's expression. He took the cigarette out of his mouth; his eyes grew curiously fixed.

"What—what's on your mind, General?"

"Only that Peggy's right in one sense. If that girl was an accomplice, then the thing would be too easy, much too easy for us. On the other hand, if that girl had been coming here to try to warn you about something. . . . I know you didn't know her, but let's suppose that's what she was doing. . . . Then the thief gets after her and thinks he's done the business. But he hasn't. Then—"

The droning engines seemed to vibrate loud above creaking woodwork, because the wind had died outside, deep tumult was subsiding, and the *Queen Victoria* was rolling almost gently as though she were exhausted by the gale. All of them were relaxed; but it did not help their nerves. Peggy jumped then as the door opened and Captain Valvick returned with the passenger-list in one hand and a quart of Old Rob Roy in the other.

"Ay told you ay only be a minute," he announced. "It wass easy to find de ports, and den de cabin numbers from inside. One is C 51 and the other C 46. Ay t'ank. . . . Hey?" he said, peering at the strained faces in the room. "What iss de matter, hey?"

"Nothing," said Morgan. "Not for a minute, anyhow. Come on, now. Set your minds at rest. You wanted to know. Find out who occupies those cabins first, and then we can go on."

With a jerk of her head, still looking at him, Peggy took the passenger-list. On the point of speaking, she said nothing, and opened the list instead. But she rose and sat on the couch this time. Under cover of Captain Valvick's talk, Warren helped him take the extra glasses off the rack and pour drinks. They all glanced furtively at Morgan, who had begun to wonder whether he were merely flourishing a turnip ghost. He lit his pipe during a queer silence while Peggy ran her finger down the list, and the ship's engines beat monotonously. . . .

"Well?" said Warren.

"Wait a bit, old boy. This takes time. . . . Mmmm. Gar—Gran—Gulden—Harris—mmm—Hooper, Isaacs mm, no—Jarvis, Jerome. . . . I say, I hope I haven't missed it; Jeston, Ka-Kedler—Kennedy. . . . Hullo!" She breathed a line of smoke past her cigarette, and glanced up with wide eyes. "What was it, skipper? C 46? Righto! Here it is. "C 46 *Kyle, Dr. Oliver Harrison.*" Fancy that! Dr. Kyle has one of those cabins. . . ."

Warren whistled.

"Kyle, eh? Not bad. Whoa! Wait a bit," said the diplomat. He struck the bulkhead. "My God! wasn't he one of the suspects? Yes, I remember now. This crook is probably masquerading. . . ."

With difficulty Morgan shut him up, for more and more was Warren impressed by the general rightness and poetic reasonableness of a crook with a taste for using the blackjack adopting the guise of a distinguished Harley Street physician. His views were based on the forthright principle that, the more respectable they looked, the more likely they were to turn out dastardly murderers. He also cited examples from the collected works of Henry Morgan in which the authors of the dirty work had proved to be (respectively) an admiral, a rose-grower, an invalid, and an archdeacon. It was only when Peggy protested that this was merely the case in detective stories that Morgan took his side.

"That's just where you're wrong, old girl," he said. "It's in real life that the crooks and killers always go in the most solidly respectable dress. Only, you see them at the wrong end—in the dock. You think of them as a murderer, not as the erstwhile churchgoing occupant of Number 13 Laburnum Grove. Whisper softly to yourself the names of the most distinguished croakers of a century, and observe that nearly all of them were highly esteemed by the vicar. Constance Kent? Dr. Pritchard? Christina Edmunds? Dr. Lamson? Dr. Crippen—"

"And nearly all of 'em doctors, eh?" inquired Warren, with an air of sinister enlightenment. He seemed to brood over this incorrigible tendency among members of the medical profession to go about murdering people. "You see, Peggy? Hank's right."

"Don't be a lop-eared ass," said Morgan. "Wash out this idea of Dr. Kyle's being a crook, will you? He's a very well-known figure . . . oh, and get rid of the notion, too, that somebody may be impersonating him while the real Dr. Kyle is dead. That may be all right for some person who never comes in contact with anybody; but a public figure like an eminent physician won't do. . . . Go on, Peggy. Tell us who's in C 51, and then we can forget it and get down to real business."

She wrinkled her forehead.

"Here we are, and this is odd, too. 'C 51. *Perrigord, Mr. and Mrs. Leslie.*' So-ho!"

"What's odd about that? Who are they?"

"You remember my telling you about a very, very great highbrow and æsthete who was aboard, and had written reams of ecstatic articles about Uncle Jules's genius? And I said I hoped for his sake as well as the kids who wanted to see the fighting that there'd be a performance to-morrow night?"

"Ah! Perrigord?"

"Yes. Both he and she are awfully æsthetic, you know. He writes poetry—you know, the kind you can't understand, all about his soul being like a busted fencer-rail or something. And I believe he's a dramatic critic, too, although you can't make much sense out of what he writes there, either. *I* can't anyway. But he says the only dramatists are the French dramatists. He says Uncle Jules has the greatest classic genius since Molière. Maybe you've seen him about? Tall, thin chap with flat, blond hair, and his wife wears a monocle?" She giggled. "They do about two hundred circuits of the promenade-deck every morning, and never speak to anybody, those people!"

"H'm!" said Morgan, remembering the dinner-table that night. "Oh, yes. But I didn't know you knew them. If this fellow has written all that stuff about your uncle—"

"Oh, I don't know them," she disclaimed, opening her eyes wide. "They're English, you see. They'll write volumes about you, and discuss every one of your good and bad points minutely; but they won't *say* how-de-do unless you've been properly introduced."

All this analysis was over the head of the good Captain Valvick, who had grown restive and was puffing through his moustache with strange noises, as though he wanted to be admitted through a closed door.

"Ay got de whisky poured out," 'he vouchsafed. "And you put in de soda. Iss it decided what we are going to do? What *iss* decided, anyway? Sometime we got to go to bed."

"I'll tell you what we're going to do," said Warren, with energy, "and we can sketch out the plan of battle now. To-morrow morning we're going to comb the boat for that girl who pulled the fainting-act in here. That's the only lead we've got, and we're going after it as hard as Whistler goes after the emerald. That is—" He turned round abruptly. "Let's have it out, Hank. Were you only trying to scare us or were you serious when you made that suggestion?"

Obviously this had been at the back of his mind from the beginning, and he did not like to face it. His hands were clenched. There was a silence while Peggy put the passenger-list aside and also looked up.

"What iss de suggestion?" asked Captain Valvick.

"It's a queer thing," said Morgan. "We don't want our pleasant farce to turn into something else, do we? But why do you think new sheets and maybe blankets were put on that berth?"

"All right," said Warren, quietly. "Why?"

"Because there may have been more blood afterwards than *we* saw there. Steady, now."

There was a silence. Morgan heard the breath whistling through Captain Valvick's nostrils. With a jerk Warren turned round; he regarded the berth for a moment and then began tearing off the bedclothes.

The cabin creaked faintly. . . .

"You may be wrong," said Warren, "and I hope you are. I don't believe anything like that. I *won't* believe it. Pillow—top-sheet—blanket—under-sheet of the bed. . . . It's all right. Look." He was holding them up, a weird figure in shirt-sleeves, with a brown blanket and a whirl of linen about him. "Look at it, damn you! Everything in order. What are you trying to scare us for? See, this sheet of the bed. . . . Wait a minute. . . !"

"Take it off," said Morgan, "and look at the mattress. I hope I'm wrong as much as you do."

Peggy took one look, and then turned away, white-faced. Morgan felt a constriction in his throat as he stepped up beside Warren and Valvick. A blanket had been neatly spread under the sheet and over the mattress; but stains were already soaking through it. When they swept off the blanket, the colours of the blue-and-white striped mattress were not very distinguishable in a great sodden patch spread for some length down.

"Is it. . . ?" asked Morgan, and took a deep draw on his cigarette. "Is it . . . ?"

"Oh, yes. It iss blood," said Captain Valvick.

It was so quiet that even across that distance Morgan imagined he could hear the liner's bell. They were moving almost steadily now, with a deep throb below decks in the ship and a faint vibration of glassware. Also Morgan imagined the pale classic-faced girl lying unconscious, with the dim light burning above her in the berth, and the door opening as somebody came in. . . .

"But what's happened to her? Where is she now?" Warren asked, in a low voice. "Besides," he added, with a sort of dull argumentative air—"besides, he couldn't have done *that* with a blackjack."

"And why should he do it, anyway?" asked Peggy, trying to control her voice. "Oh, it's absurd! I won't believe it! You're scaring me! And—and, anyway, where did he get the linen for the bed? Where is she, and why? . . . *Oh, you're trying to frighten me, aren't you?*"

"Steady, Baby," said Warren, taking her hand without removing his eyes from the bed. "I don't know why he did it, or what he expected to gain by making the bed over. But we'd better cover that up again."

Carefully putting down his pipe on the edge of the thrumming washstand, Morgan choked back his revulsion and bent over to examine the berth. The stains were still

wet, and he avoided them as much as he could. So strung
up was he into that queer, clear-brained, almost fey state
of mind that sometimes comes in the drugged hours of the
morning, that he was not altogether surprised when he
heard something rattle deep down between mattress and
bulkhead. He yanked over a corner of the sheet, wound it
round his fingers, and groped.

"Better not look, old girl," he said after a pause. "This
won't be pretty."

Shielding the find with his body so that only Captain
Valvick could see, he pulled it up in the sheet and turned
it over in his palm. It was a razor, of the straight, old-
fashioned variety, and closed; but it had recently been
used. Rather larger than the ordinary size, it was an elaborate and delicate piece of craftsmanship with a handle so
curiously fashioned that Morgan wiped the blood away to
examine it.

The handle was of a wood that resembled ebony. Down
one side ran a design picked out in thin silver and white
porcelain. At first Morgan took it for an intricate name-
plate, until, under cleaning, it became a man's standing
figure. The figure was possibly three inches high, and under it was a tiny plate inscribed with the word *Sunday*.

"Ay know," said Captain Valvick, staring at it. "It iss
one of a set of seven, one for every day of de week. Ay
haff seen dose before. But what iss dat thing on it, like a
man?"

The thin figure, in its silver and white and black, was
picked out in a curious striped medieval costume, which
recalled to Morgan's mind vague associations with steel-
cut engravings out of Doré. Surgeon, surgeon—barber,
that was it! There was the razor in the thing's fist. But
most ugly and grotesque of all, the head of the figure was
subtly like a death's head, and a bandage was across the
eyes so that the barber was—

"Blind," said Warren, who was looking over his
shoulder. "Put it away, Hank! Put it away. Blind . . .
death and barber . . . end of the week. Somebody used
that, and lost it or left it here. Put it away. Have a drink."

Morgan looked at the evil and smeared design. He

looked at the door, then at the white-painted bulkhead in the bunk, the tumbled bedclothes and the spotty brown blanket. Again he tried to picture the girl in the yellow frock lying here under a dim light, while the outside door was opening. So who was the girl, and where was she now, wrapped round in the soaked sheets that were here before? It was five miles to the bottom of the sea. They would never find her body now. Morgan turned round.

"Yes," he said, "the Blind Barber has been here to-night."

Chapter 9

More Doubts at Morning

As THE HANDS of the travelling-clock at the head of Morgan's bed pointed to eight-thirty, he was roused out of a heavy slumber by the sound of an unmusical baritone voice singing with all the range of its off-keys. The voice singing, "A Life on the Ocean Wave." It brought nightmares into his doze before he struggled awake. As he opened his eyes, the heartening bray of the breakfast bugle went past in the gangway outside, and he remembered where he was.

Furthermore, it was a heartening morning. His cabin—on the boat-deck—was filled with sunshine, and a warm salt-spiced breeze fluttered the curtain at the open porthole. It was winelike May again, with a reflected glitter of water at the porthole; and the ship's engines churning steadily in a docile sea. He drew a deep breath, feeling a mighty uplift of the heart and a sensual longing for bacon and eggs. Then somebody threw a shoe at him, and he knew Warren was there.

Warren sat across from him on the couch under the porthole, smoking a cigarette. He wore white flannels, a careless blue coat, and a sportive tie; he showed not at all the rigours of last night, nor any depression of spirit. His hair was brushed smoothly again, unpropped by sticking-plaster. He said:

"Howdy, General," and tipped his hand to his head. "Wake up, can't you? Wow! it's a beautiful morning! Even our old sea-beetle of a skipper is going to be in better temper to-day. All the sea-sick lads are beginning to creep out of their holes and say it was only something they ate, no doubt. Haaaaa!" Breathing deeply, he arched his chest, knocked his fists against it, and beamed with seraphic good-humour. "Get ready and come down to breakfast. This is an important morning in the lives of several people, including Captain Whistler."

"Right," said Morgan. "Find something to amuse yourself with while I catch a bath and dress. . . . I suppose there's some kind of story all over the boat about last night's activities, isn't there? We were doing a good deal of shouting out on that deck, now I remember it."

The other grinned.

"There is. I don't know how it happens, but there's a kind of wireless telegraphy aboard these tubs that always get a story even if it's a little cockeyed. But I've only heard two versions so far. When I came out this morning, I heard an old dame in 310 raising hell with the stewardess. She was furious. She says six drunken men were standing outside her porthole all night, having a terrible argument about a giraffe, and she's going to complain to the captain. I also passed two clergymen taking a morning stroll. One of them was telling the other some kind of a complicated story—I didn't get much of it. It was something to the effect that the boat's got in her hold a cargo of cages full of dangerous wild beasts, only they're keeping it quiet so as not to alarm the passengers. In the storm last night the cages worked loose and the Bengal tiger was in danger of getting out, but a seaman named Barnacle got it back in its cage. The preacher said A. B. Barnacle was armed only with a whisky-bottle. He said the sailor must be a very brave man, although he used horrible language."

"Come off it," said Morgan, staring.

"So help me, it's absolutely true!" the other declared fervently. "You'll see for yourself." His face clouded a little. "Look here, Hank. Have—have you thought any more about that *other* business?"

"The film?"

"Ah, hang the film! I'll trust you. We'll get it back somehow. No, I meant the—the *other* business, you know. It gives me the jitters. If it weren't for that . . . that, and the fact that when I get my hands on the lousy, low-down skunk who—"

"Save it," said Morgan.

His steward tapped on the door to tell him the bath was ready as usual; Morgan slid into a dressing-gown and went out into the breezy passage. Passing the outer door, he pushed it open a little way to put his head out and breathe the full exaltation of the morning. The warm air blew on him in a splendour of sunlight broadening along the horizon behind long pinkish-white streamers of cloud. There was a deep grey-green sea, stung with flecks of whitecaps and wrinkling under a glitter of sun that trembled up like heat haze. He looked up ahead to the long lift and fall of the bows; at the sweep of white cabins; at the red-mouthed air-funnels and brasswork of portholes awink with morning; he heard the monotonous break and swish of water past the bows, and felt that it was good. Everything was good. He even had a fleeting tenderness for Captain Whistler, who was probably now sitting with a beefsteak at his eye and sighing because he could not go down to breakfast. Good old Captain Whistler. There even occurred to him a wild idea that they might go to Whistler straightforwardly, man to man, and say, "Look here, skipper, it was a blinking shame we had to paste you in the eye last night and strew whisky-bottles all over your deck, and we're sorry; so let's forget it and be friends. Shall we?" But more sober reflection suggested to him that not all the good omens of the morning presaged enough magic to wangle this. Meanwhile, he dreamily sniffed the morning. He thought in joyous contentment of England and his wife Madeleine who would meet him at Southampton; of the holiday in Paris they would take on the money he had contrived to hypnotise out of gimlet-eyed publishers in America; of the little white hotel by the Ecole Militaire, where there were eels in the fountain of a little gravelled garden; and of other things not relevant to this chronicle.

But, while he bathed and shaved he reviewed the unpleasant side of the problem. He could still feel the horrible shock of finding that grotesque razor in the berth, and the blood under his fingers to mark the way of the Blind Barber. In a conference lasting until nearly four in the morning they had tried to determined what was best to do.

Warren and Valvick, as usual, were for direct action. The former thought it would be best to go straight to Whistler, taking the razor, and saying, "Now, you old so-

and-so, if you think I'm crazy, what do you think of *this?*"
Morgan and Peggy had dissented. They said it was a question of psychology and that you had to consider the captain's frame of mind. In the skipper's momentarily excited
state, they said, Warren might just as well tell him he had
gone back to his cabin and discovered a couple of buffaloes
grazing on the furniture. Better wait. In the morning Whistler would institute a search and find a woman missing; then
they could go to him and vindicate themselves. Ultimately,
it was so agreed.

With the razor safely locked away in Morgan's bag, and
the berth on C deck made up in case a steward should
become curious, Morgan again discussed the plan with
Warren while he dressed that morning. For the moment,
Morgan deliberately kept himself from speculating on the
hows and whys of the (alleged) murder last night. There
were things to come first. Shortly the ship would be buzzing with the news of the recovery of the emerald elephant.
Afterwards, with this weight removed from the skipper's
microscopic intelligence, they could soothe him back to
belief in a throat-cutting. Then would come the real duel
with the Blind Barber.

"What I want to know," said Warren, as they descended
to the dining-saloon, "is whether it'll be Dr. Kyle or the
Perrigords who find the emerald. I still have my suspicions. . . ."

"Of the medical profession?" asked Morgan. "Nonsense!
But I would rather like to see Dr. Kyle shaken out of his
calm. Jove! you were right! The boat's waking up. We'll
have the sick-list down to a minimum by this afternoon.
Look at all the kids. If old Jules Fortinbras has got his sea
legs—"

The dining-saloon was full of sunlight and murmurous
with an eager clatter of knives and forks. Stewards beamed
and did tricks with trays. There were more people out for
breakfast at the unholy hour of eight-thirty than there had
been for dinner last night. But at the captain's table sat
only one solitary figure—Dr. Kyle, sturdily plying knife
and fork. Dr. Kyle was a trencherman after the fashion of

the lairds in Sir Walter Scott. He could mess up a plate of fried eggs with a dispatch that would have roused the envious approval of Nicol Jarvie or that foreigner, Athelstane.

"Good morning!" said Dr. Kyle, with unexpected affability, and rolling round his shoulder, he looked up. "A fine day, a fine day. Good morning, Mr. Warren. Good morrrrning, Mr. Morgan. Sit down."

The other two looked at each other and strove to dissemble. Every morning, hitherto, Dr. Kyle had been perfectly polite, but hardly interested or communicative. He had conveyed an impression that his own society was all he cared to cultivate. A solid large-boned figure in black, with his well-brushed greyish hair and the furrows carven down his cheeks, he had devoted himself to food with the concentration of a surgical operation. Now he had an almost raffish appearance. He wore a tweed suit, with a striped tie, and his grizzled eyebrows were much less Mephistophelian as he welcomed them with a broad gesture. It was, Morgan supposed, the weather. . . .

"Er—" said Warren, sliding into his chair, "good morning, sir. Yes, indeed, it's a fine morning! Did you—er—did you sleep well?"

"Ah, like a top!" said the doctor, nodding. "Though, mind," he added, remembering his habits of thought and correcting himself cautiously, "I don't say, fra my own experience, that I should judge it a well-chosen worrrd as applied to tops. Accurately speaking (fra my own expeerience as a boy) I should say it was mair to the purpose for tops in general to refrain fra sedentary habits. However, that's as may be. I'll have more of the bacon and eggs, steward."

This was the first morning, incidentally, in which Dr. Kyle had given the letter "r" its full-wristed spin. He looked benevolently on them, and at the green glitter of the sea dancing outside the portholes.

"I mean," pursued Warren, looking at him curiously, "you didn't—that is, everything was all right when you woke up, was it?"

"Everything," said Dr. Kyle, "was fine." He paused, drawing down his brows thoughtfully. "Ah! Ye may be referring to that disturbance in the night, then?"

"Disturbance?" said Morgan. "Was there a disturbance?"

The other regarded him shrewdly, and in a way that disturbed him.

"I see, I see. You hadn't hearrd of it, then? Well, well, it didn't disturb *me,* Mr. Morgan, and all I heard was some speerited currsing on the deck. But I heard an account of it this morning, from a person of my acquaintance—which account I can't vouch for, you understand—"

"What happened?"

"Rape," said the doctor, succinctly, and closed one eye in a startlingly raffish fashion.

"Rape?" yelped Morgan. There are certain words which have a mysterious telepathic power. Although there was a buzz in the dining-room which drowned his voice, several heads were twitched in their direction. "Rape? My God! who was raped? What happened?"

"I can't say," replied Dr. Kyle, chuckling. "However, my inforrmant distinctly heard the girl's scream when set upon. My inforrmant declares that some scoundrelly dastard approached the poor girrul by telling her of his adventures while hunting big game in Africa. Weel, weel, then, that he offered her an emerald brrooch worth a fabulous sum. But, failing in his foul design, the rrascally skellum struck her over the head with a bottle o' whisky. . . ."

"Great—Cæsar's—ghost!" said Warren, his eyeballs slightly distended. "You—you didn't hear any names mentioned in the business, did you?"

"My inforrmant made no secret of it," Dr. Kyle answered philosophically. "She said the abandoned wretch and seducer was either Captain Whistler or Lord Sturton."

"And this woman's story is all over the boat?" asked Morgan.

"Oh, it will be," said Kyle, still philosophically. "It will be."

Dr. Kyle continued to talk on affably while the others attacked breakfast; and Morgan wondered what would be the ultimate version of the tale that would be humming through the *Queen Victoria* by midday. Evidently Dr. Kyle had not found any emeralds. There remained only the stony-faced Mr. Perrigord and his monocled wife. Well? The ship's miniature newspaper lay beside his plate, and he glanced over it between deep draughts of coffee, his eye slid over what appeared to be an article or essay on the back page, stopped, and returned to it. It was headed "RENAISSANCE DU THEATRE," and under it appeared, "*By Mr. Leslie Perrigord, reprinted by permission of the author from the Sunday "Times" of Oct. 25, 1932.*"

Skirling notes of harps celestial [began this effusion, with running start] sweeping one old reviewer, *malgré lui*, counterclockwise from his *fauteuil*, while *nuances* so subtle danced and slithered, reminding one of Bernhardt. Will you say, "Has old Perrigord gone off his chump this Sunday?" But what is one to say of this performance of M. Jules Fortinbras, which I journeyed to Soho to see? As Balzac once said to Victor Hugo, "*Je suis étonné, sale chameau, je suis bouleversé.*" (Molière would have said it better.) A thrilling performance, if that is consolation to the poor British public, but why speak of *that?* For sheer splendour and beauty of imagic imagery, in these subtle lines spoken by Charlemagne and Roland, I can think of nothing but that superb soliloquy in the fifth act of Corneille's tragedy, "*La Barbe,*" which is spoken by Amourette Pernod, and begins, "*Monâme est un fromage qui souffle dans les forêts mystérieuses de la nuit. . . .*" Or shall I speak of wit? Almost it approaches some of Molière's gems, say, "*Pour moi, j'aime bien les saucissons, parce qu'ils ne parlent pas français. . . .*"

"What's all this?" demanded Warren, who was reading the article also and making strange whistling noises rather like Amourette Pernod's soul. "Do you see this attack of dysentery on the back page? Is this our Perrigord?"

Morgan said, "You have no cultural feelings, I fear. As Chimène said to Tartuffe, "*Nuts.*" Well, you've got to *get* cultural feelings, old son. Read that article very carefully. If there's anything in it you don't understand, ask me. Because—" he checked himself, but Dr. Kyle had finished his last order of bacon and eggs and was rising genially from the table. Dr. Kyle bade them good morning, and said he had half a mind to play deck-tennis. Altogether he was so self-satisfied, as he strode away from the table, that in Warren's face Morgan could see newly awakened suspicions gathering and darkening. "Listen!" hissed Warren in a low voice, and stabbed out dangerously with his fork. "He *says* he didn't find any emerald when he woke up this morning. . . ."

"Will you forget about Dr. Kyle?" said the exasperated Morgan. "It's all right; it simply wasn't his cabin, that's all. Listen to me. . . ."

But an uneasy possibility had struck him. Dr. Kyle didn't find the emerald. Very well. Suppose the Perrigords hadn't found it, either? It was an absurd supposition, yet it grew on him. Assuming both parties to be entirely honest, what the devil could have happened to the emerald? They could not have missed it, either of them; he himself had heard the steel box bump on the floor. Again assuming them to be honest, it might mean that Peggy had mistaken the cabin. But this he doubted. There was shrewdness, there was certainty, in that girl's prim little face. Well—alternatively, it might mean that the Blind Barber was up to tricks. They had ample proof that he was somewhere close at hand during the wild business on C deck. He might very well have seen what happened. Later that night it would have been a simple matter to go after that emerald. . . .

Irritably Morgan told himself that he was flying at theories like Warren. Warren, taking advantage of the other's blank silence, was going on talking with vehemence; and the more he talked the more strongly he convinced himself; so that Dr. Kyle's character had begun to assume hues of the richest and most sinister black. Morgan said, "Nonsense!" and again he told himself there was no sense to this doubt. The Perrigords had found the emerald, and that was that. But his real irritation with himself was for not thinking before of a simple possibility like that of the Blind Barber's having been in attendance. If those æsthetes really hadn't found the thing, after all. . . .

"There's this that's got to be done," he said, breaking in on the other's heated discourse. "Somehow, we've got to ask Kyle a few questions, tactfully—whether he's a light sleeper, whether he keeps his door bolted at night. . . ."

"Now you're showing some sense," said Warren. "Trip him up, eh? Mind, I don't say that necessarily he's the— the barber. What I do say is that fifty thousand pounds' worth of emerald, chucked in on him like that when he thought nobody'd be the wiser. . . . Did you notice his expression? Did you hear the crazy story he told us, knowing the thing'd get so tangled up that nobody would be able to accuse . . . ?"

"Read that article in the paper," the other ordered, tapping it inexorably. "We've got to make the acquaintance of the Perrigords, even if it's only a red herring; and you've got to be able to talk intelligently about *nuances*. What's the matter with your education? You're in the diplomatic or consular service, or whatever it is. Don't you have to know French to get in that?"

He had hoped that this crack would divert Warren. It did. The young diplomat was stung.

"Certainly I know French," he returned, with cold dignity. "Listen. I had to pass the toughest examination they can dish out, I'll have you know; yes, and I'll bet *you* couldn't pass it yourself. Only it's commercial French. Ask me anything in commercial French. Go on, ask me how to say, "Dear sir. Yrs of the 18th inst. to hand, and enclose under separate cover bill of exchange, together with consular invoice, to the amt. of sixteen dollars (or perhaps pounds, francs, marks, lire, roubles, kopecks, or kronen) and forty-five cents (or perhaps shillings, centimes, pfennigs. . . .' "

"Well, what's the matter with you, then?"

"I'm telling you, it isn't the same thing. The only other French I know is some guff I remember from preparatory school. I know how to ask for a hat which fits me, and I know how to inquire my way in case I should feel a passionate desire to rush out and visit the Botanical Gardens. But I never had the least desire to go to the Botanical Gardens; and, believe me, if I ever go into a hat-shop in

Paris, no pop-eyed Frog in the world is going to sell me a lid that slides down over my ears. . . . Besides, not having a sister who's a shepherdess kind of cramps my conversational style."

"Hullo!" said Morgan, who was paying no attention. "It's begun. Good work. She thought of it. . . ."

Down the broad polished staircase into the dining-saloon came the tall and majestic figures of Mr. and Mrs. Leslie Perrigord; well-groomed, moving together in step. And between them, talking earnestly, walked Peggy Glenn.

Peggy came just a trifle above Mrs. Perrigord's shoulder. Evidently as a sort of intellectual touch, she had put on her shell-rimmed spectacles and an exuberant amount of make-up. Her frock was what looked to Morgan like a batik pattern. She was speaking with animation to the monocled Mrs. Perrigord, who seemed to convey *nuances* of reply by ghostly silent movements of eyebrow and lip. At the foot of the stairs Morgan expected her to break off and come to their table; but she did nothing of the kind. To Morgan she made an almost imperceptible signal; of what, he was not sure. Then she went on with the Perrigords to their table.

Warren muttered something in muffled surprise, after which they noted something else. Coming down the staircase a short distance behind them shuffled the big and amiable figure of Captain Valvick, whose sandy hair was brushed up straight and his leathery face once more netted with wrinkles as he listened to some tale. The tale was being told him, in fact, by Mr. Charles Woodcock. Mr. Woodcock, who freely described himself as the Bug-powder Boy, seemed excited. Invariably, when excited his thin frame seemed to hop and twist; an optical illusion, because he kept his eyes fixed on your face while he poured out a rapid string of words in a confidential undertone.

"What's Valvick up to?" demanded Warren. "All the allies seem to be working except us. Have you noticed our square-head's been keeping away from Woodcock, because they're both powerful yarn-spinners and they put each other out like a couple of forest fires? Well, then, look how quiet he's keeping and tell me what's on his mind."

Morgan didn't know; he supposed it was Mr. Woodcock's version of what had occurred last night. If so conservative a Presbyterian as Dr. Oliver Harrison Kyle had suggested rape, then he shuddered to think of the goings-on that would present themselves to the versatile imagination of the Bug-powder Boy. The dining-saloon was rapidly filling up, pulsing now with a joyous babble and clamour as of prisoners released, but they heard Mr. Woodcock's hearty voice. He said, "All right, old socks. Don't forget to tell your pals," and slapped Captain Valvick on the back as he went towards his own table.

With a puzzled expression Valvick lumbered towards their table. He beamed a good morning, swung round his chair, and uttered the word:

"Mermaid!"

Morgan blinked. "Don't," he said. "For God's sake stop! That's enough. If anybody tells me that Captain Whistler was chasing a mermaid around C deck last night, the last shred of my sanity will be gone. Don't say it! I can't bear to hear any more!"

"Eh?" said Valvick, staring. "What iss dis? Ay nefer hear anyt'ing like dat, dough ay haff a mess-boy once who say he hass seen one. Dis iss Mr. Woodcock's invention—ay tell you about it, but ay haff to listen to him a lot because he know a lot about diss crook. . . ."

Valvick sat down.

"Listen! Ay got bot' de hatches full off news. Ay tell you all about it, but first ay tell you de most important. Captain Whistler want all of us up in his cabin after breakfast, and—coroosh!—he t'ink he know who de criminal is."

Chapter 10

Dramatis Personae

AFTER THE captain had ordered porridge and the table steward had gone, a rather nervous Warren put down his coffee-cup.

"Knows who the criminal is? He's not getting any funny ideas, is he? About us, I mean?"

Chuckling, Valvick made a broad gesture. "Coroosh, no! Not at all. Dat ain't it. Ay dunno yust what it is, but he send Sparks to my cabin to say we all got to come up after mess. Sparks say de captain get a wireless message, but he will not tell me what iss in it until we see old Barnacle."

"I wonder," said Morgan.

"So dat remind, and ay say to Sparks—iss de wireless-operator; all de wireless-operators iss Sparkses, you see— ay say, "Sparks, you wass on duty yesterday afternoon, eh?" And he say, "Yes." And den ay say, "Sparks, do you remember when de old man receive dat first message about de crook, and hass a row wit' you? Wass dere some odder people in de cabin wit' you at de time?" When he says yes, den ay describe dat girl we find cracked on de head last night, and ay say, "Sparks, was *she* dere?" (All Sparkses is hawful wit' de ladies, so ay know he remember her if she wass.) Halso, if she send or receive a message, he iss going to know her name, eh?"

"Neat!" said Warren. "Swell! Who was she?"

"Ahhhh, dass de trouble. He remember her, but he dunno. Dere was several people, and halso a cousin of Sparks which is travelling as a passenger. She came in, and see dere is people in a waiting-line, so he guess she don't want to wait and she turn round and go out; he say she hass got 'ands full of papers. No matter! We find out when we know who iss missing. *Now* is de part I want to tell you. . . ."

The porridge had arrived. Captain Valvick emptied the

creamjug over it, bent his vast shoulders, adjusted his elbows in a wing-like spread, and spoke between excavations.

"Well, we get to talking, you see, and ay give him a drink of Old Rob Roy, and he say, "Coroosh! Captain, but my cousin Alick could haff use dis whisky last night." Den he tell me his cousin Alick hass suffered somet'ing hawful with de yumping toothache, and de doctor hass give him somet'ing to put on it, but it don't do no good. And ay say, "So-ho?" ay say, "den he should haff come to me, for ay know somet'ing dat cure him bing-bing." It iss composed—"

"Not to interrupt you, Skipper," said Morgan, who was keeping a wary eye out for a signal from Peggy at the Perrigords' table, "but are you sure this is strictly—"

"Ay am sure, you bet!" returned the other, with snorting excitement. "Listen. He say, "Den ay wish you would go see him," Sparks say; "he iss only round in C 47. . . .' "

"Sorry," said Morgan, and jerked his head back. "C 47, eh? Well?"

"So we go to C 47, which iss in de gangway just hopposite Dr. Kyle's. Eh? And hiss cousin is walking round in circles with de 'ot-water-bag, and sometimes he go and bump his head on de bulkhead, and say, "Coroosh! ay wish ay wass dead," and ay pity de poor fallar hawful. So ay write out what he hass to get at doctor's, and send Sparks for it. In fife minutes dat pain go, and de poor fallar can't believe it, and he got tears in his eyes when he t'ank me. Oh, ay forgot to tell you he iss a prizefighter which is called de Bermondsey Terror. He hask me if dere is somet'ing he can do for me. Ay say no, and ay give *him* a drink of Old Rob Roy, but ay got a hidea yust de same."

With a massive finger the captain tapped the table.

"Like diss. In de night ay am t'inking to myself, and all of a sudden ay yump up in my bunk, and t'ink, "Coroosh! Maybe de doctor and de odders iss honest people, but suppose diss crook sneak into de cabin where Miss Glenn t'row dat hemerald? . . .' "

Morgan nodded. The old skipper was no fool. It took some time for his clicking mind to mesh its wheels, but he arrived. This idea, bringing new implications to worry Warren, caused a silence to fall on the table.

"You don't mean"—Warren gulped—"you don't mean—?"

"Oh! no! But ay t'ank ay better ask de Bermondsey Terror. Ay say, "You wass up all night wit' de toothache?" He say yes. Ay say, "Did you hear any yumps and yitters out on de deck?" He say, "Yes, ay t'ank ay hear a woman say, "Sock him again," but ay feel too bad to go see what it iss; besides," he say, "ay haf de port closed so ay don't catch cold in de yaw, and can't hear much, but," he say, "it iss close in de cabin, and ay haff de door fastened open." Dat is de way wit de lime-yuicers. Dey iss hell on cold air. Ay wass in yail once in Boston wit' a lime-yuicer, and all he do all de time iss to squawk about dat yail because it hass got steam heat. . . ."

"And the Bermondsey Terror," said Morgan, "was up all night, and could see Kyle's door?"

"Dat iss right," agreed the captain. "And he swear nobody go down dere all night. So ay got *somet'ing* off my mind." He heaved a wheezy sigh.

Observing that Warren was about to construe this into further proof of Kyle's guilt, Morgan said, hastily: "You've accomplished lots of work before breakfast, Captain. Was there anything else? What's this you say about Woodcock knowing something?"

"Ah! Yes, yes. Ay almost forget!" The captain gave a mighty flip of his spoon. "But ay dunno yust what to make of it. Dat Woodcock iss a funny fallar, you bet. Efery time he talk business, he try to use de subtlety and den ay dunno what he iss talking about. But he say it iss a business proposition. He say he want to speak to Mr. Warren, and he got a deal to make if Mr. Warren will talk turkey. First, he knows what happen last night. . . ."

"I'll bet he does," said Warren, grimly. "What's *his* version?"

"No, no, no! Dat iss de funny part. Ay t'ank he know most of it for sure, all except about de girl."

Warren seized the edge of the table. "You don't mean he knows about Uncle Warpus or that film?"

"Well, he knows somet'ing about a film, ay tell you dat. He iss a smart man. What all he know ay dunno, but he sort of hint he know plenty about diss crook." Valvick stroked his moustache, scowling. "You better talk to him. De point iss diss. He has invented something. It iss a bug-powder gun wit' a helectric light."

"A bug-powder gun with an electric light?" repeated Morgan, rather wildly. He dismissed the idea that this might be some singular kind of nautical metaphor. "What the hell is a bug-powder gun with an electric light? This strain is gradually sapping my mental powers. I'm going mad, I tell you. Skipper, haven't we got enough on our minds without you babbling about bug-powder guns and electric lights?"

"Ay am not babbling!" said the captain, with some heat. "Dat is yust what he tell me. Ay dunno how it vurk, but it iss somet'ing you use to kill de mosquitoes in de dark. He say it will refolutionise de bug-killing profession, and he iss going to call it de Mermaid. He say it can also be used on bedbugs, cockroaches, earwigs, caterpillars, red ants, horseflies. . . ."

"I have no doubt," said Morgan, "that it will enable a good shot to bring down a cockroach at sixty yards. But get back to the subject. Whether or not it has something to do with us, we have more immediate concerns. Dr. Kyle, skipper, did *not* find the emerald in his cabin this morning. Thanks to you and the Bermondsey Terror, we've proved that the Blind Barber didn't get in to pinch it, either. . . . That leaves the Perrigords. It's got to be the Perrigords. They're our last hope. Of course the Perrigords have got it! That's why Peggy is staying so long over there. . . ."

Warren tapped his arm.

"She's giving us the high sign now," he said, in a low voice. "Don't turn round too obviously now, but have a look. No, wait a minute. It's no secret stuff. She wants us to come over to the table."

"De odder people haff got de emerald?" inquired Valvick, peering over his shoulder. "Haa! Den dat iss all right. Ay tell you ay wass worried."

"Lord! I hope so," said Morgan, fervently. "But Peggy doesn't look too pleased. Finish your breakfast, Skipper, and then join us. Get ready, Curt. Did you finish that article?"

"Sure I did," retorted Warren. He spoke out of the corner of his mouth as they moved out across the dance floor towards the other table. "And don't go making any cracks about my education either. I can tell you all about it. It seems Peggy's uncle is the goods. As a classic drama-tist he is an eight-cyclindered wow, and there's been no-body like him since Molière. If any impertinent criticism of his jewelled lines can be made by one, one would say a certain *je ne sais quoi*. I should possibly suggest the in-troduction of certain deft touches of *realism* into the speech of, say, so human and breathing a figure as the Knight Roland or the crafty Banhambra, Sultan of the Moors which would lend an element of graphic power. . . ."

"An element," said the loud, concise voice of Mr. Leslie Perrigord in the flesh, "of graphic power. And that is all."

Morgan looked him over as he sat stiffly upright at the breakfast-table, holding a fork with its prongs against the cloth and e-nun-ci-a-ting his words through stiff jaws. There was nothing effeminate or lackadaisical about Mr. Leslie Perrigord, that element which most irritated Morgan in the species intellectual. Mr. Perrigord looked as though he could pull his weight in a crew or handle a skittish horse. A tall lath with thin blond hair, a hooked nose, and a mummified eye, he simply talked. He looked at nothing in particular. He seemed far away. If you had not seen the feathery blond moustache floating as in an icy breeze, you would have sworn it was an effect of ventriloquism. But (once started) he showed no disposition to leave off talking.

A measured stream of hooey flowing from Mr. Perri-gord's lips in concise cadences was checked by Peggy only when it became necessary for Perrigord to wind himself up with ice-water. She said:

"Oh, I say, excuse me! I'm so sorry to interrupt you, but I must present two very good friends of mine. Mr. Warren, Mr. Morgan. . . ."

"De-do?" said Mrs. Perrigord, sepulchrally.

"Oh?" said Mr. Perrigord. He seemed vaguely annoyed. He had just kicked Shakespeare in the eye and mashed the hat of Ben Jonson; and Morgan felt he was ruffled at being interrupted. "Oh? Delighted, I'm sure. I was—ah—mentioning some of the more elementary points, *en passant,* in the talk I have been asked to deliver at the ship's concert to-night." He smiled thinly. "But—ah—I fear I shall bore you. It is merely a talk serving as an introductory speech to the performance of M. Fortinbras's marionettes. I fear—"

"But of course they'll be interested, Mr. Perrigord!" crowed Peggy, with enthusiasm. "Curt, I was just telling Mr. and Mrs. Perrigord about the time in Dubuque when the Knight Oliver got his pants split in the battle with the Moors, and they had to lower the curtain because all the sawdust came out of him, and he had to be sewed up again before uncle would go on with the play. Mr. Perrigord said it was charming, a charming detail. Didn't you, Mr. Perrigord?"

"Quite, Miss Glenn," said the oracle, benevolently (for him), but he looked as if he wished the others would go and let him get back to literature. He showed that heavy sort of politeness which grows acutely uncomfortable in the air. "Quite charming. These little details. But surely I am boring these gentlemen, who can have no conceivable interest. . . . ?"

"But just fancy," continued Peggy, appealing to Morgan. "Hank, you villain, I've lost my bet to you, after all. And now I'll have to stand the cocktails, and it's a terrible shame. Don't you think so, dear Mr. Perrigord?"

Warren did not like this at all.

"Bet?" he said. "What bet? Who made a bet?"

Somebody kicked him in the shins. "Because," the girl went on, "after all my tam-o'-shanter *didn't* blow in the porthole of Mr. Perrigord's cabin last night. It's beastly luck, because now I've probably lost it; but it didn't, and there's that. Just before Mr. Perrigord began talking so wonderfully"—here she raised earnest, awed, soft eyes for a moment and kept them fixed on Perrigord's countenance.

He cleared his throat. A sort of paralytic leer passed over his face. Warren saw it. So did Mrs. Perrigord—"just before Mr. Perrigord began talking so *wonderfully*, he told me he'd found nothing in the cabin at all, and I'm afraid now I *must* have lost that nice tam of mine."

"No deu-oubt," said Mrs. Perrigord, giving Peggy a nasty look through her monocle. "It was *quayte* dark on deck, wasn't it, my de-ah?"

"Quayte. And, I say, these men do take such advantage of us, don't they, Mrs. Perrigord? I mean, I think it's simply awful; but after all what can one *do*? I mean, it's much better to submit than cause a terrible lot of fuss and bother, isn't it?"

"Well, re-aolly!" said Mrs. Perrigord, stiffening. "I confess I scarcely kneow. To—to one at a time, perhaps. But —ah—reaolly, my deah, since I am olmost certain I heard at least six intoxicated men carousing out the-ah, I confess I should not have been at oll surprised to find on our floor considerably moah than a tam-o'-shanter. As I observed to the steward at the time—"

"To the steward?" asked Peggy wonderingly. "But, Mrs. Perrigord, wherever was your husband?"

Mrs. Perrigord's husband, who now seemed to despair of getting back to the serious business of sitting on literary hats, interposed:

"Most refreshing, Miss Glenn. Most refreshing. Ha-ha! I like the outspoken views, the free and untrammelled straightforwardness of our youth to-day, which is not by ancient prejudice cabined, cribbed, and confined. . . ." At this point, Mrs. Perrigord looked as though, if she were not by ancient prejudice cabined, cribbed, and confined, she would up and dot him one with a plate of kippers. "I— in short, I like it. But you must not mind my wife. Ha-ha!"

"Oh?" said Mrs. Perrigord.

"Come, come, Cynthia. *Jeunesse, jeunesse*. A trifle of exuberant 'seizing the moment,' so to speak. Remember what D. H. Lawrence said to James Joyce. Ha-ha-ha!"

"My deah Leslie," said Mrs. Perrigord coldly, "Babylonian orgies and revels of Ishtar *à la Pierre Louys* are oll very well in books. But if it is to youah æsthetic taste to have these rites peahfoahmed oll ovah the deck of a respectable linah undah youah window at 2 a.m., I must say I caon't agree. And I must insist on explaining to this young lady that muh relations with the cabin steward were—ah—puahly those of business—"

"Coo!" said Peggy.

"—and were confined," went on Mrs. Perrigord, in a louder voice, "to ringing the bell, unbolting the doah, and asking him whethah (as my husband will inform you) something could be done to stop the noise. I can assuah you that I slept no moah oll night."

Mr. Perrigord said mildly that you had got to remember what James Joyce said to D. H. Lawrence. Morgan felt that he had better do something to culminate this exchange of dirty digs before it reached the hair-pulling stage. All the same, he was aghast. The emerald had to be *somewhere*. He held no brief for either Lord Sturton or Captain Whistler, but the fact remained that they had pinched a fifty-thousand-pound jewel and thrown it through the porthole of one of those two cabins. If the emerald had somehow incredibly vanished, it meant the vanishing of Sturton's money and probably Whistler's official head. Something was wrong. Kyle said it wasn't in *his* cabin, and there was testimony to prove the Barber could not have lifted it from there. On the other hand, the Perrigords were awake; noticed the row; would certainly have noticed anything thrown in, and certainly could not have missed it this morning. His bewilderment grew, and he desperately sought for a new lead. . . .

So Morgan assumed his most winning smile (although he felt it stretch like a hideous mask) and spoke flattering, soothing, cajoling words to Mrs. Perrigord. She was not at all bad-looking, by the way; and he went to work with gusto. While Warren stared at him, he sympathised with her and apologised angrily for the behaviour of whatever disgusting revellers had disturbed her sleep. He intimated that, no matter what might have been the conversation between those two notorious old rips James Joyce and D. H. Lawrence, it had been in very bad taste.

". . . But to tell you the truth, Mrs. Perrigord," said

Morgan, leaning confidingly over her chair, "I heard that disturbance, too; and, though I can't say, since of course I wasn't there, you understand . . ."

"Oh, quayte!" said Mrs. Perrigord, relaxing a good deal and much less stiffly indicating that he had her royal ear. "Yes?"

". . . still, I should have said it sounded less like—well, shall we say Dionysian revelry?—than simply a free-for-all scrap. Er, fisticuffs, you know," explained Morgan, seeking the highbrow *mot juste*. "Especially as (if you'll forgive my saying so, Mrs. Perrigord) that a lady of your charm and knowledge of refinements in sensual indulgence would probably take a light view of men's and women's frailties if only they were staged with any degree of delicacy. Furthermore—"

"Well, no, reaolly!" said Mrs. Perrigord, looking arch. "Come now, Mr. Morgan, you can scarcely expect muh to agree *all*together with that, can you? Heh-heh-heh!"

"Sure! Absolutely, Mrs. Perrigord!" said Warren. He perceived that Hank was trying to win the old girl over, and stoutly tried to help the good work along. "We know you're a good sport. Absolutely. Remember what the travelling salesman said to the farmer's daughter."

"Shut up," said Morgan out of the corner of his mouth. "And naturally I suppose this idea of a fight occurred to you, too. Gad! I wonder you didn't get up and bolt the door, Mrs. Perrigord, in case those drunken ba—ah—in case those revellers should decide—"

"But I did!" cried Mrs. Perrigord. "Oh, the doah was bolted, I assuah you! From the very first moment I heard a woman's voice imploring someone to—to strike someone ageyne, it was bolted. I did not close an eye oll night. I can most certainly tell you that no one came into the cabin."

(Well, that tore it. Morgan glanced at his companions. Peggy looked upset. Warren angry and mystified. The puzzle was growing worse jumbled and also it was Mr. Perrigord who now seemed to be giving the nasty looks. Morgan felt that they had better go off and cool their heads before going up for the interview with Captain Whistler. He prepared some discreet words. . . .)

"But tell me," said Mrs. Perrigord, apparently struck with an idea. "Someone said—*are* you the Mr. Morgan who writes the detective stories?"

"Why—er—yes. Yes, I believe so. Thank you very much, Mrs. Perrigord, and you too, sir. It's been delightful to have made your acquaintance, and I only hope we shall have the opportunity—"

"I adore detective stories," said Mrs. Perrigord.

Her husband remained motionless. But on his glassy-eyed countenance was a curious expression. He looked as a familiar of the Spanish Inquisition might have looked if, on the morning of an *auto-da-fé,* Fra Torquemada had announced an intention of dismissing the poor blighters with a warning.

"Do you indeed, my dear?" inquired Leslie Perrigord, frostily. "Most extraordinary. Well, we must not detain them, Cynthia. Miss Glenn, I hope I shall have the pleasure of conferring with you to-day—and also your excellent uncle, to whom I look forward to meeting—and arrange matters for the performance to-night. *A bientôt!*"

"But we shall see you at the concert, of course," observed Mrs. Perrigord. On her face was a narrow-eyed smile which somehow reminded Morgan of Mr. Stanley Laurel. "Les-leh and I have bean conferring with the pursah to arrange it. I shall *so* hope to see you, deah Miss Glenn. An excellent programme has bean arranged. Madame Giulia Leda Camopsozzi will sing *morceaux* from the more modern masters, accompanied by her husband, Signor Benito Furioso Camopsozzi. I—ah—believe," she added, frowning as though this did not appeal to her, "that the pursah, a certain Mr. Macgregor, has persuaded Dr. Oliver Kyle to recite selections from the works of Robert Burns. This will of course precede M. Fortinbras's performance. *A bientôt.*"

"Cheero-ho," said Peggy, rising from the table, "and thanks most awfully for all the information. You *must* come and see me, Mr. Perrigord, and tell me all about those fascinating things—but, I say—er—if you're going to see my uncle—"

"Yes?" inquired Mr. Perrigord. He lifted his eyebrows at her worried expression.

"Don't think me foolish, but I really know him awfully well. And please promise me, if he's up and about—I mean, I know how *awful* some of you terribly intelligent people are," she really seemed to be in earnest this time, and even Mrs. Perrigord condescended to look at her as she hesitated; "but promise me you won't give him anything to drink. I know it sounds silly, but he really hasn't got a strong head; and—and you'd never believe it, but he has a most awful weakness for gin. I have to watch him, you see, because one night when we were to give a performance in Philadelphia—"

"I never touch spirits, Miss Glenn," said Perrigord, swiftly and rather curtly. " 'Why should I put a thief in my mouth to steal away my brains?' as T. S. Eliot somewhere puts it. It is abominable. I am also a vegetarian. M. Fortinbras will be quite safe in my care. Good day."

In silence the three conspirators hurried away from the table. Morgan, locked up with his own bewildering thoughts, did not speak. Peggy looked scared. It was Warren who broke the silence.

"You see?" he demanded, savagely. "Those two dumb chucks wouldn't steal anything. Now take my advice before it's too late. It's that fake doctor, I'm telling you. My Lord! the thing didn't just disappear! It's in his cabin. . . ."

"Peggy," said Morgan, "there's no other explanation. You must have mistaken the cabin."

They had reached the foot of the staircase, and she waited until a passing steward was out of earshot. "I didn't, Hank," she told him, quietly and earnestly. "I'm absolutely positive I didn't. I was out on deck again this morning, putting myself just where I stood last night. . . ."

"Well?"

"I wasn't mistaken. It was one of those two, because there are only two portholes anywhere near. It was one of those two; and I *think,* I say I think, it was Dr. Kyle's."

"As far as I'm concerned, I don't see what more evidence

you want," remarked Warren, rather querulously. "I'll do what the Brains says, and no questions asked, but I've got my own theories. Come on. We've got to go up and see Captain Whistler."

A voice just above them said: "Excuse me, Mr. Warren. I don't want to bust up anything; but if you've ten minutes to spare, I think I can make it worth your while."

Leaning over the gilt banister, tapping it with his finger, Mr. Charles Woodcock was regarding them in a very curious fashion.

Chapter 11

One Who Saw the Blind Barber

MR. WOODCOCK'S countenance wore such an expression of tense and alert seriousness that Morgan felt a new uneasiness. He remembered Valvick's remarks to the effect that Woodcock had hinted of things, nebulous but dangerous things, the man claimed to know. Never thoroughly at ease before live-wire business men, because his mind could not move as fast as theirs along their own lines, Morgan thought of several disturbing possibilities, including blackmail. And so it was that they encountered a feature of the case which (a week before) Morgan would have considered an absurdity or a frank impossibility, yet which to others was serious: one of the deadly serious things which underlay a tissue of misdirection and nonsense.

Woodcock was a wiry, restless, shock-headed man with a bony face and good-humoured eyes which were nevertheless rather fixed. Round his sharp jaw were wrinkles as though from much talking; the talking, in fact—as he strolled about the ship hitherto—had been rapid, lurid, jovial and winking. He seemed desirous of conveying the impression that he was a bouncing, engagingly mendacious good fellow with little on his mind. Now he leaned over the banister, his sharp eyes moving swiftly right and left.

"Now I spoke to the old skipper," he went on in a rapid and confidential undertone, "because I didn't have any idea of shoving myself in, you understand, where I mightn't be wanted. All right!" said Mr. Woodcock lifting his palm in a gesture as though he expected an objection. He did this each time he said, "All right!" It was a means of noting that he had made a point; and could go on from there with a certainty that, so far, everything was understood. "All right! But I know how it is with these things, and I want to make it man to man, and fair and square, so that I can convince you you'll be doing a thing you'll never regret if you come in on my proposition. All right! Now, all I want, Mr. Warren, is ten minutes of your valuable time—alone. Just ten minutes. You can take out your watch and put it on the table, and if I haven't interested you in just ten minutes—"Here he made a significant gesture of his wrist and raised his eyebrows—"then there's absolutely no more to be said."

"Not at all, not at all," said Warren rather vaguely. He was flustered at this new intrusion, and clearly had the idea Woodcock was trying to sell him something. "Glad to give you all the time you want. Well—we'll have a drink and talk it over. But not just now. My friends and I have an important date—"

Woodcock leaned closer.

"Exactly, old man. Exactly. I know. With the captain. It's all right now; it's all right," he whispered, raising his hand. "I understand, old man."

The conspirators stared at each other, and Woodcock's eyes swept from one to the other of them. "What," said Warren, "what's on your mind?"

"Ten minutes," said the other, "alone?"

"Well—yes. But my friends have got to be there. You can tell all of us, can't you?"

Woodcock seemed to scent a bluff somewhere. His eyebrows went up, but he spoke in a tone of pleasant and fatherly chiding, anxiously.

"Look, old man. Are you sure you've got it straight? Are you sure you'd like to have the young lady there?"

"Why not? Good God! what have you got into your head, anyhow?"

"All right, old man, if that's what you want!" He was affable. "I admit I'd rather talk to you alone, but I won't argue. Suppose we go up to the writing-room, where it'll be quiet."

On the way he talked steadily and with sprightly bounce of other matters, laughing heartily, amid many jocose references. The white-panelled writing-room was deserted. He led them to an embrasure of full-glass windows, where the morning sun was muffled by thick curtains, and quiet was broken only by the pounding of the engines. Here, when they were seated, he ran a hand through his bristly hair, fidgeted, and suddenly shot into action.

"Now, I want to help you, old man," he explained, still confidentially, "but you see, it's a case of mutual benefits, you see? You're young, and you don't understand these things. But when you get older and have a wife and family, ah!" said Mr. Woodcock. He made an impressive gesture. "Then you'll understand that business isn't only a matter of favours. All right! Now, frankly, you're sort of in a jam, aren't you?"

"Shoot," said Warren briefly.

"Well then. I don't know what went on on the boat last night, that everybody's talking about; I don't *want* to know. It's none of my business, see? But I do know what happened yesterday afternoon. A roll of film was stolen from your cabin, wasn't it? No, no, don't answer, and don't interrupt.

"I'm going to show you," continued Mr. Woodcock, after a pause in which he demonstrated himself an admirable showman—" 'm going to show you," he went on, rather sharply, "a little moving-picture of my own as to what might have happened. I don't say it *did* happen, y'unnastand. You wouldn't expect me to pin myself down to that, would you? I say it *might* have happened. All right! Now here's my little moving-picture. I'm coming along the gangway down on C deck, see? about ha'-past four yesterday afternoon, and I've just been up sending off a radio to my firm, and there's nothing on my mind. All of a sudden I hear a noise behind me when I'm passing one of those little offshoots of the gangway, and I turn around in time to see a guy ducking out of it, and across the gangway into the wash-room. All right! And I see this bozo's got a whole mess of movie film that he's trying to stuff under his coat—

"*U-uh,* now!" said Mr. Woodcock warningly, "don't interrupt! Well, suppose I see this guy's face so that if I haven't seen it before I'd know it again wherever I saw it; just suppose that. I wonder what it is, but I figure it's none of my business. Still, I think there may be a angle to it, see, so I sort of go down and take a peek. But all I can see is a door sort of open and a lot of film and film-boxes scattered around on the floor; and I see a guy—maybe yourself—sort of getting up from the floor with his hands to his head.

"And I think 'Whu-o, Charley! You'd better get out of this, and not be mixed up in any trouble,' see? Besides, the guy was coming round and didn't need any help, or I'd have stopped. But then I get to thinking—"

"You mean," said Warren, rather hoarsely, "you saw who—?"

"Now go easy, old man, go easy. Let me show my picture now!"

His picture, they discovered, exhibited a sort of strange interlude in which Mr. Woodcock's memory spoke to him. Apparently he was a great hand at reading the tabloids and scandal sheets, explaining also that he was a subscriber to the magazine *True Sex-Life Stories*. One of the papers, it appeared, had recently published a red-hot, zippy item straight from the capital city. It was couched in the form of innuendo, inquiring what Big Shot had a nephew who could always get a job turning a camera crank in Hollywood; furthermore, was it possible that the afore-mentioned Big Shot, in a sportive mood, had been indiscreet before a camera; and, if this were within the limits of possibility, who was the woman in the case?

"Woman?" said Warren uncontrollably. *"Woman?* There's no woman! Why, my un—"

"Steady," interrupted Morgan, his face stolid. "Mr. Woodcock's doing the talking."

Woodcock did not even smile or contradict. He probably expected this. He was still helpful, concerned; but there were tighter wrinkles round his jaw and his eyes were expressionless. "So maybe I'm thinking to myself," he pursued, jerking his wrist and shoulder with a curiously Hebraic gesture while the sharp eyes fixed Warren, "about a very funny cablegram I overhear in the wireless-room. And maybe I don't make much sense out of it, see? because I don't hear much of it; except that it's about a movie film and also about somebody being *bare*. Now, now, old man, you needn't look so funny at me—I under-

stand how these things are. But I think, 'Charley, maybe
you're wrong. Maybe it was just an ordinary stick-up job.
And if it was, then of course there'll be a noise about it
this evening, and Mr. Warren'll report he's been robbed.'
All right! Only," concluded Mr. Woodcock, leaning over
and tapping Warren on the knee, "there wasn't, and he
didn't."

During the silence they could hear some children crying
out and pelting past the door of the writing-room. The engines throbbed faintly. Slowly Warren passed his hand
over his forehead.

"There've been some funny interpretations put on all
this," he said in a strained voice, "but this is *the limit*. A
woman! . . . All right to you, old horse," he added, with
sudden crispness. "You're wrong, of course; but this isn't
the time to discuss that. WHO WAS THAT MAN WHO STOLE
THE FILM? That's what we want to know. What is it you
want? Money?"

Clearly this had never occurred to the other. He jumped
on the seat of the window. "I may not be as big as you,"
he said quietly, "but you try offering me money again, and,
by God! you'll regret it. What do you think I am, a blackmailer? Come on, old man"—his voice changed and his
eyes had a hopeful and propitiatory gleam—"come on
now. I'm a business man and this is the biggest chance of
my life. I'm only trying to do my job, after all. If I can
put this across, I'll be in line for an assistant-vice-presi-
dency. I'm giving it to you straight: if I'd thought that anything really important'd been stolen, or anything like that,
I wouldn't hold out on you for a second. But I figure it this
way. What's happened? An old guy, who ought to know
better, has played sugar-daddy and got himself into a jam
with a woman, and there's a picture of it. All right! I don't
wish him any bad luck—I sympathise, and *I offer to help*.
I offer to tell you who's got it, so's you can get it back . . .
well, whatever way you like. But I figure *I* rate a favour
in return. And if that's not fair, I don't know what is."

The man was desperately serious. Morgan studied him,
trying to understand both the man's ethics and the man's
nature. He was a problem aside from both the grim and

the comic. That a governmental stuffed-shirt had been caught in a compromosing position with a woman before somebody's moving-picture camera he thought of as neither serious nor ridiculous; in all probability he simply supposed that, if a government official got into difficulties they would *be* difficulties of that nature, to be judged solely from how he could use the fact in a legitimate business fashion. Morgan looked at Warren, and he could see that the latter considered it all fair enough.

"Good enough," said Warren, nodding grimly. "You've got a right to proposition me. Fire away. But what the devil can *I* do for you?"

Woodcock drew a deep breath.

"I want a signed testimonial, with a picture," he said, "for the newspapers and magazines."

"Testimonial? Hell, yes, I'll give you a testimonial for anything," Warren returned, staring. "But what good can I do you? What—Wait a minute. Holy smoke! You don't mean a *bug-powder* testimonial, do you?"

"I mean," said Woodcock, "I want a recommendation for a certain article which my firm is about to place on the market and which I invented. Mind, old man, if I didn't know this thing was a world-beater I wouldn't try to sell you the idea. I'm not going to ask you to accept anything sight unseen. I'm going to *show* you," said Mr. Woodcock, suddenly taking out a long package from under his coat like an anarchist who gets his victim in a corner with a bomb. "I'm going to show you that this little gadget will really do everything we claim for it in the advertising campaign. Yes, I want a testimonial, old man. . . . But not from you."

"He means, Curt," said Peggy, regarding Mr. Woodcock with a fascinated horror—"he means, you see—"

Woodcock nodded. "You get it lady. I want a testimonial of endorsement from the Hon. Thaddeus G. Warpus for the Mermaid Electrically-fitted Mosquito Gun, fitted with Swat No. 2 Liquid Insect Exterminator; saying that he personally uses it at his country home in New Jersey, and warmly recommends it. This is my chance, and I'm not going to miss it. For years we've been trying to get testimonials for our stuff from the big shots or the society women. And we can't. Because why? Because they say it isn't dignified. But what's the difference? Cigarettes, toothpaste, face cream, shaving soap—you'll get *them* recommended all right, and what's the difference? I'm not asking you to recommend a bug-powder, but a neat, sveltelooking, silver-plate and enamel job. Let me show it to you, let me explain how it works—that combines all the advantages of a double-sized electric torch with—"

Eagerly, as though to press an advantage, he began to take off the wrappings of the parcel. Morgan, as he looked at Curtis Warren, was more and more startled. This business, which had the elements of howling farce, was not farce at all. Warren was as serious as the Bug-powder Boy.

"But, man, have some sense!" he protested, waving his arms. "If it had been anything else, toothpaste, cigarettes. . . . It can't be done. It'ud make him out to look foolish. . . ."

"Yeah?" said Woodcock coolly. "Well, answer me this. Which is going to make him look more foolish, which is going to show he's more of a mug, this neat little apparatus or that film? Sorry, old man, but there you are. That's my offer. Take it or leave it."

"And otherwise you won't tell who stole that film?"

"That's what I said," agreed the other, almost cordially. "I'll tell you what, old man. You get the cablegrams working; you tell him his bare skin'll be saved if he plays ball with Charley Woodcock. . . ."

"But he'd never do it!"

"Then it'll be just too bad for him. won't it?" asked the other candidly. He folded his arms. "Now you're a nice fellow and I like you. There's nothing personal in it. But I've got to look out for myself. . . . Oh, and don't try to start anything either," he suggested, as Warren suddenly got to his feet. "You start any funny business, and I may not get my testimonial, but the story of T. G. Warpus's brief movie stardom is going to be all over the world as fast as I can broadcast it. Get me? In fact, old man," said Mr. Woodcock, trying to keep his confidential suavity, but breathing a little hard now, "if I don't get some assurance before we leave this boat that T. G. Warpus is a right guy who can take his medicine, *I* might get indiscreet when I'd had a drink too many in the bar."

"You wouldn't do that!" said Peggy.

There was a long silence. Woodcock had turned away to stare past the curtain at the sea, his hand fluttering at his bony chin. The hand dropped and he turned round.

"All right, lady," he said in a rather different voice. "I suppose you win there. No, I guess I wouldn't." He addressed Warren fiercely. "I'm not a crook. I just got mad for a minute, that was all. At least you don't have to worry about that part of it. I may try to pull some fast ones, but I'm not a lousy blackmailer. I've made you a straight proposition, and it stands. Come on, now; I apologise. What about it?"

Warren, slowly hammering his fist on one knee, said nothing. He looked at Peggy. He looked round at Henry Morgan. Morgan said:

"I'm glad you said that, Mr. Woodcock."

"Said what? Oh, about not being a crook? Thanks," the other answered bitterly, "for nothing. I'm not one of those smooth boys who can scare you into doing anything, only they call it successful salesmanship. . . . Why?"

"For instance," said Morgan, trying to keep his voice steady. He had an idea, and he only prayed that he would not bungle it. "For instance, would you like to be tried as accessory after the fact in a murder?"

"Oh, cut it," said Woodcock. "I've been wondering when the bluff would start."

All the same, his pale blue eyes briefly flashed sideways. He had got out a handkerchief and begun to mop his forehead as though he were tired of the whole business; but his bony hand stopped. The word "murder" comes rather startlingly in a business discussion. As the idea grew on Morgan—he thought that in a few minutes, if he kept his jugglery going with a steady hand, they might hear the Blind Barber's name—he had still more difficulty to keep from showing his nervous excitement. *Easy, now.* Easy does it. . . .

"Let's see. You know the name of the man who stole a piece of film from Curt Warren's cabin?"

"I could point him out to you. There's not much chance of his leaving the boat."

"He committed a murder last night. He cut a woman's throat in the cabin next to Curt's. I thought you'd better be warned, that's all. Do you want me to show you the razor he did it with?"

"For God's sake," said Woodcock, jerking round, "be yourself!"

It was dusky and stuffily warm in the white writing-room, with its parade of gold-leafed mirrors and mortuary chairs. The white glass-topped desks, the ink-wells and pen-racks rattled slightly with the slight roll of the *Queen Victoria;* and, with the motion, a drowsy curling swish of water would rise in the silence. Morgan reached into the breast pocked of his coat and took out a folded dark-smeared handkerchief. He opened it just beneath a long beam of sunlight that came through the curtains, and a dull glitter shone inside.

Again there was silence. . . .

But Mr. Woodcock was not having any. Morgan saw him sitting there very straight, his hands relaxed, and a very thin smile fluttered across his face. It was a curious psychological fact, but the very production of evidence, the very display of a blood-stained razor with such sudden convenience, was what seemed to convince Woodcock that he was being elaborately bluffed.

He shook his head chidingly.

"Oh, I remember now, Hank. old man. You're the fellow who writes the stories. Say, I've got to hand it to you at that. You had me wondering for a second." The man looked as though he honestly relished this. "It's all right. I appreciate a good try. I've done the same thing myself. But put it back, old man; put it back and let's talk turkey."

"We don't know who the girl was," Morgan went on, but with a desperate feeling that he had lost his game; "that is, not yet. We were just going up to the captain to find out. It'll be very easy to prove. . . ."

"Now listen," said Woodcock, with an air of friendly

if slightly bored tolerance. "The gag's all right, unnastand. It's swell. But why keep on with it? I've told you I'm not falling for it; I'm too old a bird. So why not talk business?"

"It's true, Mr. Woodcock!" Peggy insisted, clenching her hands. *"Won't* you see its true? We admit we don't know who was killed yet—"

"Well, well!"

"But we will know. Can't you tell us. Can't you give us a *hint?"*

"You'd never suspect," said Woodcock. He smiled dreamily, and looked at the roof with the expression of one who knows the answer in a guessing game that is driving all the players wild. It was having just that effect on these three. To know that the answer was locked up in the bony skull of the man before them, yet to be told coolly they were not to hear it. . . . "I'll give you the answer," observed the Bug-powder Boy, "the moment *I* get the right answer back from T.G. Not before."

"I'll try," began Warren, but the other pointed out *that* was no guarantee.

"You don't believe," Morgan went on grimly, "that there's been a murder by the man who stole that film. Well, suppose you were convinced of it. Wait a bit now! You had your hypothesis, so at least pass an opinion on mine. Suppose there had been a murder and we could prove it, so that you'd be withholding evidence if you kept quiet. Would you tell us then?"

Woodcock lifted his shoulder, still with the pale, tolerant smile on his face. "We-el, old man! No reason why I shouldn't concede that point—in theory. Yes, indeed. If there'd been a murder done, if somebody's been killed, that would be a different thing. I sure would tell you."

"You promise that?"

"Word of honour. Now, if we can just get back to business—"

"All right," said Warren, coming to an abrupt decision. He got up. "We're going to see the captain now. And I'll make a little deal with you. If we can convince you by to-day that a murder's been committed, then you tell what you know. If we can't, then somehow or other, I give you my solemn word I'll get that testimonial from Uncle Warpus."

For the first time Woodcock seemed a little shaken. "I don't know what the gag is," he remarked critically, "and I'm damn sure there's a gag somewhere; but my answer is, You're on. . . . Put 'er there, old man; shake on it. All right! In the meantime, just as a favour to me, you take the little Mermaid along and test it, will you? There are full directions for use inside, but maybe I'd better explain some of the salient points; some features, I'm telling you, that will make the Mermaid Automatic Electric Mosquito Gun the most talked-about item in the advertising world. For example, gentlemen! The old-fashioned, out-moded type of squirt-gun for insects you had to work by hand—working a plunger in and out by hand—didn't you? Exactly. Now, the Mermaid here is automatic. Simply twist this small enamelled button, and electricity does the rest. From the nozzle issues a fine stream of liquid insect exterminator, which can be regulated to greater or less power and range; also to spray in fan-like fashion over a wide area, all by means of buttons. Then again, gentlemen, there is our own unique feature of the electric light. How will you find those troublesome mosquitoes that, under cover of darkness, are making you loose sleep and undermining your health? I'll show you. Simply press this button. . . ."

Warren took the gift from the Greek and Morgan and Peggy hurried him out in case he grew violent in an effort to make Mr. Woodcock disgorge information. Woodcock stood teetering on his heels, smiling tightly, as they left him. In the passage outside they leaned against the wall, rather breathless.

"The low-down crook!" breathed Warren, shaking in the air the Mermaid Automatic Electric Mosquito Gun. "The dirty double-crosser! He knows! He knows, and he won't—"

"But was he serious about that testimonial?" asked Peggy, who could still not get this part of the matter untangled. "I mean, fancy! He can't really mean that he wants your uncle to appear in the newspapers saying, 'I'm wild about Woodcock's bug-powder,' can he? I mean, that would be awful!"

"Baby, that's just it. He's as serious—well, he's as serious as Uncle Warpus trying to swing an international treaty and protect somebody's neutrality. You don't know," said Warren, with some violence, "how self-complacent modern advertising is. They call it public service. Come on. Let's go up and see the old horse-thief upstairs. What Uncle Warpus would say to me if I forced him into endorsing bug-powder is more than a drinkless stomach allows me to contemplate. I have a feeling that the sooner we see Captain Whistler, the old herring, and get this business about the girl straightened out, the sooner I'm going to feel well again. Come on."

"And *I* have a feeling—" said Morgan, and stopped.

He did not continue. But he was right.

Chapter 12

Indiscretions of Curtis Warren

WHEN THEY KNOCKED at the door of Captain Whistler's cabin just abaft the bridge, it was opened by a melancholy steward who was making up the berth and clearing away breakfast dishes in a large, comfortable, rosewood-panelled cabin with curtains of rather startling pattern at the portholes.

"Commander ayn't 'ere, sir," the steward informed them, squinting at Warren in a rather sinister fashion. " 'E's gorn to see Lord Sturton, 'e said you wos to wait, *if you please.*"

Warren tried to be nonchalant, but he showed his apprehension.

"Ah," he said, "Ah! Thanks, steward. How is the old mackerel feeling this morning? That is—er—"

"Ho!" said the steward significantly, and punched at a pillow as he arranged it.

"I see," said Warren. "Well, we'll—er—sit down."

The steward pottered about the cabin, which gave evidence that the captain had fired things about in some haste, and finally doddered out with the breakfast tray. The nasty look he gave them over his shoulder confirmed their hypothesis that the beauties of nature did not induce in Captain Whistler any mood to stand on the bridge and sing sea-shanties.

"I guess he's still peeved," was Warren's opinion. "And this is kind of a delicate matter, Hank. You do all the talking now. I don't think I care to risk it."

"You bet your sweet life I'll do all the talking," agreed Morgan. "I wouldn't answer for any of us if the skipper walked in here and saw you with this razor in your hands. Especially as he's just gone to see Sturton, he is not likely to be in a playful frame of mind. Understand—you are to keep *absolutely silent* throughout the whole interview.

128

Not a word, not a movement unless you're asked to confirm something. I refuse to take any more chances. But I don't know—" He sat down in a leather chair, ruffled his hair, and stared out of one porthole at the pale sky. The sunlit cabin, swaying with drowsy gentleness in a murmurous swish of water conveyed no sense of peace. "I don't know," he went on, "that I feel altogether right about it myself. For the moment let Woodcock keep his information and blast him. *What has happened to that emerald?* That's the question."

"But after all, Hank, it isn't any business of ours," Peggy pointed out, with a woman's practical instinct. She took off her shell-rimmed glasses with a pleased air of having solved the thing, and shut them into her handbag with a decisive snap. "*I* shouldn't bother, old boy. What's the odds?"

"*What's the odds?*"

"Yes, of course I'm jolly sorry for Lord Sturton, and all that; but, after all, he's got pots of money hasn't he? And all he'd do would be to lock the emerald up in some nasty old safe, and what's the good of that? . . . Whereas this film of Curt's is really important, poor boy. I know what *I'd* do if I were a man," she declared scornfully. "I'd take that nasty little Woodcock chap and torture him until he told. Or I'd lock him up somewhere, the way they did to that baron what's-his-name, in *The Count of Monte Cristo,* and not let him have anything to eat and hold soup under his nose and laugh ha-ha until he was willing to tell me. You men *Bah!* You make me tired."

She made a gesture of impatience.

"Young lady," said Morgan, "both your ruthlessness and your logic are scandalous. I have sometimes observed a similar phenomenon in my own wife. Aside from the practical impossibility of holding soup under the bug-powder king's nose and laughing ha-ha, there's the sporting element to consider. Don't say bah. The fact remains that we have pinched old Sturton's emerald and the responsibility—What the devil's that noise?"

He jumped a little. For some moments he had been conscious of a low, steady, hissing noise somewhere about him. In his present frame of mind, it sounded exactly like the sinister hissing which Dr. Watson had heard at midnight in the dark bedroom during the Adventure of the Speckled Band. It was, in fact, the Mermaid Automatic Bug-Powder Gun.

"Curt," said Peggy, whirling suspiciously, "what are you up to *now?*"

"Handy little gadget at that," declared Warren, in some admiration. His eyes were shining, and he bent absorbedly over the elaborate silver and enamel tube. It was a stream-lined cylinder full of scrolls and flutings, with a complicated array of black buttons. From the nozzle a thin wide spray, as advertised, was flying out across the captain's papers on the centre table. Warren moved it about. "All the buttons are marked, you see. Here's "Spray"—that's what I've got on now. Then there's "Half Power" and "Full Power." . . .

Peggy put a hand over her mouth and began to gurgle. This unseemly mirth annoyed Morgan still more. Besides, the spray was peculiarly pungent.

"Turn the damn thing off!" he howled, as a thin spray began to glitter all about them. "No, don't turn it at the wardrobe, you fathead. Now you've got the captain's spare uniform. Turn it—"

"All right, all right," said Warren, rather testily. "You needn't get griped about it. I was only trying the thing out. . . . All I've got to do, you see, is press this dingus and —What's the matter with the fool thing? *Hey!*"

The pressing of the dingus, it is true, did away with the spray. It substituted what to the skilful engineers who designed it was presumably "Half Power." A thin but violent stream of liquid bug-powder ascended past Warren's shoulder as he tried to look at the nozzle and somewhat frantically twisted buttons. All he succeeded in doing was turning on the electric light.

"Give *me* the swine," said Morgan. "I'll fix it. Do something, can't you? It's raining bug-powder; the place is becoming impregnated with bug-powder! Don't turn it on yourself, you blithering idiot. Turn it. . . . O my God, *no!* Not in the captain's berth. Take it out of the captain's berth. . . . No, you can't shut it off with a pillow. Not under the bedclothes, dummy! You're—"

"Well, it's better than having it soak up the room, isn't it?" inquired Warren's hoarse voice, out of a luminous mist of bug-powder. "All right. Don't get apoplexy. I'll shut it off. I'll—" He avoided Morgan's arm, a fiendish expression on his face, and rushed to the middle of the cabin. "No, you don't. I turned this thing on and, so help me, I'll turn it off!" He gestured with the Mermaid, which was hissing like an enthusiastic cobra. "And this is the lousy thing my uncle is asked to endorse, is it? It's a cheat! It's no damn good! I'll find Woodcock and tell him so! I've turned every lousy knob. . . ."

"Don't stand there orating!" shouted Morgan, whom the clammy mist had begun to envelop. "Do something. Fire it out the port-hole. . . ."

"I know what I'll do!" said Warren, with fiendish inspiration. "I know what it is. I'll try *"Full Power."* That's probably the only thing that'll shut the swine off. That's it! If Woodcock had told the truth about it—"

Woodcock had told the truth about it, and could have exhibited a pardonable pride in its response. From the nozzle a fine stream of liquid insect exterminator shot with the force and violence of a fire-hose. Nor could Mr. Woodcock have in the least complained of its accuracy. In fact, it sizzled across the cabin full and true into the face of Commander Sir Hector Whistler just as he opened the door.

Morgan shut his eyes. In that moment of blasting and appalled silence he did not wish to look upon Captain Whistler's countenance. He would sooner have tried to outstare Medusa. Moreover, he wished he could summon his muscles to dive out of the room and run. But he could hear the Mermaid still hissing on the door-post beside the captain's head; and he risked one eye to look, not at Whistler, but at Warren.

Warren found his voice.

"I couldn't help it, Skipper!" he yelled. "I swear by all

that's holy I couldn't help it. I tried everything. I pressed every button, but it wouldn't stop. Look! See, I'll show you! Look . . . !"

There was a sharp click. Instantly the stream gurgled, fell, and died away from the Mermaid's nozzle. It stopped. The Mermaid was as innocuous as she had been before.

Morgan afterwards realised that only one thing saved them then. Peering over the captain's shoulder in the doorway he had seen the startled countenance of Captain Valvick. Only the strangled words, "So—it's—*you!*" issued from the quivering lungs of the *Queen Victoria's* commander before Valvick had shot a big hand over his mouth. With one hand over his mouth and the other impelling him by the sack of the trousers, he hustled the insane skipper into the cabin and kicked the door shut.

"Qvick!" rumbled Valvick. "You get somet'ing to gag him wit' till he cool down, or he call de chief mate and den maybe we iss all in de brig. Ay am hawful sorry, Barnacle, but ay got to do diss. . . ." Frowning, he turned a glance of angry reproachfulness on Warren. "What you want to playing for, anyway, eh? Diss iss no time for playing, ay tell you. After ay take al de time to smoot' old Barnacle down and tell him what we are doing, den it iss no time for playing. Coroosh! What iss dat stuff ay smell in de air?"

"It's only bug-powder, Skipper," insisted Warren. "After all, it's only bug-powder!"

A spasm racked the stout frame of Captain Whistler; his good eye bulged, but his internal noises beat in vain against the Gibraltar of Valvick's hand across his mouth. Nevertheless, Valvick had to use two hands to keep him quiet.

"Honest, Barnacle, diss iss for your own good!" Valvick begged, dragging him over to the chair before his desk and pushing him in. He was answered by a variety of muffled sounds like a steam-calliope heard underground. "Odderwise you are going to do somet'ing you regret. Dese yentlemen can explain; ay know it! If you promise to do not'ing, ay let you loose. Ay mean, you kin svear all you like if it reliefs your mind, but you are not to *do* not'ing. Odderwise we got to gag you, eh? . . . Ay tell you it iss for your own good! . . . Now! You iss a man of your word. What about it, eh?"

A noise of assent and an inclination of the head like the Dying Gladiator answered him. Valvick stepped back, removing his hand.

The ensuing half-hour is one of the things in Morgan's life that he likes to forget. To say that it was nerve-racking would be to employ a spiritless word, and one without those *nuances* which Mr. Leslie Perrigord declares are essential to the power of classic drama. There was much classic fire at one point in the captain's remarks—that at which he frequently clutched his throat, stabbed a shaking finger at Warren like Macbeth seeing the ghost, and kept repeating "He's mad, I tell you! He tried to poison me! He's a homicidal maniac! Do you want him to murder my passengers? Why don't you let me lock him up?"

If, eventually, more sober counsels prevailed, it was due to a circumstance which Morgan did not at the moment understand. Captain Whistler, he was compelled to admit, had certain reasonable grounds for protest. Aside from all questions of personal dignity (the Mermaid's aim had gone straight as Locksley's good clothyard shaft into the skipper's damaged left eye), there was reason for complaint in the general omnipresence of bug-powder. The cabin was haunted by bug-powder. It rose in ghostly waves from his dress uniform; it soaked his berth, pervaded his linen, clung round his shoes, made fragrant his log-book, and whispered sweet nothings from his correspondence. In short, you could safely have wagered that not for months would even the most reckless cockroach be daredevil enough to venture within smelling-distance of anything that was Captain Whistler's.

Therefore it considerably astonished Morgan that in the short space of half an hour he was prevailed on to accept their explanations. True, he placed the Mermaid Automatic Electric Mosquito Gun in the middle of the floor and jumped on it. True, he no whit retreated from his declaration that Curtis Warren was a dangerous lunatic who would shortly be cutting somebody's throat if not placed under observation. But (whether due to Peggy's blandishments or to another cause shortly to be indicated, you shall decide) he consented to give Warren just one more chance.

"Just one more chance," he proclaimed, leaning forward in the chair and bringing his hand down on his desk, "and that's ALL. If there's one more suspicious move out of not only him, but any of you— *Any of you, do you understand?*—then he goes to the brig under guard. That's my last word." Glaring he sat back and sipped the healing whisky-and-soda that had been brought him. "Now, if you don't mind, we'll get down to business. And first I'll tell you this. I promised to share any information I might get, Mr. Morgan, because I considered you at least a sane man. Well, I have some information, although I admit it puzzles me. But before I tell you, there's something I want to point out. The young maniac, and you three as well, have caused me more trouble than anybody I ever had aboard a craft of mine. *I could murder all four of you!* You've caused me more trouble than anybody except the man who stole that emerald; and, in a way, you're involved in that. . . ."

("Steady," thought Morgan.)

"But that's more important. And, if you liked, you could, I say, you *could,* help me a little in return. . . . Are you sure there's nobody listening at that door?"

His tone was so gruffly and uneasily conspiratorial that Valvick peered out the door and closed all the portholes. Peggy said, earnestly:

"I don't think, Captain, you have the least idea how glad we'd be to make it up to you. If there's anything we can do—"

Whistler hesitated. He took another sip of whisky.

"I've just seen his lordship," he went on, as though he hated to make a confession, but that Hector Whistler was a desperate man. "He's—haaa—up in the air, because the emerald wasn't insured. He *had the cheek to say I was drunk or careless, the* ??!!! £ !!!/???¾ ½ ¼ ¾ ⅜ ¼ !!!*old?* !!! £? £ ¾ !—that's what he said! He said it would never have happened if I had left it with him. . . ."

"You haven't found it, by any chance, have you?" asked Morgan.

"No! I have searched this ship with fifteen picked men from fo'c's'le-head to rudder, and I have *not* found it, young man. Now, then, be quiet and listen. I don't think he'll sue the line. But there's a question of law to be considered. That question is: Was I, or was I not, guilty of careless conduct? The emerald was technically in my possession, although I had not locked it in my safe. Show me the lubber," snarled Chaptain Whistler, glaring from one to the other of them, "who says I was guilty of careless conduct—contributory negligence—just show him to me, that's all. Let me so much as glimpse his sky-s'ls, and I'll make him regret the day his father first went courting. Am I guilty of careless conduct if four armed Dagoes take me from behind and give me the marlinspike with a bottle? Am I? *No,"* was Captain Whistler's reply, delivered with a gesture like that of the late Marcus Tullius Cicero, "no, I am not. Well, then. If somebody would tell old Sturton that I was murderously set on without a chance to defend myself. . . . Mind, I don't want you to tell him you *saw* me attacked. If there's any lying to be done, sink me! I can do it myself. But if you could tell him you are able to swear, from your own observation at the time, that you believed me to be the victim of a ruthless attack . . . well, the money don't count much with him, and I'm pretty certain he won't sue. . . . How about it?" inquired the captain, suddenly lowering his voice to a startlingly more normal tone.

There was a chorus of assent.

"You'll do it?" Whistler demanded.

"I'll do more than that, Skipper," said Warren, eagerly. "I'll tell you the name of the son of a bachelor who's got that emerald right now."

"Eh?"

"Yes. I'll give it to you straight from the table. And the man who's got that emerald at this very minute," announced Warren, leaning over and pointing his finger in the captain's face, "is none other than the dastardly crook who's masquerading on this boat as Doctor Oliver Harrison Kyle."

Morgan's spirit, uttering a deep groan, rose from his body and flapped out the porthole on riddled wings. He thought: It's all up now. This is the end. The old mackerel will utter one whoop, go mad, and call for assistance. Morgan expected many strange, possibly intricate observations from the captain. He expected him to order a strait-waistcoat. He expected, in fact, every conceivable thing except what actually happened. For fully a minute Whistler stared, his handkerchief at his forehead.

"You, too?" he said. "You think so, too?" His voice awed. "Out of the mouths of babes and—and lunatics. But wait. I forgot to show you. That was why I wanted you here. I don't believe it. I can't believe it. But when even the maniacs can see it, I've got to hard my helm. Besides, it may not mean that. I don't believe it. I'm going insane myself. Here! Here! Read this!" He whirled to his desk and rummaged. "This was what I wanted you to see. It came this morning."

He held out a radiogram, delicately scented with Swat Number 2 Instantaneous Insect Exterminator, and handed it to Morgan.

Commander, S.S. *Queen Victoria,* at sea [it ran]. Federal agent reports unknown man picked up supposedly dying Chevy Chase outside Washington March 25. Thought victim auto accident concussion of brain. No identification no papers or marks in clothing. Patient rushed to Mercy Hospital in coma. Two weeks delirious until yesterday. Still incoherent but claims to be person aboard your ship. Federal agent thinks crook responsible Stelly and MacGee jobs. Federal agent thinks also physician is impostor on your ship. Well-known figure and must be no mistake made or trouble, and medical profession influential care all sides. . . .

Morgan whistled. Warren uttered an exclamation of triumph as he read the message across the other's shoulder. "You've come to that, have you?" demanded Captain

Whistler. "If that message is right, I don't know what to think. There's no other physician than Dr. Kyle aboard the ship—except the ship's doctor, and he's been with me seven years."

> Will not be definite case trouble. Arrest nobody yet. Am sending man Inspector Patrick knows accused personally. Patrick sailed S.S. *Etrusca* arrive Southampton one day before you. Afford him facilities. Advise.
> ARNOLD, COMMISSIONER N.Y.P.D.

"Ha-ha!" said Warren. He threw out his chest. He took the radiogram from Morgan and flourished it over his head. "Now say I'm crazy, Skipper! Go on, say it—if you can. By God! I knew I was right. I had him figured out. . . ."

"How?" demanded Captain Whistler.

Warren stopped, his mouth slightly open. They all saw the open trap into which, with cheers and wide eyes, Warren had deliberately walked. To tell why he thought Dr. Kyle guilty was exactly the one thing he could *not* do. Morgan froze. He saw his companion's eyes assume a rather glassy look in the long silence. . . .

"I'm waiting, young man," said Whistler, snappishly. "Sink me! I'd be eternally blasted if I'd let the police get all the credit for a capture on *my* ship, sink me! provided I could think of a way to trap that—Go on! Speak up! Why do you think he's guilty?"

"I tell you I've said it from the first. Ask Peggy and Hank and the captain if I haven't! I've sworn he was posing as Dr. Kyle, ever since he batted me over the head in my cabin. . . ."

He stopped suddenly. Captain Whistler, who had started to take a healing pull at his whisky-and-soda, choked. He put down the glass.

"Dr. Kyle batted you over the head in your cabin?" he said, beginning to look curiously at the other. "When was this?"

"I mean, I was mistaken. That was an accident! Honest it was, Captain. I fell and hit my head—"

"Then I'll give you the benefit of the doubt, young man.

I will not be trifled with any longer. You made an accusation, and it seems—I say it *seems*—to be right. Why did you accuse Dr. Kyle?" Warren ruffled his hair. He gritted his teeth feverishly.

"Well, Captain," he said, after a pause, "I knew it! He *looked* guilty. He—had a kind of guilty look about him when he was so pleasant at breakfast and said somebody'd been raped; that's why. . . . You don't believe me, do you? Well, I'm going to show you, and I'm going to prove that he's got to be put under lock and key! So I'll tell you why I came up here to see you. There was a murder committed aboard this boat last night, you old sturgeon! Hank," said Warren, whirling around, *"give me that razor."*

It is a literal fact that Captain Whistler shot at least six inches into the air. Without doubt this was due partly to the extraordinary power in his sea-legs that uncoiled him from his chair like a spring; but behind this materialistic explanation there surged a stronger spiritual ecstasy. And he did not forget what to do. Even as he was descending, his hand flashed into the drawer of the desk and emerged levelling an automatic pistol.

"All right," he said. "Steady, me lads. . . ."

"Captain, it's absolutely true," said Morgan, seizing his arm. "He's not mad and he's not joking. This criminal did commit a murder; I mean, the impostor on the boat. If you'll give me one minute, I'll prove it. Come on, Valvick. To hell with his gun. Let's hold him back in his chair and sit on him until we can jam the truth down his throat. By this time your second officer will have made the rounds of the boat, and he'll find a woman missing. That woman was murdered last night, and she's overboard now—"

There was a knock at the door.

Everybody froze; why, none of them knew, except that it may have been some latent idea they were all making outstanding asses of themselves. A silence fell while Whistler gibbered a command to come in.

"Beg leave to report, sir," said the crisp voice of the second officer. "And"—his eyes flashed over—"*and* to Mr. Morgan, as you ordered. Two of us have made a complete round of the ship. We have investigated every passenger and member of the crew. There was nobody hurt last night."

A vein was beginning to beat in Morgan's temple. He controlled his voice. "Right-ho, Mr. Baldwin. But we're not looking for a person who was merely hurt. We're looking for a woman who is murdered and missing. . . ."

Baldwin stiffened. "Well, sir, you may be," he said in a tone of regret. "But you won't find her. *I have checked over personally everybody on this ship, and there is nobody missing, either.*"

"Is that so, Mr. Baldwin?" inquired Whistler, almost genially. "Well, well."

Warren was escorted to the brig, under heavy guard, at exactly 11:45 Eastern daylight-saving time.

Observations of Dr. Fell

IN THE GREAT book-lined room above Adelphi Terrace the warm May sun threw flat shadows on the floor and the river glittered under its blaze. Through the open windows they could hear the distant bang of the clock in Westminster Tower beating out twelve. Cigar stumps had accumulated, and Morgan was growing hoarse from his recital.

Sitting back in the chair, his eyes half-closed behind the eyeglasses on the ribbon, his chins upheaving in chuckles under the bandit's moustache, Dr. Fell shifted his gaze from the distant traffic along the Embankment.

"Noon," said Dr. Fell. "Now, break off for a minute and I'll order up some lunch. A long cool draught of beer will do you an uncommon amount of good." Wheezing, he pulled a bell-cord. "First, my boy, allow me to say that I would have given a year of my already wasted life to have been with you on that voyage. Heh! Heh-heh-heh! And at the moment I will ask only one question. Is there more to come? Is it really possible for any given group of people to get in *more* trouble than your excellent band has already done?"

Morgan croaked slightly.

"Sir," he said, with a deep gesture of earnestness, "what I've already told you is a—a microscopic atom, an invisibility, a microbe concealed in a drop of water in the vast comprehensive ocean of trouble which is to come. You have heard nothing yet, nothing. That my brain is still whole I am prepared to admit, but why it is still whole I can't tell you. After the sinister episode of the gold watches . . . but that's yet to come."

He hesitated.

"Look here, sir. I know your interest in detective plots, and if I came to ask your aid, I'd want to get everything straight first. That is, I like my own plots to be clean-cut. If it's going to be really a murder story, in spite of all entangled nonsense, I want to know that so that I can be prepared, and not have the whole thing sprung on me as a hoax. I like to see the body on the floor. When somebody disappears in a story, you've nothing solid to go on. It might be—and generally is—a dastardly trick to prove that there's been no murder, or that the wrong person's been murdered, or something that only annoys you. . . . That's from the analytic side, you understand, and not the human side. But, as to the murder, if you ask me at this moment whether there's really been a murder, I've got to admit I can't tell you."

Dr. Fell grunted. He had a pencil in one hand, with which he had been tapping some notes.

"Well, then," he said, blinking over his eye-glasses, "in that case, why don't you ask *me*?"

"You—er—think—?"

"Yes, there's been a murder," replied Dr. Fell. He scowled. "I dislike having to tell you that. I dislike having to think of it, and I hope I may be wrong. There is one thing that, inevitably, you have got to tell me, which will settle any doubts. But one thing I insist on. Don't be afraid of the nonsense. Don't apologise for the vast Christian joy of laughing when an admiral slips on a cake of soap and sits on his own cocked hat. Don't say that it has no place in a murder case, or that a murderer himself can't laugh. Once you set him up as a waxworks horror, leering over his red hands, you will never be able to understand him and you will probably never see who he is. Damn him if you will, but don't say that he isn't human or that real life ever attains the straight level of ghastliness to be found in a detective-story. That's the way to produce dummy murderers, and dummy detectives as well. And yet—"

He stabbed at the notes with his pencil.

". . . and yet, my lad, it's both logical and ironical that this particular case should produce what is in a sense a dummy murderer. . . ."

"A dummy murderer?"

"I mean a professional criminal; an expert mimic; a mask. In short, a murderer who kills for the sake of expediency. How can a person who's playing a part as somebody else be anything more or less than a good or bad copy of the original? So he eludes us in his own personality, and all we've got to judge by is how well he speaks stolen lines. H'm! It makes for better analysis, I dare say, and the mask is undoubtedly lifelike. But, as for seeing his real self in the mask, you might as well question one of M. Fortinbras's marionettes. . . ." He stopped. The small, lazy eyes narrowed. "You jumped a little there. Why?"

"Well—er," said Morgan, "as a matter of fact, they've —er—they've got old Uncle Jules in the brig."

For a moment Dr. Fell stared, and then his vast chuckle blew a cloud of sparks from his pipe. He blinked thoughtfully.

"Uncle Jules in the brig?" he repeated. "Most refreshing. Why?"

"Oh, not for murder or anything like that. I'll tell you all about it. Of course they're going to let him out to-day. They—"

"Humf. Harrumph! Now let me see if I understand this. Let him out to-day? Hasn't the boat docked yet?"

"That's what I was getting at, sir. It hasn't. Thank the Lord for what you've said, anyhow, because that's why I'm here. . . . You know Captain Whistler, don't you? And he knows of you?"

"I have had some experience," replied Dr. Fell, shutting up one eye meditatively, "with the old—um—cuttlefish. Heh! Heh-heh-heh! Yes, I know him. Well?"

"We were to dock early this morning. The trouble was that at the last minute there was a mix-up about our dock or berth or whatever they call it; the *Queen Anne* didn't get under way so that we could move in, and we were left lying in the harbour, with no chance of docking until about two o'clock this afternoon. . . ."

Dr. Fell sat up. "And the *Queen Victoria* is still—?"

"Yes. Due to something you shall hear of in due course, I was able to persuade Whistler to let me go ashore with the pilot; I had to sneak it, of course, or the others would have been wild. But," he drew a deep breath, "Whistler knowing you, I contrived to convince him that, if I could get to you before the passengers left that ship, there might be *kudos* in it for him. Actually, sir, you'll say I had the hell of a nerve, but what I did was practically promise him you'd land him an outstanding crook with credit for it if I could get to you before the passengers left the *Queen Victoria.*"

He sat back and shrugged his shoulders; but he watched Dr. Fell closely.

"Nerve? Ha! Heh-heh-heh!" Nonsense!" rumbled the doctor, affably. "What's Gideon Fell, for, I ask you, if not for that? Besides, I owe Hadley one for doing me in the eye over that Blumgarten business last week. Thank'ee, my boy, thank'ee."

"You think—?"

"Why, between ourselves, I rather think we'll land the Blind Barber. I have rather a strong suspicion," said Dr. Fell, scowling, with a long rumbling sniff through his nose, "who this Blind Barber is. If I'm wrong, there'll be no harm done aside from a little outraged dignity. . . . But, look here, why is it necessary? What about this New York man who was supposed to arrive on the *Etrusca* this morning?"

Morgan shook his head.

"I suppose it's bad to run ahead of my story," he said, "but we've had so many mix-ups, setbacks, and dizzy confusions that one more out of place is comparatively small. The *Etrusca* arrived right enough, but Inspector Patrick isn't on her. He didn't sail at all. I don't know why; I don't make any sense of it at all; but the fact remains that if something isn't done the Barber will walk off that ship a free man in exactly three hours."

Dr. Fell sat back in his chair and for a moment he sat looking vacantly, and in a cross-eyed fashion, at the notes on the table.

"Um! H'm, yes! Hand me that A.B.C. on the tabouret there, will you? Thanks. . . . What train d'jou take this morning? Seven fifty-three to Waterloo? So. Now, then. . . . H'm yes! This would do it. I don't suppose by any chance you have a passenger-list of that ship with you?"

"Yes. I thought—"

"Hand it over." He flicked the pages rapidly until he found a name. Then he went very slowly through it, his fingers following the list of cabins. When he found what he seemed to want, he made a comparison; but it was on the other side of the table and Morgan could not see precisely what had been done. "Now, then, excuse the old charlatan a moment. I am going to make some telephone-calls. Not under torture would I reveal what I intend to do, or where's the fun of mystifying you, hey? Heh! There's no pleasure like mystification, my boy, *if* you can pull it off. . . . As a matter of fact, I'm just going to wire the name of the murdered woman to Captain Whistler, with a few suggestions. Also it would be a good idea to ring up a branch of Victoria 7000 and make other suggestions. Have another bottle of beer."

He lumbered across the room, chuckling fiendishly and stamping his cane. When he returned, he was rubbing his hands in exultation behind a woman laden with the largest, most elaborately stocked lunch-tray Morgan had seen in a long time.

"Mash and sausage," he explained, inhaling sensuously. "Down here, Vida. . . . Now, then. Let's get on with our story. There are several points on which I want to be enlightened, if you feel up to talking over the food. Your case, my boy, is the best surprise-package I've opened yet. With each separate event, I discover, there is no telling whether the thing is a water-pistol or a loaded automatic until you pull the trigger. In a way it's unique, because some of the best clues are only half-serious. . . ."

"Question," said Morgan.

"Exactly. Have you ever reflected," boomed Dr. Fell, tucking a napkin under his chin and pointing at his guest with a fork in the serene assumption that he had never reflected, "on old proverbs? On the sad state of affairs which makes old proverbs so popular, and so easy to quote, precisely because those old platitudes are the only maxims which to-day nobody believes? How many people really believe, for instance, 'honesty is the best policy'?—particularly if they happen to be honest themselves. How many people believe that 'early to bed and early to rise' have the effect designated? Similarly, we have the saw to the effect that many a true word is spoken in jest. A true application of that principle would be too exciting; it would call for much more ingenuity and intelligence than most people are able to display; and it would make social life unendurable if anybody for a moment believed that a true word *could* be spoken in jest—worse, for instance, than going out to dinner with a crowd of psycho-analysts."

"What's all this?" said Morgan. "You can't hang a man on a joke."

"Oh, they're not jokes. You have no idea as to the trend of this?"

"No."

Dr. Fell scribbled rapidly on a sheet of paper, and passed it over.

"Here, for your further enlightenment," he said, frowning, "I have tabulated eight clues. Eight suggestions, if you will. Not one of 'em is direct evidence—it's the direct evidence I'm looking for you to supply in your next instalment of the story. I feel fairly certain you will mention the evidence I want; and my hunch is so strong that I—like several others—will risk Whistler's official head on it. Eh?"

Morgan took the paper, which read

1. The Clue of Suggestion.
2. The Clue of Opportunity.
3. The Clue of Fraternal Trust.
4. The Clue of Invisibility.
5. The Clue of Seven Razors.
6. The Clue of Seven Radiograms.
7. The Clue of Elimination.
8. The Clue of Terse Style.

"It doesn't mean a devil of a lot to me," said Morgan. "The first two you could apply in any way you like. . . . Wait! Don't puff and blow, sir!—I say 'you,' meaning myself. And I don't like to consider the suggestion of the third. . . . But what about seven razors? We didn't find seven razors."

"Exactly," boomed the doctor, pointing his fork as though that explained it. "The point is that there probably *were* seven razors, you see. That's the point."

"You mean we ought to have looked for them?"

"Oh, no! The Barber would have got rid of the others. All you should have done was remember that they were seven. Eh?"

"And then," said Morgan, "this point about seven radiograms. . . . What seven radiograms? There are only two radiograms I mentioned in my story."

"Ah, I should have explained about that," said Dr. Fell, skewering a sausage. "Seven—mystic number; rounded, complete, suggestive number with a curious history. I use it advisedly in place of the word 'several,' because we assume there were several. The interesting thing is that I am not referring to any radiograms you saw. You didn't see 'em. That's very significant, hey?"

"No, I'll be damned if it is," said Morgan, somewhat violently. "If we didn't see 'em—"

"Proceed, then," requested the doctor, waving a large flipper. "I feel positive that before you have finished I shall have noted down eight more clues—sixteen, say—by which we finish and round out our case."

Morgan cleared his throat and began.

PART TWO

Chapter 13

Two Mandarins

AMONG unthinking chroniclers it is much the fashion, at certain movements of mysticism, to embark on a reflection as to how, if it were not for such-and-such a small thing happening, then such-and-such a larger thing would not have happened, and so on until they have ultimately proved King Priam's bootblack responsible for the fall of Troy. Which is, demonstrably, nonsense.

Doubtless such a historian would say that all would yet have been well, when Curtis Warren was installed in a padded cell on D deck, if it were not for two tiny circumstances harmless in themselves. In proof of this he would point out that—if they had only known it—the conspirators were within an ace of catching the Blind Barber himself at least once that day; and there would have been no more lurid happenings aboard the *Queen Victoria*. The present chronicler does not believe it. Men go straight as a stream of liquid exterminator from the nozzle of the Mermaid Automatic Electric Bug-Powder Gun along the line that is determined by their characters, nor can any horseshoe nail affect their destinies. Curtis Warren, as may have been observed from time to time, was a fairly impetuous young man much influenced by the power of suggestion. If he had not got into more trouble one way, it would have been in another; and only a thoughtless quibbler could lay the blame on such excellent articles as a detective novel and a bottle of Scotch whisky.

Sic volvere parcæ! To solace him in captivity they could not share, Peggy Glenn presented him with a bottle of whisky (full size) and Henry Morgan with one of his old detective-novels.

Thereby, incidentally, they showed their own characters. If anybody says Morgan should have known better, it will

149

shortly be indicated how much he had on his mind. Morgan was fighting mad at the perverse orneriness of the Parcæ, and his own none-too-good sense reduced to a minimum. Besides—as he agreed with Peggy—if that stormy petrel, Curtis Warren, were not safe from causing trouble when locked and bolted in a padded cell, where the devil *would* he be safe?

Now let's quit this philosophising and get down to business.

There had been an almost touching scene of farewell after Warren had been shot into the padded cell by three sturdy seamen, of whom two had to undergo considerable repairs in the doctor's office immediately afterwards. It would also take too much time to dwell on their progress down from the captain's cabin to D deck, which resembled an erratic Catharine wheel of arms and legs whirling down companionways and causing pale-faced passengers to bolt like rabbits. With a last heave he was fired into the cell and the door slammed; yet, damaged but undaunted, he still continued to shake the bars and hurl raspberries at the exhausted sailors.

Peggy, in a tearful frenzy, refused to leave him. If they would not let her stay with him, she made a loyal attempt to kick Captain Whistler in a vital spot and get locked up herself. Morgan and Valvick also loyally insisted that, if the old sea-cow thought Warren off his onion, they were loony, too, and demanded their rights of being imprisoned. But this Warren—either with a glimmer of sense or a desire to make a gallant gesture—would not hear of.

"Carry on, old man!" he said, grimly and heroically, shaking hands with Morgan through the bars of the cell. "The Barber's still loose, and you've got to find him. Besides, Peggy's got to help her uncle with those marionettes. Carry on, and we'll nail Kyle yet."

That Whistler did not accede to their demands for a uniform imprisonment, both demand and consent being made in the heat of rage, Morgan afterwards attributed solely to his desire to produce them as witness to Lord Sturton that he had been treacherously attacked. This did not occur to him at the time, or he would have made use of it as a threat; and Captain Whistler would have been saved trouble, as shall be seen, with the choleric peer. All the three consiprators knew was that their ally had been locked away in the bowels of the ship: down a dark companion-way, through a steel-plated corridor pungent with oil and lit by one sickly electric bulb which quivered to the pounding of the ship's engines, and behind a door with a steel grill through which he stared out like King Richard in exile. A sailor with a whistle, reading *Hollywood Romances,* had been stolidly posted on a chair outside, so that the possibility of a jail-break was *nil*.

There was, however, one consolation. The rather sardonic ship's doctor—who believed not at all in Warren's insanity, but found it prudent from long experience not to cross Captain Whistler before his temper subsided—made no objection to supplying the maniac with cigarettes and reading-matter. If he saw the bottle of whisky which Peggy smuggled through in a roll of magazines, he made no sign.

Morgan's contributions to the captive were a box of Gold Flake and a copy of one of his earlier novels called, *Played, Partner!* Now, if you are a very prolific writer of detective-stories, you will be aware that the details of earlier ones tend to fade from your mind even more quickly than they do from the reader's. Morgan remembered in a general way what the book was about. *Played, Partner!* was the tale of Lord Gerald Derreval, known to West End clubland as a wealthy idler, *dillettante,* and sportsman; but known to Scotland Yard under the enigmatic and terrible pseudonymn of The Will-o'-the-Wisp. As a gentleman burglar, Lord Gerald was hot stuff. His thrilling escapes from captivity under heavy guard made Mr. Harry Houdini look like a bungler who had got out of clink only with a writ of *habeas corpus*. Of course, there was never anything really crooked about Lord Gerald. All he did was pinch the shirt off any old reprobate who had been low-minded enough to get rich, thereby qualifying Lord Gerald for a high place in the Socialist literature which is so popular nowadays. Besides, he was redeemed by his love for the beautiful Sardinia Trelawney. In the end he trapped the real villain who had tried to saddle a murder on him; and made it up with Inspector Daniels, the man who had sworn to get him and was in general so weak-minded and got the bird so often that even in the midst of pitying him you wondered how he contrived to hold his job.

These were the details that had faded from Morgan's mind, but such was the dynamite placed in the hands of Mr. Curtis Warren along with an imperial-quart of Old Rob Roy. It would, perhaps, have been wiser to give him a Bradshaw or a volume of sermons; but the moving finger writes, and, having writ, moves on; and, besides, philosophical remarks on this question have already been made. After Peggy had bidden him a tearful good-bye, and Morgan and Valvick had shaken hands with him, they went up in a thunder-fraught mood to see the captain.

"Honest, now," said Valvick rather broodingly, as they crossed the boat-deck in the sunlight that Warren was forbidden to see, "do you t'ank we are right, or iss dere a mistake? Dat wass no yoke, what dey tell us. If dey say dere is nobody missing, den ay don't see how dere is somebody missing. Maybe we talk about a murder and dere is no murder."

"I tell you we're right!" snapped Morgan. "We're right, and it's got to be proved somehow. First thing, I'll tackle Whistler in as cool a frame of mind as I can. I'll challenge him to get that blood on the razor and in the berth tested. The ship's doctor can do it, or maybe Dr. Kyle. . . ."

"Kyle?" said Peggy, staring at him. "But Dr. Kyle—"

"Will you get your mind off that tedious joke?" said Morgan, wearily. "Let's dispose of it once and for all. Don't you realise that Kyle is the one person on the whole ship who can't possibly be guilty?"

"Why?"

"Because he's the one man who's got an alibi, old girl. Look here, Skipper. You're pretty sure your friend with the toothache, the Bermondsey Terror, is honest; aren't you?—all right. And what did he say? He said that he didn't lose sight of Kyle's door all night; that he heard the row on deck from the beginning.. . . Wait a bit. You didn't know about that, did you, Peggy?" He rapidly sketched out the Bermondsey Terror's information, and also gave Valvick the evidence of the Perrigords. "So what? The Blind Barber stole the rest of that film and killed the girl while the row was going on out on deck. Nobody went in or out of Kyle's door all night. So how did Kyle get out and back? It won't wash, I tell you."

"It's you that's the blind one, Hank," she informed him, scornfully. "He needn't have been in his cabin at all, need he? Alibis! Bah! What's the good of an alibi. They always turn out to be fakes, anyway."

Morgan gestured.

"All right. It's easily settled. We're going into action at once, and by the Lord we're going to prove our case. Here's a commission for you, Skipper. Go down and see your friend the Bermondsey Terror and question him. Also see the cabin steward and make any inquiries you think of. . . ."

"Now?" asked Valvick, scratching his head.

"Now. We'll prove it one way or another. To continue," he said to Peggy, as the other muttered a few reflections and lumbered off, "I'll tackle Whistler about that blood. I'll swear it's human blood; and, if it is, we can safely point out to him that nobody could have lost so much and still show no sign of being hurt this morning. Nobody, old girl! Then we'll make the whole round of the ship ourselves, if necessary. And we'll show 'em."

He looked rather malevolently about the boat-deck, which was crowded and noisy. Warren's triumphal progress to the brig had taken place belowdecks and by a devious way, but the news was already flying, so that there was a note of shrillness in the clatter of talk. Somnolent figures in deck chairs, set out to dry themselves under the sun, were sitting up from their rugs; a game of shuffleboard had been suspended and two deck-tennis players came up to the net for a conference. The ship's reigning belle—there is always one—had stopped her professional smiling, her beret pushed over one ear and a cigarette half-way to her mouth, and was bending to listen in a whispering group of admirers. She stood on a raised platform by a lifeboat, her gaudy green scarf blowing against the sky. Far above their heads, on one of the three vast black funnels that showed a faint stain of smoke, the liner's whistle emitted a sudden hoarse *Whooo!* as though it were giving an alarm. A suggestion of lunch was now in the air. There was a good deal of laughter. Morgan scowled.

They found Whistler getting his cabin set to rights and being particularly rough on the steward.

"I won't discuss it," he said, "any more. Maybe I was hasty. I won't say I wasn't. But I acted within my rights, and I'll let that young drunkard or lunatic stop there until I damned well get ready to let him out. We'll say nothing of his story. But take a look around my cabin, just *look* at it, and then tell me whether I didn't do the right thing.' He thrust out his jaw, the good eye narrowed in his battered face, and the gold stripes on his sleeves gleamed as he jammed his fists on his hips. But there was something curiously conciliating about him. "Come now!" he said suddenly. "We're alone. There's no need for you to defend your friend. What's the truth of the matter?"

They could hear the breath whistling from his nose.

"Does this mean, Captain," said Peggy, after a pause in which she seemed taken aback, "that you really don't think Curt is mad, after all? Oooh, you villain! After you ordered those nasty men to *manhandle* and," she gasped, "and mistreat—"

"I want the truth, madam. The truth, that's all. In my position—"

"I say, Captain," said Morgan, after another pause in which Whistler shut his teeth hard, "does this mean something new has happened?"

"Why should it?"

"Oh, I only wondered. . . ." He was looking quickly round the cabin, searching a clue, and then he saw it. Rolled into a wad at one side of the wardrobe lay what looked very much like a sheet tied round stained blankets. "So," said Morgan, "do you mean to tell us a steward saw something queer about the cabin next to Curt's? And went in and found the berth full of bloodstained sheets? And then reported to you? Excellent. Here's the razor that was used in the killing." He took it out of his pocket and laid it on the table, while Whistler stared at him fixedly. "Now everything is fine. All you've done is accuse the wrong man of being a liar and a lunatic, and locked him up under guard. If old Sturton can only get you convicted of criminal negligence to the extent of fifty thousand pounds, the officials of this steamship line will be in an even better humour."

As a matter of fact, he was (despite himself) feeling sorry for the old mackerel. A persistent voice told him that the whole mess was their own fault. All that made him wild was that circumstances seemed conspiring to prevent belief in something he still fiercely felt to be true.

"Murder!" said the captain, in a sort of gulp. "Murder! You have the nerve to stand there and talk to me of murder when there's nobody not accounted for on the whole ship? Where's the murdered person? . . . And don't try to talk to me about what my superiors will think. I put that young lunatic in confinement for an offence against discipline. That's all. An offence against discipline, and that's my right. My word is *law,* and any maritime court—"

"It would make a good story, though," the other pointed out, "printed in the newspapers. Impassioned Defence of Captain Whistler. 'The Dastardly Villain Set on Me with a Bug-powder Gun.' That also would gratify the Green Star Line. Yes, it would. In your eye."

The captain seemed slightly awed.

"Isn't there any justice?" he inquired suddenly. and looked rather blankly about the cabin. "In all God's green earth, isn't there any justice? What have I done to deserve this?"

It was only the beginning of a genuinely powerful, if rather pathetic, oration, for which there was undeniably some justification. It was pitched in a rather Biblical strain. Captain Whistler pointed out and enumerated his afflictions. Masked foreigners, he said, attacked him with stilettos and bottles. Uninsured jewels belonging to ?!£&/!! viscounts were stolen while murdering thieves posed as Harley Street doctors at his table. Blood-stained blankets and razors mysteriously appeared in the cabins; women vanished but did not vanish; the nephews of eminent American administrators first went mad and gibbered of bears and geography then ran amok with bug-powder guns, tried to poison him and finally threatened him with razors. Indeed, an unprejudiced listener would have decided that the situation aboard the *Queen Victoria* was past hope. An unprejudiced listener would have said this boat had been chosen for the annual convention of the Ancient Order of Sorcerers, and that the boys must have been showing off a bit. Captain Whistler said it was too much. He said he was a strong man, but he would rather be thrown to the sharks.

"I know it, Captain," Morgan agreed, uncomfortably, when the typhoon began to die and the skipper went to pour himself a drink with shaking hands. "And, believe it or not, we feel as badly about it as you do. So the first thing we must do—"

"There is nothing to do," said the other, with finality, "except maybe get drunk."

". . . is to join forces and start to unwind this tangle. So here's a guarantee of good faith. We'll go with you to Sturton and clear you absolutely. We'll say we saw you suddenly struck down without a chance to defend yourself; for all you know, it may be true. . . ."

"You'd do that?" demanded the skipper, sitting up. "I was damned if I'd ask a favour of you, but if you would— could . . . man, I'll do anything. I'll even let that madman out of the brig."

Morgan reflected. "As a matter of fact," he said, hesitantly, "for the next few hours I'd rather you didn't."

"HANK!" said Peggy. But she stopped.

"Yes, you see how it is," nodded Morgan, after some thought. "When we thought the captain wouldn't listen to reason, we'd have blown the wall down to get him out. But if we do have co-operation—have we Captain?"

"To the water-line, man."

"Then it may be much the best thing to leave him where he is for the moment. He's thoroughly comfortable, and we have a breathing-space while he's in a place where he can't possibly get into trouble. At least," Morgan amended, rather doubtfully, "I don't *see* how he can get into trouble. The whole thing was in your attitude, Captain. If you'd like us to talk to Sturton now, we're ready."

They met storm signals at the door of the peer's large and rather elaborate suite of cabins on B deck. The door to the drawing-room was on the latch, and they penetrated into a stuffy finery of curtains drawn at the portholes, gilt furniture disarranged, and an array of medicine-bottles sprawled round a chaise-lounge on which Sturton had evidently taken his hitherto sea-sick rest. Whether his recovery had been due to smooth weather or the loss of the emerald they did not know; but he had definitely recovered. From behind the door of the bedroom rose a dry, quick, high-pitched voice in a sort of pounce.

". . . and take a radiogram. Ha. Now. 'Messrs. Kickwood, Bane, and Kickwood, Solicitors.' . . . Spell it? Damn it, Miss Keller, you spell it the way it's pronounced: K-i-c-k-w-o-o-d, Kickwood. Ha. '31B King's Bench Walk.' Or is it 31A? Why can't these confounded lawyers make up their minds? How should *I* remember their infernal addresses? Wait a minute, wait a minute. . . ."

The door popped open in the gloom. A lean figure in a shabby grey dressing-gown, with a worsted plaid shawl wrapped round its shoulders, stared at them. Even indoors it wore a broad-brimmed black hat, and the greyish face underneath had so queer a look, in the midst of Lord Sturton's costly trinkets strewn about the drawing-room, that it reminded Morgan of one of those pictures of wizards in an Arthur Rackham illustration. Also, Morgan wished somebody would open a porthole.

The figure said, "Hah!" and stalked over. It was observable that before this man Captain Whistler looked exactly as Warren had looked before Captain Whistler.

"Well?" said Lord Sturton. "I'm waiting, I'm waiting." He took a thin finger and thumb and flicked at one of his side burns. "Have you got that emerald?"

"If you'll only be patient, sir," replied Whistler, as

though he were trying to swell himself out with affability and be his public beaming self, "I—ha-ha! Of course we shall get it."

"Then you haven't got the emerald. Very well. Why don't you say so?"

"I only wished to say—"

"Rubbish, rubbish, rubbish! Answer me, yes, or no. If you haven't got the emerald, why are you here?" Sturton shot out his neck.

"It was about that little matter we were discussing—ha-ha!" returned Whistler, with a broad gesture of paternal friendliness. "You know I said, your Lordship, that I could bring witnesses to show I had behaved within my duties. You said I was responsible—"

"So you are, so you are. I have your signed receipt. Here."

"The great line of which I have the honour to be one of the senior commanders has always wished, your Lordship, to avoid unpleasantness," began the captain, in a rolling voice. "However, having its best interests at heart. . . ."

"Pfaa!" snapped the other, suddenly sitting down against the back of the chaise-longue and hunching his shawl round his shoulders. "Why don't you say what you mean? You mean that you've been caught fair and square; but what you want is a sporting run. Eh? Eh?"

"That, your Lordship, is putting it harshly. . . ."

Sturton thrust his finger out of the shawl and pointed. "I'll give it you. Damn no man without proof. Bible says so. Prove it to me; no damage suit. There."

Morgan got the impression that he immensely enjoyed being arbiter of somebody's official head; that it tickled a nerve of perverted humour under his dry ribs. He could humour a whim—but the whim had to have its compensations. Morgan realised that, with this sharp-eyed old lad questioning, a lie had to be good. Well, he should be beaten. In a way, Morgan thought, that was incentive enough to save Whistler's bacon! Sturton was leaning back, hugging the shawl round his head. On the table at his elbow was a curious trinket of his own: a Mandarin-head that would wag on its pedestal, and had two rubies for eyes. At intervals he would reach out and set it wagging.

"Well?" he said, abruptly. "Anything to say?"

"A while ago, your Lordship, you intimated to me—as I told this lady and gentleman—that, if I could offer you the proof I said I could," Whistler cleared his throat, "you would not—ah—"

"Well? Well? Where's the proof? I don't see it?"

"These witnesses, you see—"

Morgan got ready, steadying himself. It was unnecessary.

"Who are *you,* young man? Are you the nephew of a friend of mine? Are you Warpus's nephew? Eh?"

"No, your Lordship," interposed the captain. "This is Mr. Henry Morgan, the very distinguished writer, who I thought would offer evidence acceptable. . . ."

Sturton laughed. It was not a pleasant sound. Morgan glanced at Peggy, who had begun to grow frightened. Sturton laughed again.

"Fail first count. *You'd* make no lawyer. I want witnesses I know of. Er—Commander, you stated to me, I think, that you believed you could produce this nephew. Where is he?"

He leaned out and flung the question with a snap of impatience.

The Parcæ were at it again. Morgan could have whistled in admiring astonishment, or sworn from the same situation.

"This morning," continued Sturton, "you stated to me that you could bring him. Why isn't he here? Won't he come?"

Whistler jerked himself out of his hypnotised stare. "Yes, yes, of course. Your Lordship. I—ah—that is, I'm sure he'll be glad to come."

"I repeat to you," squeaked the other, snapping his finger on the Mandarin's head until the rubies winked demoniacally. "that, as this little trial by the court may cost me fifty thousand pounds, I must insist on a direct answer. Don't quibble with me. Don't spoil my entertainment. He was the witness I especially asked for, and the only witness I especially asked for. Why didn't you bring him?"

"It was not exactly *convenient*. . . ." said Whistler, his voice beginning to rise to a roar despite himself. His eye rolled round at Morgan, who could only shrug.

"Ah!" said Sturton. "Signals, eh? Signals. Now then. . . ."

"If you will allow me to go and find him, your Lordship—"

"Once and for all, I demand, I insist on an answer! Where is he?"

All caution boarded the Flying Dutchman and sailed away. "He's in the *brig*; you dried-up lubber!" roared Captain Whistler, exploding at last. *"He's in the brig.* And now I'm going to tell you what I think of you and your ruddy elephant and your—"

Sturton was laughing again.

It was an unholy noise in that gloomy, ill-smelling place, with the rubies winking on the table and Sturton's head bobbing under the broad hat. "Ah." he said, "that's better! That's more like yourself. I'd heard the news, you see. He's in the brig. Yes, yes, Exactly. Why did you put him there?"

"Because he's stark, raving mad. that's why! He attacked me with a razor. He tried to poison me. He gabbled about bears. He—"

"Indeed?" said Sturton. "Mad, is he? Well, well. And this is the man, I think, you wished to call as a witness to your spotless behaviour? This is your star witness, who was to testify how you lost the emerald? . . . Captain Whistler, are you sure that you yourself are entirely in your right mind?"

Peggy went over and patted the skipper on the back, speaking soothing words to him. Her feminine instincts were deeply aroused, for he was almost at the point where there were tears in those honest old eyes. And again he was speechless before the evil weaving of Lachesis. He must now be beginning, Morgan fancied, to have a faint conception of how Warren had felt.

"I am waiting," said Sturton.

Again the mirth tickled his rusty ribs. But he was watching Whistler wind himself up for a few sulphurous remarks, and forestalled him by holding up a scraggy hand.

"Rubbish rubbish rubbish. Wait. Don't say it, Commander. You'd regret it. *I* have something to say. It is only fair to you. The joke has been excellent, excellent. excellent. It has amused me, although, as a lawyer, Commander —tut, tut! But it is time to end it now. I have enjoyed myself long enough. . . . Captain, there will be no suit."

"No suit?"

"None. My secretary informed me of the rumour in the ship. That the nephew of my old friend had been imprisoned for trying to kill somebody. I could not resist amusing myself. Well! Time's ended. Joke's up. I have business. . . . No suit. Finished, ended, done. Don't want to hear of it again."

"But that emerald . . . !"

"Oh, yes! Yes, yes. The stone, of course. Very funny things go on aboard this ship. But why should there be a suit? Maybe the thief reformed; got qualms of conscience. How should *I* know? Anyhow—"

He fumbled in the pocket of his dressing-gown.

He laughed again, shaking his lean shoulders.

Before their astounded eyes he held up, twisting on its gold chain and glittering as it slowly revolved, the emerald elephant.

Chapter 14

Can These Things Be?

"DON'T KNOW how it happened," continued Sturton, rather carelessly, "and don't care, now I've got it back. I know *you* didn't recover it. Ha! . . . Found it lying on the middle of the table there," he stabbed his finger, "half an hour ago. Saw nobody, heard nobody. There it was. Somebody walked in and put it down—Here's your receipt back, Commander. You won't get this elephant again."

Again his squeaky mirth rose as he blinked at their faces. The receipt fluttered out and fell at Whistler's feet.

Morgan only half heard him. He was getting to the point where too many surprises were as deadening as too much pain. Staring at the little Mandarin-head smirking and wagging on the table, he heard Whistler gabbling something, the peer assuring him there would be no trouble, and the end of the latter's squeaky tirade:

". . . find out who stole it? Go on, if you like. *I* won't stop you. But I've got it back, and that's all I care. *I'm* not going to prosecute anybody. Ha! Got enough lawsuits as it is. Let the beggar go. Why bother? Shouldn't be surprised if it got stolen by mistake, and somebody returned it. Never mind. Now get out. Get out! . . ."

He was flailing his arms at them like a banshee, with the emerald gleaming on its chain from one hand. They were shooed into the gangway and the door closed behind them. Then they stood in the corridor on B deck and looked at one another.

"You're quite right, Captain," agreed Morgan, after listening thoughtfully to the skipper's rather weak-voiced comments. "If anything, I should think the adjectives were conservative. But the question remains, who, how, and why?"

After Whistler had recovered himself. swabbing his face with a handkerchief, he was weakly jubilant. He had the air of one who had endured blessed martyrdom in the arena, and suddenly sees ahead of him not the cruel countenance of Nero Ahenobarbus, but a cheering St. Peter at the head of a celestial brass band. The captain drew himself up. His face subtly altered. Taking his receipt for the emerald, he tore it into small pieces and blew them away. Over the battered face, with its plum-coloured eye, there spread a benevolent smile.

"My friends," he said, placing an arm around the shoulders of Peggy and Morgan, "I don't know who returned that ruddy elephant, and I don't care. Whoever it was, he did me a good turn that Hector Whistler will never forget. I could forgive him anything, I could almost forgive him"—momentarily the face darkened, but only for a moment—"*this*. Yes, even the foul blow. foully struck when I wasn't looking. If old Sturton doesn't care—My friends, to-morrow night, our last night at sea, is the captain's dinner. My friends, I will give such a dinner as has never been seen on blue water since the days of Francis Drake. Champagne shall bubble at every table, and every lady shall wear a corsage. And this, my friends, reminds me. I think, I say I *think* that I have in my locker at this moment a bottle of Pol Roger 1915. If it will now please you to come with me and accept the hospitality of an old, rough sea-dog—"

"But, hang it, Captain," said Morgan, "the difficulties aren't one-tenth over. Not a tenth. There's the little matter of a murder. . . ."

"Murder?" inquired the old, rough sea-dog genially. "What murder, lad?"

Mysterious are the ways of psychology.

"But, Captain Whistler!" cried Peggy, "that poor girl . . . down in the cabin beside Curt's . . . that awful razor. . . ."

"Ah, yes, my dear!" agreed the captain tolerantly benevolent. "Yes, of course. You mean that little joke of yours. Of course. Yes. Ha-ha-ha!"

"But—"

"Now, my dear," the other pursued, with radiant kindliness, "you listen to me. Come! You take a bit of advice from a rough old seafaring man old enough to be your father. From the first I've liked the cut of your jib, Miss Glenn, and the swing of your spanker-boom. Aye, lassie, I might have had a daughter like you if the Mrs. W. that was hadn't been dead and gone these twenty years, rest her sweet soul. It was in a sou'wester off Cape Hatteras, I mind. . . . But you don't want to hear of that. This is my advice, lassie. When a murder's been committed, in my experience, there's somebody dead," Captain Whistler pointed out, with irrefutable logic. "And if somebody's dead, that person can't be breathing heaven's free air on my deck. There's nobody missing, and nobody's complained, which they generally do in case of a murder. So— come, now; until somebody complains, I'm a free man. Just between ourselves, wasn't somebody having you on?"

"But you promised, Captain, that you'd co-operate and help us and—"

"And so I will, Miss Glenn," he told her, heartily, patting her shoulder. "You two—and old Sharkmeat also, if he likes—shall have the freedom of the ship, to question whom you like, and say I sent you. If you have news, ha-ha-ha! come to me. . . . By the way, would you like me to release that poor lad from his cell? No? Well, remember that I offered. I'll tell you what I'll do. I'll send him a fine basket of fruit, with my compliments, and a specially cooked capon for his dinner. How's that? Then, when we touch England day after to-morrow, we'll see what can be done about obtaining the services of the finest mental-specialist in London. . . ."

He stopped.

"Yes," said Morgan, seizing the opportunity, "and that reminds us all of Dr. Kyle, doesn't it? Not that I believe he's the Blind Barber, but it takes us back to that radiogram from the Police Commissioner, and the fact that— whatever else you believe or don't believe—there's a damned dangerous criminal aboard."

"H'm!" said Whistler. "H'm! Possibly. In any case, I've been instructed not to do anything, haven't I, in case there's a mistake, eh? And the more I think it over, sink me!" he said with a happy flash of inspiration, "the more I'm convinced there *has* been a mistake. Why? I'll tell you. Because dangerous criminals don't steal fifty-thousand-pound jewels and then *return* 'em, do they? Sink me! you know, if I hadn't been assured by old Sturton that the emerald was returned to him while young Warren was in the brig—well I'd be fairly sure it was more of his mad vapourings. But I know it couldn't have been young Warren. . . ."

"Thank God for *that*," said Morgan.

"Anyhow," continued Whistler, assuming his hearty manner again, "I'll think it over. I believe it's a mistake and there's no crook aboard at all. Though—h'm—it would be a feather in the cap of the Green Star Line if I could have the honour of nabbing a notorious criminal before that New York detective arrived. I'll think it over. So, if you won't drink a health in Pol Roger—eh—no? Well, good day, good day, good day!"

He was off, saluting jauntily, before the stupefied allies could stop him. He swung his shoulders, his thumbs hooked in his pockets, and he was hoarsely humming a tune to the effect that Captain Ball was a Yankee slaver, blow, blow, blow the man down! His smile was radiant.

When he had gone, Peggy looked about hopelessly.

"Hank," she said, "it's no good. We can't beat Providence. Let's give it up. Let's go to the bar and get screamingly drunk."

Morgan replied grimly: "We will not. Give it up, I mean. But a couple of quick ones in the bar might fortify us before we comb this boat from stem to stern. . . . Why's the place so quiet, anyway?" He peered round. "They're all at lunch, that's it! We've missed lunch, and I didn't even hear the bugle. Never mind; we can get a sandwich in the bar. Come on. This thing has got to be thrashed out. Girl, that emerald's turning up puts the absolute lid on it! . . . What do you suppose could have happened?"

"Oh, drat the emerald!" she sniffed, with some pettishness. "Who cares about their nasty old emerald, anyway?

We'll find out about this girl, if you like. But, honestly, Hank, I'm beginning to think we must be wrong, after all. H'm! I'll bet she was a hussy, anyway. . . ."

"She was calling Curt's name," her companion reminded her. He was determined not to lose his last ally. "She knew something that concerned him, don't you see? So if you want to help him, she'll be your first concern. It probably concerns the film; remember *that* my wench! Besides, have you forgotten another thing? Curt promised that chap Woodcock—definitely gave him his word—that he'd demonstrate by to-day there'd been a murder committed, or else force a bug-powder endorsement out of old Warpus."

She put her hand to her forehead. "Oh, I say, but I'd forgotten all about that awful little man! Oh, Hank, this is dreadful! And when I think of my poor Curt languishing behind prison bars, sitting there forlornly with his poor head in his hands. . . ." A sob caught her throat; she choked, and the tears overflowed here eyes. "Oh, it's awful, awful, awful!"

"Well, my God! don't cry about it!" said Morgan, waving his arms desperately. He peered round to make sure there was nobody in sight. "Look here. I didn't know you felt like that about it. Listen! *Stop* yowling, will you? It's all right. You heard what the skipper said. We'll go right down and get him out—"

"Oh, I w-wouldn't g-get him out f-for anything!" she gulped, forlornly, over the handkerchief she was jabbing at the corners of her eyes. Her breast heaved jerkily. "He —h-he'd only d-do some perfectly m-mad thing straight-away and g-get p-put right—right b-back in again. But, oh, d-dear! when I think of the p-poor d-darling l-languishing, p-positively—l-languishing—in—in a—foul d-dun— *bubuloo!*" choked Peggy, and burst into a spasm of weeping.

These, reader, are the times that try men's souls: when tears flow by reason of some inexplicable logic that escapes you, and all you can do is to pat her shoulder whilst desperately wondering what is wrong. He tried remonstrance —an error. He pointed out that it was not as though Warren had been shoved in the Bastille, never again to see the light of day; adding that the maniac was quite comfortable there and had been promised a specially cooked capon for his dinner. She said she wondered how Morgan thought the poor boy would have the heart to eat it. She said he was a cruel, callous beast ever to think of such a thing; and went off the deep end again. After this crushing retort, all he could think of was to rush her to the bar for a couple of stiff drinks as quickly as possible.

That her tears were dried was due to a new cause for worry, which he saw presented itself to her as soon as they entered the bar.

The bar (quaintly called smoking-room) was a spacious oak-panelled cathedral at the rear of B deck, full of stale smoke and a damp alcoholic fragrance. There were tables in alcoves of deep leather lounges, and a number of gaunt electric fans depending from the pastoral-painted ceiling. Except for one customer, who stood at the bar counter with his back towards them, it was deserted. Sunlight streamed through windows of coloured mosaic glass swaying gently on the floor; only peaceful creakings of woodwork and the drowsy murmur of the wake disturbed its cathedral hush.

Peggy saw the one customer, and stiffened. Then she began to advance stealthily. The customer was a short, stocky man with a fringe of black hair round his bald head, and the arms and shoulders of a wrestler. He was just raising his glass to his lips when he seemed warned by some telepathic power. But before he could turn Peggy had pounced.

"*Ah!*" she said, dramatically. She paused. She drew back as though she could not believe her eyes. "*Tiens, mon oncle! Qu'est-ce que je vois? Ah, mon Dieu, qu'est-ce que je vois, alors?*"

She folded her arms.

The other started guiltily. He turned round and peered up at her over the rim of his glass. He had a reddish face, a large mouth, and an enormous curled grey-streaked moustache. Morgan observed that the moment Peggy fell into the Gallic tongue her gestures corresponded. She became a whirlwind of rattling syllables. She rapidly smacked her hands together under the other's nose.

"*Eh bien, eh bien! Encore tu bois! Toujours tu bois! Ah, zut, alors!*" She became cutting. "*Tu m'a donné votre parole d'honneur, comme un soldat de la France! Et qu'est-ce que je trouve? Un soldat de la France, hein! Non!*" She drew back witheringly. "*Je te vois en buvant le* GIN!"

This, unquestionably, was Uncle Jules sneaking out with the laudable purpose of knocking off a quick one before his niece caught him. A spasm contorted his face. Lifting his powerful shoulders, he spread out his arms with a gesture of extraordinary agony.

"*Mais, chérie!*" he protested in long-drawn, agonised insistence like a steamer's fog-horn. "*Mais, ché-é-riii-e! C'est un très, très, très petit verre, tu sais! Regards-toi, cherié! Regards!! C'est une pauvre, misérable boule, tu sais. Je suis enrhumé, chérié*—he coughed hollowly, his hand at his chest—"*et ce soir*—"

"*Tu parles! Toi,*" she announced, pointing her finger at him and speaking in measured tones, "*toi, je t'appelle dégoutant!*"

This seemed to crush Uncle Jules, who relapsed into a gloomy frame of mind. Morgan was introduced to him, and he followed them to a table while Morgan ordered two double-whiskies and a milk-and-soda. Uncles Jules appealed in vain. He said he had never had so bad a cold in his life, coughing hideously by way of demonstration, and said that if nothing were done about it he would probably be speechless by five o'clock. Peggy made the obvious retort. She also adduced examples from a long list of Uncle Jules past colds, including the time in Buffalo when he had been brought back to the hotel in an ash-cart.

He brightened a little, however, as he described the preparations for the performance that night. Preparations marched, he said, on a scale superb. Three hand-trucks had been provided to convey his fifty-eight separate marionettes (housed in a cabin of their own adjoining his, although they were *not* sea-sick, happy *gosses*) together with all the vast machinery of his theatre, to the hall of concert.

The three costumes, one in which he spoke the prologue, and two for his extras, the French and Moorish warrior, were now being given a stroke of the iron; the piano and violin for off-stage music were installed behind the scenes as the theatre was set up in the hall of concert. A hall of concert magnificent, situated on B deck, but with a back-stage staircase leading up from the dressing-room on C deck. Which reminded him that, while investigating the dressing-room. he and his assistant, Abdul, had met M. and Mme. Perrigord.

"A husband and his wife," pursued Uncle Jules, excitedly, "very charming, very intelligent, of whom the cabin finds itself near by. Listen, my dear! It is he who has written of me those pieces so magnificent which I do not understand. One thousand thunders, but I am enchanted! Yes, yes, my dear. Among us we have arranged the order of the performance. Good! Also we have met a Dr. Keel, a medicine Scottish, who will make recitations. Good! All is arranged. Two professors of a university who voyage shall shall be our warriors; M. Furioso Camposozzi at the piano and M. Ivan Slifovitz at the violin have arranged for accompanying my sitting with music of the chamber which I do not understand, see you? but, ah, my dear, what a triumph of intelligence. For me, I shall be superb? I—"

"Dear uncle," said Peggy, taking a soothing draught of whiskey neat and sighing deeply afterwards, "it is necessary that I speak with this monsieur. Go to your cabin and couch yourself. But attend! It is I who speak! *Nothing to drink*. Nothing! Is it understood?"

M. Fortinbras swore that an old soldier of France would cut his throat sooner than break his promise. He finished his milk-and-soda with a heroic gesture, and doddered out of the bar.

"Listen, Hank," said Peggy, dropping the language of Racine. She turned excitedly. "Seeing the old boy has just brought me back to business, I've got to see that he keeps sober until after the show; but it's given me an idea. . . . You're determined on questioning everybody on this boat, seeing everybody face to face. . . ."

"I'm letting nobody by," returned Morgan grimly, "except the people we *know* to be aboard. I'm going to take a passenger-list, and get a crew-list from the captain, and check everybody if it takes all afternoon. It would be devilish easy for somebody to conceal an absence when that first officer went round. 'Oh, no, she wasn't hurt—sorry she isn't here; she's lying down; but I can give you my word. . . .' Peggy, that girl hasn't vanished. She's somewhere on the boat. She's a real person! Hang it, we saw her! And she's going to be found."

"Righto. Then I'll tell you your pretext."

"Pretext?"

"Of course you've got to have a pretext, silly. You can't go roaring about the ship after somebody who was murdered and starting an alarm, can you? Fancy what Captain Whistler would say, old dear. You've got to do it without arousing suspicion. And I've got the very idea for you." She beamed and winked, wriggling her shoulders delightedly. "Get hold of your dear, dear friend Mrs. Perrigord—

Morgan looked at her. He started to say something, but confined himself to ordering two more whiskies.

". . . and it's as easy as shelling peas. You're looking for volunteers to do amateur acts at the ship's concert. *She's* in charge of it. Then you can insist on seeing everybody without the least suspicion."

Morgan thought it over. Then he said:

"Ever since last night, to tell the truth, I have been inclined to scrutinise any idea of yours with more than usual circumspection. And this one strikes me as being full of weak points. It's a comparatively simple matter if I encounter a lot of shy violets who are averse to appearing in public. But suppose they accept? Not that I personally would object to an amateur mammy-singer or a couple of Swiss yodellers, but I don't think it would go well with the chamber-music. How do I persuade Mrs. Perrigord to accompany me, in the first place, and to put all my crooners on the programme, in the second?"

Peggy suggested a simple expedient, couched in even simpler language, to which Morgan rather austerely replied that he was a married man. "Well, then," Peggy said excitedly, "it's even easier than *that,* if you're going to be fussy and moral about it. Like this. You tell Mrs. Perrigord that you're after material for character-drawing, and you want to get the reactions of a number of diversified types. On Being Approached to Make Exhibitions of Themselves in a Public Place. . . . Now don't misunderstand me and get such a funny look on your face! She'll eat it up. All you've got to do is suggest getting somebody's reactions to some loony thing that nobody's ever thought of before, and the highbrows think it's elegant. Then you might jolly her along and sort of make goo-goo eyes at her. As for the volunteers, bah! You can turn 'em all down after you've heard 'em rehearse, and say it won't do. . . ."

"Woman," said Morgan, after taking a deep breath, "your language makes my gorge rise. I will *not* make goo-goo eyes at Mrs. Perrigord, or anybody else. Then there is this question of rehearsing. If you think I have any intention of sitting around while amateur conjurers break eggs in my hat and wild sopranos sing "The Rosary," you're cockeyed. Kindly stop drivelling, will you? I've been through too much to-day."

"Can you think of any better plan?"

"It has its points, I admit; but—"

"Very well, then," said Peggy, flushed with triumph and two whiskies. She lit a cigarette. "I'd do it myself with *Mr.* Perrigord, only I have to help uncle. I'm the Noises Offstage, you know: the horses, and Roland's horn, and all that, and I've got to get my effects set up this afternoon. I'l get it over as quickly as I can, because we *must* find that film. What I really can't understand is why our crook returned that emerald and yet didn't—I suppose he really didn't put the film back in Curt's cabin, did he? Do you think, we ought to look?"

Morgan made an irritable gesture.

"Don't you see that it wasn't the barber who did that? Off-hand, you'd say that there was only one explanation of it. When we chucked it away, it landed either in Kyle's cabin or in the Perrigords'. The obvious answer is that one of 'em found it in the cabin, meditated keeping it, then got scared at the row and sneaked it back to Sturton. But, damn it all! I can't believe that! Does it sound like Kyle? It does NOT. Conversely, if Kyle is a masquerading crook you can lay a strong wager that a cool hand like the Blind Barber wouldn't return that emerald—as Whistler said. Wash out Kyle either because he's a crook or because he isn't. If he's genuinely a great brain specialist he wouldn't do one thing, and if he's genuinely a great crook he wouldn't do the other. . . . And what have we left?"

"You think," demanded Peggy, "that nasty Mrs. Perrigord—?"

"No, I don't. Or friend Leslie, either. I can see Leslie handing over the emerald to Sturton with immense relish, and giving a long dissertation on the bad taste of gaudy baubles, but— Ah! News! Enter our squarehead."

He broke off and gestured to Captain Valvick, who had just shambled into the bar. The captain was puffing hard; his leathery face looked redder than ever, and, as he approached, he distilled like a wandering oven a strong aroma of Old Rob Roy.

"Ay been talking wi' Sparks and de Bermondsey Terror," he announced, somewhat unnecessarily and wheezed as he sat down. "And, ay got proof. Dr. Kyle iss not de crook."

"You're sure of that?"

"Yess. De Bermondsey Terror iss willing to swear. He iss willing to swear Dr. Kyle has gone into his cabin last night at half-past nine and he hass not left it until de breakfast bugle diss morning. He know, because he hass heard Dr. Kyle iss a doctor, and he wonder whedder he can knock on de door and ask him if he can cure de bad toot'. He didn't do it because he hass heard Kyle is a great doctor who live in dat street, you know, and he iss afraid of him. But he knows."

There was a silence.

"Hank," Peggy said, uneasily, "more and more—that radiogram from New York, where they were so sure— don't you think there's a dreadful mistake somewhere?

What *can* be happening, anyhow? Every time we think we know something, it turns to be just the other way round. I'm getting frightened. I don't believe anything. What can we do now?"

"Come along, Skipper," said Morgan. "We're going to find Mrs. Perrigord."

Chapter 15

How Mrs. Perrigord Ordered Champagne, and the Emerald Appeared Again

CLEAR YELLOW EVENING drew in over the *Queen Victoria* moving steadily, and with only a silken swishing past her bows, down towards a horizon darkening to purple. So luminous was the sky that you could watch the red tip of the sun disappear at the end of a glowing path, the clouds and water changing like the colours of a vase, and the crater of glowing clouds when the sun was gone. The dress bugle sounded at the hush between the lights. And the *Queen Victoria,* inspired for the first time by that mild fragrance in the air, woke up.

Sooner or later on any voyage this must happen. Hitherto-blank-faced passengers rouse from their deck-chairs and look at one another. They smiled nervously, wishing they had made more acquaintances. The insinuating murmur of the orchestra begins to have its suggestion on them; they see broad Europe looming, and lamps twinkling in the trees of Paris. A sudden clamour of enjoyment whips the decks like the entrance of a popular comedian. Then they begin by twos and threes to drift into the bar.

Activity had begun to pulse this night before it was quite dark. The beautiful, mongoose-eyed shrew who was going to Paris for her divorce searched out her shrewdest evening-gown; so did the little high-school teacher determined to see the Lake Country. Love affairs began to flicker brightly; two or three bridge games were started; and the disused piano in the screened deck off the bar was rolled out for use. The dining-saloon was in a roar of talk. Diffident ladies had come out with unexpected rashes of jewels, optimists ordered from the wine-list, and the orchestra was for the first time encouraged. When Henry

Morgan—tired, disgusted, and without energy to dress for dinner—entered with his two companions towards the close of the meal, he saw that it was the beginning of what for the sedate *Queen Victoria* would be a large night.

His own ideas were in a muddle. After four exasperating hours of questioning, he was almost convinced that the girl with the Greek-coin face had never existed. She was not aboard, and (so far as he could ascertain) had never been aboard. The thing was growing eerie.

Nobody knew her, nobody remembered having seen her, when at length in desperation he had dropped the pretext of searching for music-hall talent. On the tempers of some already harassed people, in fact, this latter device had been ill-timed. Its effects on Lord Sturton, on an Anglo-Indian colonel and his lady not yet recovered from *mal-de-mer,* on a D.A.R. from Boston and kindred folk, had been a bouncer's rush from the cabin before the request was fully out of his mouth. Even Captain Valvick's easy temper was ruffled by receptions of this kind.

Mrs. Perrigord, on the other hand, had been invaluable. Although she must have been aware that there was more in the tour than Morgan would admit, she had been impassive, helpful, even mildly enthusiastic. She took on herself a duty of cutting things short in a way that the easygoing novelist admired but could not imitate. When a proud mother eagerly went into long explanations of how her daughter Frances, aged nine, could play "Santa's Sleigh-Bells" on the violin after only six lessons, and how Professor E. L. Kropotkin had confidently predicted a concert future, then Mrs. Perrigord had a trick of saying, "I reolly don't think we need waste your time," in a loud, freezing voice which instantly struck dumb the most clamorous. It was an admirably frank trait, but it did not add to Morgan's comfort through those long, hot, gabbling, foodless hours in which he acquired a distaste for the entire human race.

Mrs. Perrigord did not mind at all. She said she enjoyed it, chatting volubly all the while, and coyly taking Morgan's arm. Moreover, she took quite a fancy to Captain Valvick, who, she confided to Morgan in a loud side-whisper, was so fresh and unspoilt, a definition which the skipper seemed to associate vaguely with fish, and which seemed to fret him a good deal. Another curious, puzzling circumstance was the behaviour of Warren, when they looked in on him in the padded cell just before going down to dinner.

It was growing dark, but he had not switched on the light in his cell. He was lying at full length on the bunk, his face turned to the wall as though he were asleep. In one hand was a closed book with his finger marking the place in the leaves. He breathed deeply.

"Hey!" said Morgan, whistling through the bars. "Curt! Wake up! Listen . . . !"

Warren did not stir. An uneasy suspicion assailed his friend, but he thought he could see the whisky-bottle also, and it appeared to be only slightly depleted: he could not be drunk. Mrs. Perrigord murmured, "Pooah lad!" The sailor on guard duty, who had respectfully risen, said the gentleman 'ad been like that all afternoon; was exhausted-like.

"Ay don't like dis," said Valvick, shaking his head. "Ahoy!" he roared, and pounded at the bars. "Mr. Warren! Ahoy!"

The figure moved a little. It raised its head cautiously in the gloom and there was a fiendish expression on its face. Placing a finger on its lips, it hissed *"Sh-h-h!"*, made a fierce gesture for them to go away, and instantly fell somnolent again.

They went. Whatever the meaning of the episode, it was driven from Morgan's mind by the prospect of food and drink. The fragrance and glitter of the dining-room soothed his rattled nerves; he breathed deeply once more. But— there was nobody whatever at the captain's table, not even Dr. Kyle. In the middle of the crowd and clatter, every chair remained ominously empty. He stared.

". . . Now you *must,"* Mrs. Perrigord was saying, "you really *must* come and dine at ouah table to-night, you kneow. Whatevah is worrying you, Mr. Morgan, I must insist on youah forgetting it. Come!" Her smile became mysterious as she took her rather dazed guests across the room. "Les-leh will not be with us to-night. He will dine on milk and dry biscuit, and prepare himself foah his talk." She leaned close to Morgan. "My husband, you know, has rather extrooordinry principles, Mr. Morgan. But I, on the othah hand—"

Again she smiled. That was how she came to order champagne.

After the soup, Morgan felt a warmth steal through him. After the fish, his wolfish silence began to wear thin and his spirits stirred from their depths. In the midst of a tender steak, done rare between crisp marks of the grill and smoking between those smooth-slipping chipped potatoes whose edges have no hardness, he suddenly felt a pleased sense of relaxation. The music of the orchestra did not sound far away, and he rather liked the appearance of the faces about him. Life looked less like a heap of unwashed dishes, and the warm lights were comforting. Champagne nipped warm and soothing. Captain Valvick said, "Ahh-h!" on a long-drawn note. When the steak disappeared, to be replaced by mysteriously tinted ice-cream and smoking black coffee, his spirits commenced to soar. He appreciated the noise that people were making around him. The champagne nestled through his innards, causing him to beam round on Mrs. Perrigord and the captain; to find himself keeping time with his foot when a reckless orchestra ventured into Gilbert and Sullivan.

"Ta-ti-ta-ta-ta-, ti-ta-ta-ta-*ti*; sing, 'Willow, tit-willow, tit-wilow,' " murmured Henry Morgan, wagging his head expansively. He smiled, and Mrs. Perrigord spread effulgence in reply. " 'Iss it veakness of intellect, birdie, ay cried—!' " whoomed Captain Valvick, drawing back his chin for a thoughtful rumble; " 'Or a tough worm in youah little in-side—' " gently speculated Mrs. Perrigord, beginning to giggle; and all three together, inspired with a surge of mirth, whirled out together:

> "With a shake of his poor little head he replied,
>   " 'Willow,
>   " 'Tit-willow,
>   " 'Tit-willow!' (WHEE!)"

"Oh, I say, you know," protested Mrs. Perrigord, whose face was growing rather flushed and her voice more loud, "we reolly shouldn't be doing this at oll, should we? Oh, I *say!* Heh-heh-heh! Shall we have anothah bottle?" she beamed on them.

"You yust bet we do!" boomed Captain Valvick. "And diss one iss on me. Steward!" A cork popped, pale smoke sizzled, and they raised glasses. "Ay got a toast ay like to giff. . . ."

"Oh, I say, you know, I reolly mustn't!" breathed Mrs. Perrigord, putting her hand against her breast; "just fancy! What would deah Les-leh ay? But if you two positively outrageous people positively insist, you know. . . . Heh-heh-heh! Here's loud cheeahs!"

"What I mean to say is this," said Morgan vigorously. "If there's any toast to be drunk, first off there ought to be a toast drunk to Mrs. Perrigord, Skipper. She's been the best sport in the world this after, Skipper, and I'd like to see anybody deny it. She came with us on a fool's errand, and never asked one question. So what I propose—"

He was speaking rather loudly, but he would not have been heard in any case. The entire dining-saloon had begun to converse in an almost precisely similar vein, with the exception of one or two crusty spoil-sports who stared in growing amaze. They could not understand, and would go to their graves without the ability to understand, that mysterious spirit which suddenly strikes and galvanises ocean liners for no reason discernible to the eye. Laughter in varying tones broke like rockets over the tumult; sniggers, giggles, guffaws, excited chuckles growing and rushing. More corks popped and stewards flew. It being against the rules to smoke in the dining-saloon, for the first time a mist of smoke began to rise. The orchestra smashed into a rollicking air out of *The Prince of Pisen;* then the perspiring leader came to the rail of the balcony and bowed to a roar of applause, dashed back and whipped his minions into another. Jewels began to wink as total strangers drifted to one another's tables, made appointments, gesticulated, argued whether they should stay here or go up to the bar;

and Henry Morgan ordered a third bottle of champagne.

". . . Oh, no, but I say, reolly!" cried Mrs. Perrigord, sitting back in a sort of coy alarm and talking still more loudly, "you mustn't! You two outrageous people are positively outrageous, you know! It's simply dreadful how you take advantage of a pooah, weak woman who"—gurgle, gurgle, gurgle—"it's reolly lovely champagne, isn't it?—who can't defend herself, you know. Just fancy, you wicked men, I shall be positively *tight,* you know. And that would be owful, wouldn't it?" She laughed delightedly. "Simply screamingly, deliciously owful if I am tight when I am tight, and—"

"What ay say iss diss," declared Captain Valvick, tapping the table and speaking in a confidential roar. "De champagne iss all right. Ay got not'ing against de champagne. But it iss not a man's drink. It do not put hair on de chest. What we want to drink iss Old Rob Roy. Ay tell you what. After we finish diss bottle we go up to de bar and we order Old Rob Roy and we start a poker game. . . ."

". . . but I say, you mustn't be so owfully, owfully *formal,*" said Mrs. Perrigord chidingly. "*Henry.* Theah! I've said it, haven't I? Oh, deah me! And now you'll think I'm positively"—gurgle, gurgle, gurgle—"positively *dreadful,* won't you? But I have so *many* things I should like to discuss with you, you know. . . ."

A new voice chirped:

"Hullo!"

Morgan started up, rather guiltily, to see Peggy Glenn, in a green evening gown that looked rather disarranged, negotiating the last step of the staircase and bearing down on them. She was beaming seraphically, and something in her gait as she moved through the layers of smoke struck Morgan's eye even out of a warmth of champagne. Mrs. Perrigord turned. "Why, my deah!" she cried, with unexpected and loud affection. "Oh. how reolly, reolly *wonderful!* Oh, do, do come heah! It's simply wonderful to see you looking so spic hic, so sick and span after oll those owful things that happened to you last night whee! And—"

"Darling!" cried Peggy ecstatically.

"Peggy," said Morgan, fixing her with a stern eye, "Peggy, you—have—been—drinking."

"Hoo!" cried Peggy, lifting her arm with a conquering gesture by way of emphasis. Her eyes were bright and pleased.

"*Why* have you been drinking?"

"Why not?" inquired Peggy, with the air of one clinching a point.

"Well then," said Morgan magnanimously "have another. Pour her a glass of fizz, Skipper. All I thought was after all that bawling and screaming this afternoon—"

"You did. You bawled and screamed this afternoon about Curt being shut up in a foul dungeon with the rats, and—"

"I hate him!" Peggy said passionately. She became tense and fierce, and moisture came into her eyes. "I hate and loathe him and despise him, that's what I do. I don't ever want to hear his name again, ever, ever, ever! Gimme a drink."

"My God!" said Morgan, starting up. "What's happened *now*?"

"Ooo, how I loathe him! He wouldn't even speak to me, the f-filthy w-wretch," she said, her lip trembling. "Don't ever mention his name again, Hank. I'll get blind, speechless drunk, that's what I'll do, and *that'll* show him, it will, and I hope the rats gnaw him, too. And I had a big basket of fruit for him, and all he did was lie there and pretend he was asleep, that's what he did; and I said, "All right!", so I went upstairs and I met Leslie—Mr. Perrigord—and he said, would I like to listen to his speech? And I said yes, if he didn't mind my drinking, and he said he never touched spirits, but he didn't mind if I did; so we sort of went to his cabin—"

"HAVE ANOTHER DRINK, MRS. PERRIGORD—CYNTHIA!" roared Morgan, to drown out the possibilities of this. "Pour everybody a drink. Ha-ha!"

"But, Henry!" crowed Mrs. Perrigord, opening her eyes wide, "I think it's p-perfectly wonderful, reolly, and so screamingly funny, don't you know, because oll deah Leslie evah does is tolk, you see, and the pooah darling must have been most dreadfully disappointed. Whee!" Gurgle, gurgle, gurgle.

"Ay like to see de young foolks have a good time," observed Captain Valvick affably.

". . . and for Curt to act like that just when everything was nice and arranged for the performance to-night, when I'd finally succeeded in keeping Uncle Jules sober! And it *was* such a ghastly task, you know," explained Peggy, wrinkling up her face to keep back the tears, "because four separate times I caught him trying to sneak out after that horrible old GIN!" The thought of that horrible old gin almost overcame her with tears, but she turned a grim if wrinkled face steadily towards them. "But at last I made him see reason, and everything was all right, and he came down here in lovely shape to the dining-room to eat his dinner, and everything is nice—"

"Your Uncle Jules," said Morgan thoughtfully, in the midst of a curious silence, "came down *where* to eat his dinner?"

"Why, down here! And—"

"No, he didn't," said Morgan.

Peggy whirled round. Slowly, painstakingly, with misted eyes and lips slowly opening, she scanned the dining-saloon inch by inch. Babble and riot flowed there under a fog of smoke; but Uncle Jules was not there. Peggy hesitated. Then she sat down at the table and burst into sobs.

"Come on!" said Morgan, leaping to his feet. "Come on, Skipper! There's a chance to salvage the wreck if we work fast. He'll be in the bar if he's anywhere. . . . How long's he been on the loose, Peggy?"

"Th-thrree-qu-quarr*bolooo*!" sobbed Peggy, beating her hands against her forehead. "And only an hour unt-t-il the *bolooo*. Oh, w-why w-was the aw-ful st-stuff ever invented, and w-why do beastly m-men drink—?"

"Can he drink much in three quarters of an hour?"

"G-gallons," said Peggy. *"Whoooo!"*

"My de-deah," cried Mrs. Perrigord, the tears starting to her own eyes, "do you reolly mean that that*cher* M'skieux Fortinbras has really m'uskic, hic, has reolly got himskehelp *tight?* Oh, my deah, the horrible, owful, drunken—"

"Lady, lady," thundered Captain Valvick, hammering the table, "ay tell you diss is no time for a crying yag! Come on, Mr. Morgan; you take care of one and ay take care of de odder. Stop it, bot' of you! Come on now. . . ."

By dint of holding firmly to Mrs. Perrigord's arm while the captain took Peggy's, they slid through the rollicking, friendly crowd that was now streaming upstairs for a head-long rush on the bar before the hour of the ship's concert. The bar, already crowded and seething with noise, seemed even more crowded and noisy to Morgan. Each of his trio had consumed exactly one bottle of champagne; and, while he would have scorned the imputation that he could be-come the least sozzled on a quart of fizz, he could not in honesty deny certain insidious manifestations. For example, it seemed to him that he was entirely without legs, and that his torso must be moving through the air in a sin-gularly ghostly fashion; whereas the more lachrymose be-came the two ladies over Uncle Jules going off on the razzle-dazzle, the more it impressed him as an excellent joke. On the other hand, his brain was clearer than normal; sights, sounds, colours, voices took on a brilliant sharpness and purity. He felt in his pores the heat and smoke and alcoholic dampness of the bar. He saw the red-faced crowd milling about leather chairs under the whirring fans and the pastoral scenes of the roof. He saw the amber lights glittering on mosaic glass in the windows, and heard some-body strumming the piano. Good old bar! Excellent bar!

"Come on!" said Captain Valvick. "Shovf de ladies into chairs at de table here and we make de round. *Coorosh!* Ay vant to see that marionette show myself. Come on. We start along de side and work ofer. You see him anywhere? Ay dunno him at all."

Morgan did not see him. He saw white-coated stewards shuttling in and out of the crowd with trays; but everybody in the crowd seemed to get in his way. Twice they made the circuit of the room: and no Uncle Jules.

"It's all right, I think," said Morgan, mopping his fore-head with a handkerchief when they drew back towards a door giving on B deck. "He's probably gone down to take a last look at the marionettes. It's all right. He's safe, after all, and—"

" 'When chapman-billies leave the street,' " intoned a sepulchral voice just behind them, " 'and drouthy neighbours neighbours meet—When market-days are wearin' late, and folk begin to tak the gate.' . . . Not bad, not bad," the voice broke off genially. "Guid evening to ye, Mr. Morgan!"

Morgan whirled. A hand was raised in greeting from a leather alcove in a corner, where Dr. Oliver Harrison Kyle sat bolt upright in a solitary state. On Dr. Kyle's rugged face there was an expression of Jovian pleasure; a trifle frozen, it is true, but dreamy and appreciative. He had stretched out one hand levelly, and his eyes were half-closed as he rolled out the lines. But now he gestured hospitably.

Dr. Kyle was full of reaming swats that drank divinely. Dr. Kyle was, in fact, cockeyed.

" 'Auld Ayr, wham ne'er a town surpasses,' " announced Dr. Kyle, with a gesture that indicated him to be a local boy and proud of it, " 'for honest men and bonnie lasses'! Aye! A statement ye ken, Mr. Morgan, frae the wairks o' the great Scottish poet, Rabbie Burrrns. Sit down, Mr. Morgan. And perhaps ye'll tak a drap o' whusky, eh? 'The souter tauld his queerest stories—' "

"Excuse me, sir," said Morgan. "We can't stop now, I'm afraid, but maybe you can help us. We're looking for a Frenchman named Fortinbras; short, stocky chap—perhaps you saw—?"

"Ah," said the doctor reflectively. He shook his head. "A guid horse, Mr. Morgan, a guid horse, but ower hasty. Weel, weel! I could ha' tauld him frae his ain exuberance at clearing the firrst sax hurdles he wadna gang the courrse. Ye'll find him *there*," said Dr. Kyle.

They hauled Uncle Jules out from under the lounge, a pleasant far-off smile on his red face, but unquestionably locked in slumber. Peggy and Mrs. Perrigord arrived just as they were trying to revive him.

"Quick!" Peggy gulped. "I knew it! Stand round, now,

so nobody sees him. The door's right behind you . . . carry him out and downstairs."

"Any chance of reviving him?" inquired Morgan, rather doubtfully. "He looks—"

"Come *on!* Don't argue! You *won't* say anything of this, will you, Dr. Kyle?" she demanded. "He'll be perfectly all right by curtain-time. Please don't mention it. Nobody'll ever know. . . ."

The doctor assured her gallantly the secret would be safe with him. He deplored the habits of inebriates, and offered to give them assistance in moving Uncle Jules; but Valvick and Morgan managed it. They contrived to lurch out on the deck and below without more than the incurious observation to stewards. Peggy, stanching her tears, was a whirlwind.

"Not to his cabin—to the dressing-room at the back entrance to the concert-hall! Oh, be careful! Be careful! Where can Abdul have been? Why wasn't Abdul watching him? Abdul will be furious; he's got a fearful temper as it is. . . . Oh, if we can't revive him there'll be nobody to speak the prologue; and Abdul will have to take *all* the parts himself, which he probably won't do. . . . Listen! You can hear the hall filling up already. . . ."

They had come out into the corridor in the starboard side of C deck aft, and Peggy led them up a darkish side-passage. At its end was a door opening on a steep stairway, and beside it the door of a large cabin whose lights she switched on. Faintly, from up the staircase, they could hear an echoing murmur which seemed to come chiefly from children. Panting hard, Morgan helped Valvick spill on a couch the puppet-master, who was as heavily limp as one of his own puppets. A small whistle escaped the lips of Uncle Jules as his head rolled over. He murmured, *"Magnifique!"* and began to snore, smiling sadly.

Peggy, weeping and cursing at once, rushed to an open trunk in one corner of the cabin. It was a cabin fully fitted up as a dressing-room, Morgan saw. Three superb uniforms, with spiked helmets, broadswords, scimitars, chain mail, and cloaks crusted in glass jewels, hung in a wardrobe. A scent of powder was in the air; on a lighted dressing-table were false whiskers of varying hues, wigs in long fighting-curls, face creams, greasepaints, spirit gum, make-up boxes, and pencils of rich soft blackness. Morgan breathed deeply the air of the theatre and liked it. Peggy snatched from the trunk a large box of baking-soda.

"You neffer do it," said Captain Valvick, looking gloomily at Uncle Jules. "Ay seen lots of drunks in my time, and ay tell you—"

"I will do it!" cried Peggy. "Mrs. Perrigord, please, *please* stop crying and pour out a glass of water. Water, somebody! I got him round once in Nashville when he was nearly as bad as this. Now! Now, if somebody will—"

"Oh, the poah *deah!*" cried Mrs. Perrigord, going over to stroke his forehead. Immediately, with a deep snore which rose to crescendo in a reverberating whistle, Uncle Jules slid off the couch on the other side.

"Up!" wailed Peggy. "Hold him—lift him up, Captain! Hold his head. That's it. Now tickle him. Yes, tickle him; you know." She dropped a lump of baking-soda into a glass of water and advanced warily through an aroma of gin that was drowning the odour of grease-paint. "Hold him now. Oh, *where* is Abdul? Abdul knows how to do this! Now, hold him and tickle him a little. . . ."

"*Gla-goo!*" snorted Uncle Jules, leaping like a captured dolphin. An expression of mild annoyance had crossed his face.

"*Viens, mon oncle!*" whispered Peggy soothingly. Her steps were a little unsteady, her eyes smearily bright; but she was determined. "*Ah, mon pauvre enfant! Mon pauvre petit gosse! Viens, alors. . . .*"

The *pauvre enfant* seemed vaguely to catch the drift of this. He sat up suddenly with his eyes closed; his fist shot out with unerring aim, caught the glass full and true, and carried it with a crash against the opposite bulkhead. Then Uncle Jules slid down and serenely went on snoring. "Haah, whee!" breathed Uncle Jules.

There was a knock at the door.

Peggy nearly screamed as she backed away. "That can't be Mr. Perrigord!" she wailed. "Oh, it can't be! He'll ruin us if he learns this. He *hates* drinking, and he says he's going to write an account again for the papers. Abdul! Maybe it's Abdul. He'll have to do it now. He'll have to. . . ."

"Dat," said Captain Valvick suddenly, "is a very funny knock. Lissen!"

They stared, and Morgan felt a rather eerie sensation. The knock was a complicated one, very light and rapid, rather like a lodge signal. Valvick moved over to open it, when it began to open of itself in a rather singular and mysterious way, by sharp jerks. . . .

"Ps-s-sst!" hissed a voice warningly.

Into the room, after a precautionary survey, darted none other than Mr. Curtis Warren. His attire was much rumpled, including torn coat and picturesquely grease-stained white flannels; his hair stood up, and there was some damage done to his countenance. But a glow of fiendish triumph shone from it. He closed the door carefully and faced them with a proud gesture.

Before they could recover from the shock of stupefaction and horror, he laughed a low, satisfied, swaggering laugh.

Thrusting his hand into his pocket, he drew it forth and held up, winking and glittering on its gold chain, the emerald elephant.

"I've got it back!" he announced triumphantly.

Chapter 16

Danger in Cabin C46

MORGAN SAID NOTHING. Like Captain Whistler on several occasions too well known to cite, he was incapable of speech. His first sharp fear—*viz.*, that his eyes were deceiving him, and that this might be a grotesque fantasy of champagne and weariness—was dispelled by sombre reality. Warren was here. He was here, and he had the emerald elephant. What he might have been up to was a vision which Morgan, for the moment, did not care to face. All he distinctly remembered afterwards was Valvick saying, hoarsely, "Lock dat door!"

"As for you—" continued Warren, and made a withering gesture at Peggy. "As for you—that's all the faith and trust you put in me, is it? That's the help I get, Baby! Ha! I put through a deep-laid plan; but do you trust me when I'm shamming sleep? No! You go rushing off in a tantrum. . . ."

"Darling!" said Peggy, and rushed, weeping into his arms.

"Well, now—" said Warren, somewhat mollified. "Have a drink!" he added, with an air of inspiration, and drew from his pocket a bottle of Old Rob Roy depleted by exactly one pint.

Morgan pressed his fists to his throbbing temples. He swallowed hard. Trying to get a grip on himself, he approached Warren as warily as you would approach a captured orang-outang, and tried to speak in a sensible tone.

"To begin with," he said, "it is no use wasting time in futile recriminations. Beyond pointing out that you are intoxicated as well as off your onion, I will say nothing. But I want you to try, if possible, to collect yourself sufficiently to give me a coherent account of your movements." A horrible suspicion struck him. "You didn't haul off and paste the captain again, did you?" he demanded. "O God!

you didn't assault Captain Whistler for the third time, did you? No? Well, that's something. Then what have you been up to?"

"You're asking *me*?" queried Warren. He patted Peggy with one hand and passed the bottle to Morgan with the other. Morgan instantly took a healing pull at it. "You're asking *me*? What did Lord Gerald do in Chapter Nine? It was your own idea. What did Lord Gerald do in Chapter Nine?"

To the other's bemused wits this was on a par with that cryptic query touching the manifesto said to have been thundered forth by W. E. Gladstone in the year 1886.

"Now, hold on," said Morgan, soothingly. "We'll take it bit by bit. First, where did you pinch that emerald again?"

"From Kyle, the dastardly villain! I lifted it out of his cabin not five minutes ago. Oh, he had it, all right! We've *got* him now; and if Captain Whistler doesn't have me a medal. . . ."

"From KYLE? . . . Don't gibber, my dear Curt," commanded Morgan, pressing his hands to his temples again. "I can't stand any more gibbering. You couldn't have got it from Kyle's cabin. It was returned to Lord—"

"Now, Hank, old man," interposed Warren with an air of friendly reasonableness. "*I* ought to know where I got it, oughtn't I? You'll at least admit that? Well, it was in Kyle's cabin. I sneaked in there to get the goods on the villain, the way Lord Gerald did when Sir Geoffrey's gang thought they had him imprisoned in the house at Moorfens. And I've *got* the goods on him. . . . Oh, by the way," said Warren, remembering something exultantly. He thrust his hand into the breast pocket of his coat and drew out a thick bundle. "I also got all his private papers, too."

"You did *what*?"

"Well, I sort of opened all his bags and trunk and brief-cases and things. . . ."

"But, I say, howevah did the deah boy get out of gaol?" inquired Mrs. Perrigord. She had dried her tears, adjusted her monocle again, and she watched breathlessly with her hands against her breast. "I think it's most, owfully, screamingly, delightfully clevah of him to. . . ."

There was a quick knock at the door.

"They're after him!" breathed Peggy, whirling round with wide eyes. "Oh, they're a-after the p-poor darling to p-put him back in that horrible brig. Oh, *don't let them take—*"

"Sh-h-h!" rumbled Valvick, and made a mighty gesture. He blinked round. "Ay dunno what he done, but he got to hide. . . ."

The knock was repeated. . . .

"Dere iss no cupboard—dere iss no—Coroosh! Ay got it! He hass got to put on de false whiskers. Come here. Come here, ay tell you, or ay bust you one! You iss cuckoo! Don't argu wit' me," he boomed as a spluttering Warren was hauled across the cabin. "Here iss a pair of red whiskers wit' de wires for de ears. Here iss a wig. Mr. Morgan, get a robe or something out of dat locker. . . ."

"But why, I ask you?" demanded Warren. He spoke with a difficult attempt at dignity from behind a threatening bush of red whiskers with curled ends, and a black wig with long curls which Valvick had jammed over one eye. When he began to shake one arm and declaim, Morgan wrapped round him a scarlet bejewelled robe. "I've got proof! I can prove Kyle is a crook. All I've got to do is to go to Whistler and say, 'Look here, you old porpoise—' "

"Shut up!" hissed Valvick, clapping a hand over the whiskers. "Now. We iss ready. Open dat door. . . ."

They stared tensely, but the sight, as Morgan opened the door, was not very alarming. Under ordinary circumstances they would have deduced that their visitor was, if anything, a shade more nervous than they. A stocky A.B. in dungarees and a striped jersey was pulling at his forelock, shifting his feet, and flashing the whites of his eyes. Before anybody could speak, the A.B. burst out rapidly, in a hoarse confidential voice.

"Miss! Wot we want to 'ave clearly understood, my mates and me, which I was delegyted 'ere to sy, is that my mates and me is in naow wy responsible. Miss! Stryke

me blind, so 'elp me, miss, if we're responsible! Like this.
Not that we didn't feel like it, wot with 'im ordering us
abaht like we wos dirt, and 'im only a ruddy Turk, yer see
—but it's abaht that bloke Abdul, miss—"

"Abdul?" said Peggy. "Abdul! Where is he?"

"Right 'ere, miss, yer see. I've got 'im outside, miss. In
a wheelbarrow, miss."

"In a wheelbarrow?"

"Like this, miss. So 'elp me! All dy me and my mates
wos a-working wheeling them ruddy dummies, miss, and
a-working *'ard,* so 'elp me. And Bill Pottle, my mate, says
to me, 'e says, 'Gawd lummy, Tom, d'you know 'oo we've
got on this 'ere tub?' 'e says. 'It's the Bermondsey Terror,
Tom, the bloke we see knock out Texas Willie larst year.'
So all of us thought we'd go and tyke a look at 'im, and a
real top-notch good sport 'e wos, miss, 'oo said 'ed been
a-drinking, wiv a Swede, and, 'Come in,' 'e says, 'all of
yer!' So 'e begins a-telling us 'ow 'e beat the Dublin Smasher
in eighteen seconds. And just when we wos all interested,
miss, in walks this 'ere Abdul, yer see, miss, and starts
rysing a row. And somebody says, 'Gorn' yer ruddy frog-
eater,' 'e says, 'gorn back to yer ruddy 'arem,' 'e says.
Then Abdul gets narsty and says, 'Ow, well, 'e'd rather be
a frog-eater than a ——— Britisher a-stuffing fuller roast
beef,' 'e says. And the Bermondsey Terror gets up and
says, 'Ow, yerce?' And Abdul says, 'Yerce.' So Bermondsey sorter reaches out and taps him a couple, yersee,
miss. . . ."

"But he's all *right,* isn't he?" cried Peggy.

"Sure, 'e's all right, miss!" the other hastened to assure
her, with a gesture of heavy heartiness. "Except 'e can't
talk, yer see. Bermondsey 'it 'im in the vocal cords, once,
yer see, miss. . . ."

With her eyes brimming over, Peggy glared. "Oooh,
you—oh, you nasty, brawling fighting. . . . Can't *talk?* You
take him back, do you hear? You work over him, do you
hear? If he isn't in shape in half an hour I'll walk straight
up and tell the captain, and I'll—"

She herself was incapable of speech. She dashed at the
door, the thoroughly scared A.B. ducking out before her

wrath. He was mumbling something rather defiantly to the effect that that was what Abdul had croaked out, and the Bermondsey Terror said *he* didn't care, and if any games was tried on *him*—Peggy slammed the door.

"Coroosh!" said Captain Valvick, wiping his forehead. He shook his head despondently. "Ay tell you ay seen roughneck ships before, but diss one of Old Barnacle's iss de worst. It iss hawful. Ay haff a cook once on de old *Betsy Yee* which get mad and chase de whole fo'c's'l round and round de deck wit' a carving-knife; and ay t'ank now ay could get him a job on diss ship and he be right at home. Coroosh! what iss going to happen next?"

A faint, pleasant, gurgling noise behind them caused them to turn. The neck of a bottle had been tilted up among a brush of savage red whiskers. It descended. Red-whiskered and black-wigged, Curtis Warren regarded them affably.

"Good for the old Bermondsey Terror!" he said. "I'd like to meet that fellow. He'd make a good addition to our crowd. It reminds me a little of the way I served old Charley Woodcock about an hour ago. . . . What does Abdul weigh, Peggy? Woodcock's fairly light."

Cool despair settled on Morgan, so that he felt pleasant and collected now. Nothing more, he was certain, could happen. They might as well bow before the Parcæ and enjoy the gyrations of those relentless sisters.

"Ha-ha-ha!" he said. "Well, old boy, what did you do to Woodcock? What's Woodcock got to do with this?"

"How do you think I got out of the jug, anyhow?" demanded Warren. "It was a stratagem, I'm telling you, and a damned good stratagem, if you ask me. I asked you before, What did Lord Gerald do in Chapter Nine? And I'll tell you. The trick was this. If they thought he was safely locked up, then he could prowl as he liked and get the evidence that would hang the guilty man. That was *my* position. . . . So I had to have a substitute to take my place so they wouldn't suspect anything. And if I do say it myself, I worked it pretty well—though I'll have to hand the real credit to you, Hank." He removed his whiskers to talk the better.

"Woodcock was definitely the one person I could summon to me so that he'd come any time I liked, wasn't he? Right. Well I carefully prepared my ground by seeming to sleep all afternoon, so they'd get used to it; I refused dinner and everything. Then I wrote a note to Woodcock. I said I had news from my Uncle Warpus, and to come down to the brig at exactly seven o'clock. Just before this, I told him to have a message sent in the captain's name to the sailor on guard—I'd learned his name—to get him away for ten minutes, so there'd be nobody to hear when we talked business. I asked the sailor whether I could send a message, and he said he supposed it was all right, but he couldn't leave to take it; so they sent a pageboy. The only thing was, I was afraid somebody might read it, so—" Warren glanced round with triumphant glee, rubbing his hands.

"Masterly," said Morgan in a hollow voice.

"So what did I do? I ripped the book apart. There's always the heavy mucilage sticking the cover to the inside flaps of the book; and I tore out one of the flaps and sealed it. *And it worked!* Good old Charley came through. The sailor didn't like to leave when the fake message came through; but he saw there were bolts on the outside of the door I couldn't move, and I was asleep, anyway." Warren made a gesture. "Down comes Woodcock and says, 'You've got it, have you?' And I said, 'Yes; just pull back those bolts and open the door for a second; I don't want to get out, but I'll have to give you this.' So he opened the door. And I said, 'Look here, old man, I'm damned sorry, but you know how it is,' and I let him have it in the jaw. . . ."

"Darling!" said Peggy. "Oh, you poor dear idiot. Why didn't you make him *tell* before you hit him? . . . Oh, confound it all, if you'd only done what I wanted you to, if you'd only tortured him before you hit him! Oh, dear . . . and now look what's happened, with all this nasty fighting and torturing!" She wrung her hands. "Abdul and Uncle Jules, look at them! And unless we can get them on their feet there'll be no performance. Listen! I can hear the crowd upstairs already. . . ."

She snatched the bottle from Warren's hand and strengthened herself with a draught. A wheel seemed to go round behind her eyes. "The n-nasty d-drunken b-beasts!" said Peggy; "the——"

"My deah!" said Mrs. Perrigord, "Oh, I say, I don't know what has kick-happened, but I think it was most owfully clevah of Mr. Joyce to torture oll those people, and get out of gaol, I do, reolly, especially as it was Henry's idea, and I think we reolly might have the courtesy to offer Mr. Lawrence a glass of champagne. . . ."

"SILENCE!" roared Morgan. "Listen, Peggy, the performance doesn't matter now; hasn't that occurred to you? Have you realised that we're saddled again with that blasted emerald . . . which Curt swears he got out of *Kyle's* cabin? Curt, come to your senses. You couldn't have got it out of Kyle's cabin, I tell you! Lord Sturton——"

Warren shook his head tolerantly, agitating the curls of the savage black wig that was jammed over one ear.

"No, no, old man," he said. "You don't understand. Not Lord Sturton—Lord Derreval. Lord Gerald Derreval. If you don't believe me, go down to Kyle's cabin—it isn't far from here—and look behind the wardrobe trunk just under the porthole. The steel box is there; I left the box there so the crook would maybe think the emerald was still in it. . . ."

Valvick whirled on Morgan.

"Maybe," he said, "maybe it been dere all de time! Coroosh! You t'ink dere is *two* emeralds, and one of dem a fake, and somebody hass returned de fake to dat English duke, eh?"

"Impossible, Skipper," returned Morgan, who was feeling queerly light-headed. "Don't you think Sturton would know a real emerald from a fake? Unless, somehow, the real emerald was returned to him. . . . I don't know! The thing's driving me insane. Go on, Curt. Go on from the consummation of your crafty scheme to entice Woodcock to the brig. What then?"

"Well, I got in a neat upper-cut, you see. . . ."

"Yes, yes, we know that. But afterwards?"

"I tore the sheet up, bound and gagged him securely,

and tied him to the berth so he couldn't move; then I put a blanket over him, so when the sailor came back he'd only look into the cell and think I was there. . . . Neat, eh?"

"I have no doubt," agreed Morgan, "that at the present moment Mr. Woodcock thinks very highly of your forethought. If the idea had ever previously occurred to him to tip over the beams concerning your Uncle Warpus. I should think it would recommend itself strongly to him now. You're a wonder, you are. Carry on."

"So I sneaked away and made straight for Kyle's cabin to get the goods on him. I wasn't afraid of running into Kyle because I looked through a porthole and saw him in the bar; besides, I knew he was due at the concert. And—there you are. The proof! Also, I've got his papers. All I was afraid of was what Captain Whistler had said about maybe catching Kyle, but everything was fine. Now all we've got to do is examine his papers, and we'll find evidence that he's really the crook who's impersonating Dr. Kyle. . . ."

"Yess, dere is de papers, too," rumbled Captain Valvick. "It is a hawful offence, ay tell you. Worst offence on de high seas to steal a man's papers. What we going to do *now*?"

Morgan stalked up and down the cabin, slapping his hand against the back of his head.

"There's only one thing. We've got to get Curt back to the brig before the captain learns he's on the loose. I don't see how it's to be done without—*Mrs. Perrigord*," he said whirling round, *"what are you doing?"*

"But, my own Henry," protested Mrs. Perrigord, jumping involuntarily. Her face wrinkled up in anguish. "Oh, I do so hope I didn't offend you! Reolly, I was only ringing the bell for the steward. Pierre Louys wants a bottle of champagne, you know, and you know it would be dreadfully rude if we didn't kick-offer. . . . But I reolly didn't know which was the b-bell, so what could I do but ring *oll* the bells, you see. . . ."

Morgan reeled. He dived and caught her arm just as she

was about to press a last push-button, hitherto overlooked, and labelled *"Fire Alarm."*

"Peggy," he said, "if you ever showed any sense and speed, show 'em now. If those bells don't bring down a mob, at least there'll be a crowd of highbrows swarming in to see if things are all ready for the performance. At the moment, this is the safest place on the ship for Curt if you'll do as I tell you. Black his face—fit him out in wig and whiskers. . . ."

"I will, Captain!" said Peggy grimly. "The poor darling sha'n't go back to that horrible old brig if *I* can help it. But what—?"

Morgan took her hands and looked her steadily in the eye.

"Can I trust you and Curt here for just five minutes—just five minutes, that's all I ask—without your getting in more trouble. You *can* stay out of more trouble for five minutes, can't you?"

"I swear it, Hank! But what are you going to do?"

"The skipper and I are going to take those papers back to that cabin before anybody discovers they're gone. There's no chance of being caught; the only chance and danger is here. Give me that emerald, Curt. I don't know what's happened or what it is, but we'll take it back and be quit of the responsibility. Hand it over!"

"Are you stark, raving crazy?" shouted Warren. "I risk life and limb and my position in the Diplomatic Service to get the goods on a murdering crook, and now you ask me to hand back—"

Morgan lowered his voice, perceiving this was the only way of handling the matter, and fixed him with a hypnotic eye.

"This is subtle, Curt. A subtle, deep scheme, you see. We only pretend to do it. But the moth is in our net now. A pin, a cork, and a card, and we add him to our Baker Street collection! You see? You trusted the wit and resource of Lord Gerald in a tight spot; now trust it again. . . . Eh? Ah, that's it. That's it, old chap. Papers all here? Good! And—er—go light on the whisky, will you, or what there is left of it, until we get back? Stout fellow. . . . Now, remember, Peggy, you've promised there'll be no trouble. I rely on you. Come on, Skipper. . . ."

He backed away gingerly, as a lion-tamer might swerve to get out of a cage. Mrs. Perrigord said she wanted to go with Henry. She insisted on going with Henry. Exactly how she was dissuaded from this intention Morgan never knew, since he and Valvick slid out a fraction of a second before the closing door.

The gangway was empty, although a more confused buzzing and laughing, mingled with the deep note of people shuffling chairs, swept down from the staircase up to the stage.

"Well, remarked the skipper musingly, "we is de only two people left wit' any sense, and ay don't t'ink much of diss Lord Gerald, whoever he iss. Coroosh! Ay don't believe de government off de United States need to care much about dat movie-film. Ay dunno if dey know it, but dey have bigger worries. All dey got to do iss send dat young Warren out in de Diplomatic Service and dey are going to have a war every week. It iss up to us. We got to save de situation."

"We'll save it, Skipper. Easy, now! . . . Damn it! Don't walk like a crook! We're only out for a stroll. Take these papers. Round the corner here. At least, thank the Lord *we've* kept out of trouble so far. If anybody saw Curt sneaking back to Kyle's cabin, he'd be pounced on in a second. We haven't got a chance to put Kyle's papers back where they were—he'll know there's been a burglary—but at least there'll be nothing missing. In the ensuing search *this* emerald. . . . Look here, do you think somebody's pinched it *back* from Sturton?"

"Ay not be surprised. Ay not be surprised at anyt'ing. Sh-h-h, now! Here is where we turn off. Listen!"

At a dim side-passage off the main corridor they stopped and peered down. All the noises of the ship were away from them, in the dim tumult of the throng milling up on B deck towards the concert-hall. Here it was so quiet the sea's rush and murmur became again discernible, and the low creaking of woodwork. But there were voices somewhere. They listened a moment before they could place them as coming from behind the closed door of C 47 in the passage.

"It iss all right," whispered the captain, nodding. "Dat iss ony Sparks and hiss cousin, de Bermondsey Terror. Ay haff start de Bermondsey Terror off on Old Rob Roy, and ay bet he don't want to stop. But don't disturb 'em, or we haff to explain. Walk soft. . . . !"

C 46, Dr. Kyle's cabin, had its door closed. They tiptoed down, and Morgan felt his heart rise in his throat, growing to an enormous pounding, as he softly turned the knob. He pushed it open. . . .

Nobody inside.

One danger passed. If there had been somebody. . . .

Again he felt hot fear as he switched on the light, but there was nobody. It was a large cabin, with what he supposed to be a bathroom attached, and now in a wild state of confusion. Not even a private detective could have called Warren's methods in the least subtle.

Under the porthole stood a large wardrobe trunk with its leaves apart, its lid propped up and top shelf streaming ties. He pointed.

"Look there, Skipper. If that steel box were thrown in *this* porthole last night, it would land behind that trunk and nobody would ever see it unless the trunk were moved. . . ."

Valvick closed the door softly. He was peering at two valises open on the floor, and an unlocked brief-case lying across the berth.

"Come on," he said; "we haff to work fast. Take a handful of these papers and shove 'em somew'ere. Coroosh! Ay feel like a crook! Ay don't like diss. What you doing?"

Morgan was groping behind the trunk. His fingers touched metal, and he withdrew the circular box with the hinged lid. He stared at it a moment, and handed it to Valvick.

"There it is, Skipper. And here's the elephant"—he stared at Warren's trophy in his hand and shivered. "Come on; let's put it back. The less we have to do. . . ."

"*Listen!*" said Valvick, cocking his head.

Nothing. The porthole was open; they heard the curtain thrumming in the breeze, and the multitudinous rustlings of the sea. Also, very faintly, they could hear the murmur of voices from the gangway opposite, where sat Sparks and the Bermondsey Terror. Nothing else.

"Come on," whispered Morgan. "You're getting nerves, Skipper. Stuff those things away somewhere, and let's get out of here. We'll put this little job through without any hitch, and they'll never suspect us. . . ."

A voice said:

"You think so?"

Morgan felt his skin crawl, and his head bump forward against the trunk as he knelt. The voice was not loud, but it brought the universe to a standstill like a dead clock. After it the silence was so heavy that he seemed unable to hear the sea or the thrumming curtain.

He looked up.

The door to the bathroom, previously closed, was standing open. Captain Whistler stood with one hand on the knob and the other on a trigger. He was wearing full-dress uniform, an arabesque of gold braid against the blue, from which the breeze (Morgan noticed even in that glassy, frozen moment) brought a wave of Swat Number 2 Liquid Insect Exterminator. Captain Whistler's good eye had a malignant gleam as at the realisation of some obvious fact that had hitherto escaped him. . . . Behind him, Second-Officer Baldwin was looking over his shoulder. . .

His glance travelled to the emerald in Morgan's hand.

"So you two," said Captain Whistler, *"were* the real thieves, after all. I might have known it. I was a fool not to see it first off last night. . . . Don't move! All right, Mr. Baldwin. Move out and see if they're armed. Steady now. . . ."

Chapter 17

Bermondsey Carries On

THERE WERE, as they afterwards reflected, several courses that thoughtful men might have pursued. Even thoughtful men, however, would have conceded that these two conspirators were fairly in the soup. If at one time explanations might have been made to Captain Whistler, both Morgan and Valvick realised that by this time the Parcæ had so tangled matters up that it was practically impossible to explain *anything*. Morgan himself doubted whether even half an hour's lucid thought would enable him to explain the situation to himself. Yet there are certain courses which thoughtful men deplore—those courses are elementary, like a reflex action, and spring to the muscles from a prompting older than reason. Captain Valvick, for instance, might have held out the steel box. He might have thrown the box on the floor at Whistler's feet, and surrendered in explanation.

Captain Valvick did nothing of the kind.

He threw that steel box, in fact, straight at the light in the roof of Cabin C 46, where it spattered glass and extinguished the same in one reverberating pop. Then he nearly yanked Morgan's arm from his socket swinging him out before himself into the passage and slamming the door behind.

Morgan dimly heard Whistler's avenging yell. Flung against the opposite bulkhead, he bounced back in time to hear a weight of bodies thud against the door inside.

"Dat old Barnacle!" roared Valvick, whose powerful hands were firmly clamped on the knob at the door as he held it. "Dat!&—£/&???(!! *ay show him!* He t'ank we iss t'ieves, eh? By yumping Yudas, ay show him; Nobody effer tell me dat before; NOBODY! Ay show him. Qvick, lad; rope! Ve got to get rope and tie de door shut. . . ."

"Wassermarrer?" inquired a voice behind Morgan.

The voice had to speak loudly and hoarsely, because insane riot banged at the door inside, mingled with baffled bellowings from the *Queen Victoria's* skipper. Morgan spun round, to see that the door of Cabin C 47 was open. Framed in the doorway, his shoulders filling it and wriggling out at either side, stood a young man who was likewise so tall that he had to bend his head to peer out. He had a flattened countenance and a ruminating jaw like a philosophical cow.

"Coroosh!" roared Valvick, with a blast of thankfulness. He panted. "Bermondsey! Iss dat you?"

"Ho!" said the Bermondsey Terror, his face lighting up. "Sir!"

"Bermondsey—qvick—dere is no time to argue. Ay haff done you a good turn wit' de toot-ache, eh?"

"Ho!" said the Bermondsey Terror.

"And you say you like to do me a good turn? Good! Den you do diss, eh? You hold diss door for me until we can go for help and get aw—can get rope to tie dem up. Here, you hold. . . ."

Uttering his significant monosyllable, the other leaped from the door with a crack of his head on the doorpost which he seemed to mind not at all, and lent his weight to the knob.

"Wot's up?" he inquired.

"Dey iss robbers," said Captain Valvick.

"Ho?"

"Dey steal my pearl cuff-links," rumbled Captain Valvick, with rapid pantomime, "and de platinum studs which my old mudder gave me. Dey steal dis yentleman's watch and his pocket-book wit' all de money. . . ."

"Robbed *you*?"

"Yess. All ay want you to do iss hold de door v'ile—"

"Ho!" said the Bermondsey Terror, letting to the door to hitch up his belt. "Lemme at 'em!"

"No!" roared the captain, with a hideous insight of what he had done with his burst of poetic fancy. "No! Not dat! Only hold de door! Ay tell you it is de capt—"

The Bermondsey Terror's somewhat diminutive mind was concentrated on business. He hurled his fifteen stone at the door without pausing for explanation or protest. There was a thud and crackle; then a sound suggesting that two rather heavy bodies had been catapulted back across the cabin like bowling-pins. Then Bermondsey plunged into the dark cabin.

"We've got to stop him!" panted Morgan, trying to get through the door. He was stopped by Valvick's arm. "Listen! he'll—"

"Ay don't t'ink we can do not'ing but run," said Valvick. "*No!* Stay back. Ay am sorry for old Barnacle, but—"

From the cabin issued hideous muffled noises, language reminiscent of King Kong, and the clean inspiriting crack of knuckles against bone and flesh. A large suit-case sailed out of the darkness, as though from a lively spiritualist séance; banged against the opposite wall and showered underwear, socks, shirts, and papers. The passage began to be inundated with Dr. Kyle's possessions. Morgan, breaking loose, made another effort to dive in at the door. It was a gallant attempt, which might have succeeded if at that moment somebody had not thrown a chair.

Then he had a vague impression that somebody was dragging him away. Dimly he heard the Bermondsey Terror's hoarse voice announcing in muffled accents, between cracks, that he would teach people to steal pearl cuff-links and gold watches that their mothers gave them. When Morgan's wits cleared a second or more later, he was some distance from the scene of tumult. A new sound struck him—a deepening, gathering buzz and laughter. They were in the passage leading to the back stairs of the concert-hall.

"You ain't hurt!" Valvick was saying in his ear. "It yust bump you. Brace up! Qvick, now! De hunt be up in a second, and we got to find a place to hide if we don't want to be put in irons. . . . Sh-h-h! Walk careless! Here iss somebody. . . ."

Morgan straightened up, feeling his eyes crossed in a buzzing head, as somebody stalked round the corner into the narrow gangway. It was a steward bearing a large tray on which there were six tall gilt-foil bottles. Paying no attention to them, the steward swung past and knocked at the door of the dressing-room. In response to his knock there was poked out a face of such appalling hideousness that Morgan blinked. It was a brown face with tangled black hair, murderous squint-eyes, and whiskers.

"Champagne, sir," said the steward, crisply, "for a Mr. D. H. Lawrence. That'll be six pounds six, sir."

The cut-throat leered. On his head he placed rather rakishly a spiked helmet of brass set with emeralds and rubies; so that he could the better reach under an elaborate green robe, where he fumbled a moment, and then laid on the tray two American twenty-dollar bills. The bottles were mysteriously whisked inside by what appeared to be feminine hands behind the warrior. Then, as the steward hastened away, the warrior drew from its scabbard a broad curved scimitar and squinted evilly up and down the passage. Seeing Valvick and Morgan, he beckoned.

"Well?" inquired the voice of Curtis Warren, as the two conspirators tumbled into the dressing-room and Valvick locked the door. "Did you get it back all right? Did you . . . ?" The warrior stared. Thoughtfully he pushed his helmet forward and scratched his wig. "What's the idea, Hank? You've still got the emerald! Look. . . ."

Morgan nodded wearily. He glanced round. Uncle Jules was on the couch again, sprawled wide, while Peggy was trying to raise his head and insinuate a second dose of baking-soda under his twitching nose. There was a sharp plob as Mrs. Perrigord dexterously opened a bottle of champagne.

"You explain, Skipper." said Morgan, sadly juggling the emerald in his palm. "Suffice it to say that the game is up. U-up. Go on, Captain."

Valvick sketched out a rough outline. "You mean," said Warren, quakes and bubbles beginning to show under his ferocious moustache—"you mean the Bermondsey Terror is down there murdering the old sardine for stealing Hank's watch? Why, oh *why* wasn't I there to see it? Yee-ow! I'd have given anything to see it! Curse the rotten luck, why do I have to miss every good thing. . . ?"

Tears had come into Peggy's eyes again.

"But," she protested, "why, oh *why* can't you lay off the poor old captain? What have you got against him, anyway? Why must you go about assaulting the poor dear captain every time you get out of my sight? It isn't fair. It isn't just, after he said he almost had a daughter like me off Cape Hatteras. It—"

"Owful!" said Mrs. Perrigord, clucking her tongue reprovingly. "You owful, naughty boys, you. Have some champagne."

"Well, why hass he got to *be* dere, anyway?" demanded Valvick, hotly. "Ay tell you de old Barnacle call me a t'ief, and now ay am mad. Ay going to find out who iss at de bottom of diss business if ay haff to sving from de yardarm for it. And ay mean it."

"He was only trying to do his duty, Skipper," said Morgan. "We ought to have been warned. You heard what he said this afternoon: he wanted to have the honour of nabbing Kyle for himself. He and the second officer were probably there searching the cabin when they heard us coming. They ducked into the bathroom and when they opened the door and saw us they thought . . . well, what would *you* have thought? Skipper, it's no go. They'll be having a search party out for us in five minutes. The only thing to do is to go to Whistler, try to explain, and take our medicine. God knows what they'll do to us; plenty, I should think. But . . . there you are."

Valvick brought his arm down in a mighty gesture. "Ay will not! Ay am mad now, and ay will NOT! Barnacle iss not going to put me in de brig like a drunken A.B. while diss crook laughs ha-ha. We are going to hide somewhere, dat iss what, so he don't catch us, and den—"

"What's the good of that?" Morgan wanted to know. "Calm yourself, Skipper. Even if we could hide, which I doubt, what good would it do? We land day after tomorrow, and they'd be bound to catch us. We couldn't stay on the ship. . . ."

"Haff you forgotten dat de New York detective iss coming aboard at Southampton to identify diss crook, eh?"

"Yes, but—"

"And de charge we got to avoid iss stealing de emerald. . . ."

"With others, including Curt's jail-break, assault and battery of Woodcock; to say nothing of—"

"Bah! What iss Woodock? All you got to do iss promise him de bug-powder testimonial and he be all right. As for de odders, what iss dey? When dat detective point out de right man, do you t'ink Whistler going to get away wit' accusing us of stealing? Ay bet you not. Dey only t'ink he iss cuckoo, and den we threaten to tell de newspapers about dat bug-powder gun and dey will giff him de bird something hawful if he open his mouth about de rest! Coroosh! It iss easy. Ay will not be put in dat brig! Dat iss my last word. *'For God. For de cause! For de Church! For de laws!'* Liberty for ever, hooray! Are you wit' me, Mr. Warren?"

"Man, you never said a truer word!" said the Moorish warrior, and gripped his hand. "We'll show 'em, we will! Let 'em try to put me back in that brig!" He flourished his scimitar. Peggy rushed into his arms, beaming through her tears. He burst into song.

> *"May the serr-vice united ne-'er se-ver,*
> *But hold to its co-oolours so true!"*

sang the Moorish warrior, enthusiastically, and Valvick took it up,

> *"Theee ar-my and naaa-avee forever—*
> *Three cheers for the red—white—and blue!"*

"Sh-h!" howled Morgan as the three of them clasped hands in a dramatic gesture. "All right! Have it your way. If you must do it, I suppose I can be as mad as anybody else. Lead on; I'll follow. . . . The point is, where do you propose to hide? . . . Yes, thanks, Mrs. Perrigord, I *will* have some champagne."

Peggy slapped her hands together. "I've got it! I've got it! I know where you'll hide so they won't put you in that nasty brig. You'll hide with the marionettes."

"With the marionettes?"

"Of course, silly! Listen! The marionettes have a cabin of their own, haven't they? Adjoining Uncle Jules's, isn't it? And the stewards are all afraid to go in there, aren't they? And you have three uniforms like the marionettes, haven't you, and false whiskers? And food can be passed in to you from Uncle Jules's cabin, can't it? And if they did look in they'd only see marionettes lying in the berth. Darling, it's wonderful and it'll work, too. . . ."

"I'm glad to hear that," said Morgan. "Without wishing to be a spoil-sport, it would damp my ardour considerably if I had to hang on a hook all day and then found it *didn't* work. Besides, I think enough strain has already been put on Captain Whistler's reason without having a marionette sneeze in his face when he looked into the cabin. YOU'RE MAD, PEGGY. Besides, how can we get away with it? We're wasting time. The highbrows will be roaring down on this cabin in a minute, asking if Uncle Jules is ready to begin performing, and then we're discovered. This cabin is probably surrounded at the moment, and we can't even get to our hideaway. I also think it probable that a searching-party would feel considerable curiosity concerning three full-panoplied Moorish warriors seen strolling arm in arm down C deck."

Peggy pointed her finger at him.

"No, we're not caught, either! Because you three will climb into those clothes this minute, *and we'll put on the whole performance ourselves.* They won't know you in disguise, and you can help wheel the marionettes back to the cabin and stay there."

There was a silence. Then Morgan got up, with his head in his hands, and danced helplessly.

"Baby, the idea is a knockout!" breathed Warren. "But how are we going to work it? I can stand in front of the stage with a battle-axe right enough; but what about the rest of it? I can't even work those marionettes, to say nothing of what they say. . . ."

"Listen to me. Quick, champagne, somebody!" She snatched a bottle from the beaming Mrs. Perrigord, and after a moment, brilliant with inspiration, she con-

tinued: "We'll save Uncle Jules's bacon yet. To begin
with, there isn't a real Frenchman aboard this ship, with
the exception of Uncle Jules and Abdul. The audience will
be mostly kids, or else people with only a smattering of
French, out to see the fighting. . . ."

"What about Perrigord?" inquired Warren.

"I'm not forgetting him, darling. That's where Hank
comes in. Hank will be the Emperor Charlemagne and
also the crafty Banhambra, Sultan of the Moors. . . ."

"Good for you, old man!" applauded Warren, radiating
kindliness and slapping the Emperor Charlemagne on the
back.

". . . because I've heard his accent, and it's at least
good enough to deceive Perrigord. People will think he *is*
Uncle Jules, because we'll stuff him with pillows and disguise him; and when he speaks the prologue it's behind a
lighted gauze screen at the back of the stage, and nobody
can tell who it is. Yee, this is wonderful, now I think of it!
The rest of the time he's out of sight. I have a typewritten
copy of his part, and all he has to do is read it. . . . As
for working the marionettes, you can master that in ten
minutes while Madame Camposozzi is singing and Kyle's
reciting and Perrigord is talking. All you need is to be
strong in the arms, which is where Curt and the skipper
excel, and you can make 'em *fight,* can't you? Well—"

"Yess, but where do ay come in?" asked Valvick. "Ay
dunno no French except one or two words. Ay can juggle
plates, dough," he suggested hopefully, "and play de
piano. . . ."

"You can play the piano? Then," declared Peggy excitedly, "we're absolutely all right. Because, you see, the
only other speaking parts are very small—the Knight
Roland, the Knight Oliver, and Bishop Turpin. Those
parts will be taken by Curt. I'll prompt him roughly. just
a few words; but it won't matter what he says, because the
skipper will be playing the piano, loud and hard, with
appropriate music.. . ."

Morgan roared. He couldn't help it. The strengthening
sizzle of champagne cried, "Whee!" along his windpipe;
weariness dropped from him. He looked round at the

radiant Mrs. Perrigord, who was now seated on the stomach of the prostrate Uncle Jules and looking coyly at him. Again plans began to twist and shift in his brain.

'Right you are!" said he, slapping his hands together. "By Gad! we'll go down in a burst of glory if we do nothing else! It's mad, it's risking a thunderbolt from above, but we'll do it. Up and at 'em! Come on, Skipper; into those uniforms we go—there's no time to be lost. . . ."

There was not. From above began to sound now a measured and steady clapping; a deeper buzz and hum which rattled the lights of the dressing-table. Stopping only to execute a brief gleeful round-the-mulberry-bush with Warren, Peggy rushed to set out the cosmetics.

"And this," continued Morgan, excitedly stripping off his coat, "is where Mrs. Perrigord comes in. Sing your prayers, lads, to the blessed stars that sent her to us to-night. . . ."

"*Gloo!*" crowed Mrs. Perrigord. "Oh, you positively owful man, you mustn't say things like that! Whee!"

". . . because," he said, tapping Warren on the chest, "she's going to get rid of the people who were to be extras in our places to-night. Don't you see? We can't have anybody behind the scenes but ourselves. Wasn't this Madame Camposozzi to play the piano, and some Russian the violin; yes, and a couple of professors to be warriors . . . ?"

"O Lord! I'd forgotten that!" cried Peggy, freezing. "Oh, Hank, how can we—?"

"Easy! Mrs. Perrigord simply puts on one of those chilly stares of hers when they come down here, and says the places have been filled. We have the organiser of the concert talking for us, and she'll be obeyed; otherwise there'd be a row and we could never wangle it. . . . Listen!" he whirled round to her. "That's all right, isn't it? Mrs. Perrigord—CYNTHIA—you'll do it for me, won't you?"

There was a world of pleading in his voice. The organiser of the concert did not give him a chilly stare. She said, "Oh, you owful man!" and got up and put her arms round his neck.

"No, listen! Wait a bit—listen, Cynthia!" said Morgan desperately. "Listen to what I have to say. Let go, damn it!

I tell you we can't lose time! Let me get my waistcoat off. . . ."

"I don't think you're making yourself quite clear," observed Warren critically. "Suppose your wife could see you now, you old rip? Let the poor woman go, can't you?"

"You've *got* to get her in shape to face 'em, Hank!" cried Peggy, flying across the room. "Oh, it's p-perfectly a-aful the w-way we're p-persecuted and t-tortured with these n-nasty drunken p-people . . . !"

"Who's a nasty drunken people, may I ask?" inquired Mrs. Perrigord, suddenly raising a flushed face from Morgan's shoulder.

"All I was saying, darling—"

A fusillade of knocks on the door froze the conspirators where they stood.

"Signor Fortinbras!" exclaimed a voice with a broad rolling accent. The knocks were redoubled.

"Signor Fortinbras! It ees-a me, Signor Benito—Furioso—Camposozzi! Signor Perrigord he weesha to know eef you are alla-right. He—"

Peggy raised a quavering voice. "He is quite all right, Signor Camposozzi. He ees-a—I mean, he is dressing now. Please come back in five minutes. Mrs. Perrigord wishes to speak to you."

"Ah! Good! Tenn-mee-*noots* and we start. Good! Good! I am averraglad to hear it. Signor Ivan Slifovitz hasa tolda me," bawled Signor Camposozzi, with deplorable Latin lack of reticence, "that he thought you might hava drink too moocha *Gin*. . . ."

"*Gin?*" repeated a sudden, thoughtful, sepulchral voice just behind Morgan. It seemed to come from deep down in the earth. "Gin?"

Uncle Jules abruptly sat up. He slid off the couch. With eyes half-closed and face intent, as though some illuminating idea had come to him, he walked straight to the door.

"*Je vais chercher le gin,*" he explained hurriedly.

Valvick was after him at a bound, but, since his hand was on the knob of the door, nothing less than a full-sized miracle could have prevented discovery if Signor Camposozzi's attention had not been momentarily distracted.

"Eee!" squeaked Signor Camposozzi, for a reason they could not discern. *"Sangua della madonne,* who are you? Go away! You been-a fighting; you area onea begga crook. . . ."

"Now look 'ere, Guv'nor," protested a hoarse voice, "don't run awy, will yer? *'Ere!* Come back! I've got 'ere," continued the Bermondsey Terror, "two gold watches, two sets of cuff-links, two pocket-books, but only one set o' studs. I'm looking for a chap nymed Cap'n Valvick, 'oo owns part of it, and I wants ter 'ave 'im tyke his choice. 'Ere! Come back—I only wanted to ask where I could find—"

There were two sets of frantic footsteps rushing away as the Bermondsey Terror pursued him.

Chapter 18

Gold Watches and Disappearance

"A LITTLE more larceny, of course," said Morgan, "added to the list of our other offences won't matter a great deal. All the same, Skipper, you'd better stop the Bermondsey Terror and give him time to think up some excuses. Also, it mightn't be a bad idea to retrieve Captain Whistler's best studs and cuff-links."

Valvick took Uncle Jules, who was smiling vacantly, and propped him against the wall with one hand while he unlocked the door. He called "Bermondsey!" and one set of footfalls stopped. Then Valvick set up Uncle Jules like a sign on a couch just beside the door.

"He's coming round," said Warren, inspecting the red face of the puppet-master. "Look here, Baby, what happens to our new scheme if the old geezer wakes up? He may not be too tight to play, after all. Better give him another drink."

"We'll do nothing of the kind!" snapped Peggy. "We don't need to abandon our scheme. If he does come round, we can still hide in the back of the stage. Take off your helmet, Curt, and fill it with water. We'll slosh him down, and then maybe——"

She stopped as the Bermondsey Terror, laden with his plunder, stooped his head under the door. Except for a torn necktie and a scratch down one cheekbone, the Terror was undamaged. A drowsy smile went over his face.

"Ho!" said the Terror. " 'Ere's the stuff, sir. You and t'other gentleman just pick out whatcher want."

Valvick peered out hastily, drew him into the cabin, took the booty from his hands and slid it out of sight along the couch.

"Listen, Bermondsey," he growled, wiping his forehead: "Ay am afraid dere has been a mistake. Ay 'tank you haff smack de wrong men. Ay——"

"Ho?" inquired the Terror. His smile deepened. He wagged his head and closed one eye portentously. 'I sorter thought so, d'yer see, when I see 'oo they wos." Shaken by hoarse mirth, he winked again. "Never yer mind, Guv'nor. Did me good, that workout. Wot's the game? I sorter thought there wos something up when first I see somebody go into the sawbones' room and come out with the green jule thing as *that* gentleman's got now," he nodded at Morgan, who had disentangled himself from Mrs. Perrigord, "and then I see you two take it back. None o' my ruddy bursness, yer see, till you asks for 'elp."

Again he laughed hoarsely. Morgan, to whom had come a glimmer of hope that might avert Peggy's insane idea, took it up.

"Look here, Bermondsey. About those two robbers—just how much damage did you do to them?"

The Terror smiled complacently. He counted a few imaginary stars, closed his eyes, and uttered a snore.

"Out," inquired Morgan.

"Cold," said the Terror.

"Did they see you? Would they know you again, I mean?"

"Ho!" said the Terror. "Not them! Wosn't no light, yer see. 'Ad ter strike a match ter tear the watches orf 'em. Ho-ho-ho!"

"Bermondsey," said Warren, enthusiastically, as the other stared dully at his costume, "I want to shake your hand. I also want to offer you a drink of champagne. . . . What's on your mind, Hank?"

Morgan had begun to stalk about excitedly. He picked up the watches and examined them. Then he put them down on the couch with the emerald elephant.

"If this idea works out," he said, swinging round, "then there'll be no need to lie under a heap of marionettes and play dead for two days. Nor will there be any need to go to the brig, either, for any of us except Curt. . . ."

"That's fine," said Warren. "That's great. Well, all I've got to say is, and I take my oath on it, I am not going back to that damned padded cell, whatever happens! Get me? Furthermore—"

"Shut up, will you?—and listen! You'll need to go back for not more than an hour. The whole point is, Captain Whistler doesn't know you're *out* of the brig, does he? Right. Now don't interrupt. So what have we got? We've got in Bermondsey a witness who can definitely prove we were not stealing that emerald out of Kyle's cabin, but were *returning* it, together with Kyle's papers. Our witness needn't say anything about Curt's having taken it from there. Then—"

"Ahoy dere!" protested Valvick. "Coroosh! you are not going to try to see Barnacle *now,* are you?"

"Listen! Then this is the way it's to be done:

"Peggy takes the note-cases, watches, and the rest of it, including the emerald. She goes to Whistler and says, 'Captain, do you know what the two people you thought were thieves have done? They've saved your bacon and saved the emerald when it was nearly stolen a second time.' She then tells a story of how, as we were passing by, the skipper and I saw a mysterious masked stranger—"

"Horse feathers!" said Warren, with some definiteness. "You're drunk."

Morgan steadied himself. "All right, we'll omit the mask then. We saw this stranger sneaking out of Kyle's cabin laden with Kyle's papers and the emerald. We set on him; and, although he got away without our learning who he was, we retrieved the whole thing. . . ." A howl of protest arose, and Morgan regarded them sardonically. "Actually, the reason why you oppose it is that you want to hide in with the marionettes and put on that damned show, don't you? Isn't that true?"

"Yes, ay know," Valvick growled stubbornly, "but what about dem getting beaten up?"

"That's part of it. You don't honestly imagine even old Whistler would believe *we'd* pinch his watch and cuff-links, do you? Very well: Admittedly we were in a bad position and acted hastily when we ran out on him. But our mythical crook, who was ever in attendance, is on the watch; and, thinking Whistler's got the emerald from us, bursts in. By the use of a bottle as a weapon—that's Whistler's own story, remember, and he's got to stick to it whether he believes it or not—the crook lays low the captain and the second officer, and he makes a clean haul of everything. . . ."

He stopped, feeling that the story sounded thin even to his own ears; yet also convinced that their own plan was even more impracticable. It was a case of Mephistopheles or deep water, a toss-up of two insanities, but at least his scheme might do something towards soothing the gigantic wrath of Captain Whistler. Warren grunted.

"And then you and Valvick attack this crook again, I suppose?" he asked. "Hank, it's the bunk. I'm surprised at you."

"No! You don't understand. The crook, groggy from Captain Whistler's powerful smashes, staggers away to fall. We, roused by the noise, return. We find the plunder again. At first we daren't take it to Whistler, knowing what he'll think. But Peggy, seeing we have nothing to fear from our noble conduct, persuades us—"

He saw that Valvick was wavering and scratching his chin, and said desperately:

"Let's put it to a vote. We do this, while Curt returns to the brig and pacifies Woodcock by a definite promise to get him the testimonial. *Listen!"* An inspiration struck him. "Do you realise that, while Captain Whistler's authority only extends over the high seas, Woodcock is a private citizen and can prosecute in the civil courts? He can get a thousand pounds damages for that, and *he's* not got any false dignity to restrain him. Do you want to go to jail, Curt? Well, if you leave Woodcock tied up there much longer—and they may not discover him until to-morrow— he'll be so wild that a bug-powder testimonial from the President himself wouldn't keep him quiet. For God's sake, get the champagne out of your brains for three seconds and think! You needn't stay in the brig any longer than you like, Curt. Whistler's promised to let you out."

"I still vote No," said Warren. A babble of voices arose, while they got together in the middle of the cabin waving their arms and shouting. Mrs. Perrigord said it was oll owfully clever, and she voted as Henry did.

"Eee! Stop it!" cried Peggy, clapping her hands to her

ears. "Listen. Let *me* talk. I'll admit I think it would be rather nice to go to the captain and make goo-goo eyes at him, sort of. Wait! But we'll let it rest on Uncle Jules and —I don't care what you say, he's my uncle, and I won't have him g-guyed because they s-say he's too drunk to—"

"Steady now!" said Warren, as she shook her fists desperately.

". . . to play. And we'll let it rest at that. If he's sober enough to play inside of, say fifteen minutes or half an hour, we can hold the curtain until then; we'll adopt Hank's idea. If not, then we'll carry on as we'd intended. . . . What's that noise?" She broke off suddenly. Her smeary eyes travelled past Morgan's shoulder and widened. Then she screamed.

"Where," said Peggy, *"is Uncle Jules?"*

The door of the cabin was lightly banging with the slight roll of the ship.

Uncle Jules was gone. Also missing were the watches, the cuff-links, the note-case, the studs, and the emerald elephant.

Chapter 19

Indiscretions of Uncle Jules

THE Moorish warrior removed his spiked helmet and flung it on the floor.

"Sunk!" he said wildly. "Sunk! Done brown. Come on, take our vote if we want to, but we can't do either one thing or the other now. I'm getting sick of this. What's the matter with the old soak? Is he a kleptomaniac?"

"You let him alone!" cried Peggy. "He can't help it. He's drunk, poor darling. Oh, *why* didn't I think? He's done it before. Only mostly it's only motor-car keys, and there's not an awful lot of harm done, in spite of what awful people say. . . ."

"What do you mean, motor-car keys?"

Her eyes wrinkled up. "Why, the keys of the cars, you know; things you turn on the ignition with. He waits till somebody goes away, leaving the key in the car, and then he sneaks up ever so softly and pinches the key out. Then he goes away somewhere until he can find a fence, and throws the key over it. After that he goes on to find another car. There was a most horrible row in St. Louis because he got loose in a ground where they park cars, and pinched thirty-eight keys at one haul. . . . But why don't you *do* something? Go after him! Get him back before they find—"

"HAH!" cried a furious voice.

The door was flung open. Fat-faced, with vast trembling cheeks, sinister beetle brows and vast moustachios, a tubby little man stood in the doorway. He pointed at Peggy.

"So! So! You have trieda to de-ceive me, eh? You have a trieda toa deceive Signor Benito Furiosa Camposozzi, eh? *Sangua della madonne,* I feex you! You tella me he eesa all-right, eh? Haah! What you call all-aright, eh? I tell you, signorina, to youra face, he ees-a DRUNK!" Signor Camposozzi was breathing so hard that he choked. Peggy hurried up to him.

"You saw him? Oh, please tell me! Where is he?"

Signor Camposozzi raised one arm to heaven, slapped his forehead, and the whites of his eyes rolled up horribly.

"Sooah? You aska me if I see heem? Haah! I weela tella you! Never have I beena so *insulted!* I go up to him. I say, 'Signor Frotinbras!' He say, 'Shhh-h!' In heesa hands he hasa got fourteen gold watches and pocket-books. He open theesa pocket-books and handa me—ME—he handa me wan pound *note*. He say, 'Sh-hh! You buya me onea bottle of gin, eh? Sh-h!' Den he go off asaying, 'Shhh-h!' and a pooshing wan pound note under every door he see. I say—"

"There goes the old swordfish's dough," said Warren, staring from under his villainous eyebrows. "Look, Mr. Sozzi, listen. Did you see—I mean, did he have a kind of a jewel thing with him? A sort of green thing on a gold chain?"

"Haah! Dida I *see* it?" inquired Signor Camposozzi, with a withering leer. "He hasa fasten it around his neck."

Morgan turned to Valvick. "The fat's in the fire now anyway, Skipper," he said. "Whatever else we do, we can't be marionettes. But if it occurs to Uncle Jules to give that emerald away to somebody . . . well, we can't be in more trouble than we are. We'd better go after him. No, Curt! No! You're not coming, do you hear?"

"Certainly I'm coming," said Warren, drawing his scimitar again and placing a bottle of champagne in the pocket of his robe. "Think I'm going to miss this? It's absolutely safe. My own mother wouldn't recognise me in this outfit. If we run into the old haddock or anybody, I can simply gesture and say, 'No speeka da Eenglish.' See?"

As a matter of fact, he was the first one out the door. Nobody protested. The fat was now sizzling and flaring in the fire anyway; and, Morgan reflected, at least three people were better than two at nobbling Uncle Jules—provided they could find him—before he gave away Captain Whistler's watch to somebody and left a trail of Captain Whistler's money all along C deck. Also, they were joined by the Bermondsey Terror.

"Head for the bar!" said Morgan as the three of them

charged up the passage. "He'll go in that direction by instinct. No, not that way. Turn round and go by the port side, or we may run into Whistler and his crowd. . . ."

They stopped. A confused noise was beginning to bellow down in the direction of cabin C 46; the patter of running feet, excited voices, and a stentorian ocean-going call to arms. The four allies instantly shifted their course and made for the forward part of the boat—a fortunate circumstance, since they picked up Uncle Jules's trail within a few seconds. Indeed, nobody but Messrs. Lestrade, Gregson, and Athelney Jones could have missed it. Two or three doors were open, and infuriated passengers, clad only in dress trousers, and dress shirts hanging out over them, were dancing stockingless in the doors while they bawled at a dazed steward.

"I couldn't 'elp it!" protested the steward. "I tell you, sir—"

"You!" said Warren, presenting the point of his scimitar at the steward's breast, an apparition which nearly brought a scream bubbling from between the other's lips. "You!" he repeated, as the steward strove to run. "Have you seen him? A bald-headed drunk with a prizefighter's shoulders and his hands full of stuff?"

"Yes! Y-yes, sir! Take that thing away! Just gone! Did he get yours too?"

"My what?"

"Shoes!" said the steward.

"I'll have the law on this line!" screamed one maddened passenger, laying hold of the steward's collar. "I'll sue 'em for the biggest damages ever awarded in a court. I'll complain to the captain. I put my shoes outside my door to be polished, and when I go to get 'em what do I see but—"

"He's stolen every damn shoe that was outside a door!" snorted another, who was sniffing after shoes up and down the passage like a terrier. "Where's the captain? Who was it? Who—"

"Come *on*," said Captain Valvick. "Out on de deck and go round."

They found a door forward, and plunged out on C deck —on the same deck and the same side that had seen the hurricane of the night before. As before, it was dimly lighted, but this time peaceful. They paused and stared round, breathing cool air after the thick atmosphere inside. And Morgan, as he peered down a companion-way leading to D deck, came face to face with Mr. Charles Woodcock.

Somebody swore, and then there was silence.

Mr. Woodcock was coming slowly and rather painfully up the steps. Aside from rumpled clothes, he was undamaged, but every joint was cramped from his long trussing in torn sheets. His bush of hair waved in the breeze. He writhed his shoulders, cracking the knuckles of his hands; and on his bony face, as he looked up and saw who stood there, was an expression—

Morgan stared as he saw that look. He had expected many things from the unfortunate bug-powder representative, triumph, threats, rumpled dignity swearing vengeance, sinister joviality, at all events hostility. But here was an expression which puzzled him. Woodcock had stiffened. His tie was blown into his face and seemed to tickle his nose and terrify him like the brushing of a bat in the dark. His bony hand jerked. There was a silence but for seething water. . . .

"So it's *you* again," said Warren, and slapped the scimitar against his leg.

Woodcock recognised the voice. He glanced from Warren to Morgan.

"Listen!" he said, clearing his throat. "Listen! Don't fly off the handle now. I want you to unnastand something. . . ."

This looked inexplicably like retreat. As startled by Woodcock's appearance as he had evidently been by theirs, Morgan nevertheless cut in before Warren could speak again.

"Well?" he demanded, and assumed by instinct an ominous tone. "Well?"

The pale smile fluttered on Woodcock's face. "What I wantcha to unnastand, old man," he said, writhing his shoulders again and speaking very rapidly, "is that *I* wasn't responsible for you being stuck in that brig, even if you think I was; honest to God I wasn't. Look, I'm not mad at

you, even if you've hurt me so bad I'll maybe have to go
to the hospital. That's what you've done—but you can see
I'm not mad, can't you, old man? Maybe it was right for
you to take a sock at me—from what you thought, I mean.
I know how it is when you get mad. A guy can't help himself. But when I told you—you know, what I did tell you—
it was absolutely in good faith. . . ."

There was something so utterly suspicious and guilty-
seeming about the man that even the Bermondsey Terror,
who had evidently no idea what this was all about, took a
step forward.

" 'Ere!" he said. "Oo's *this?*"

"Come up here, Mr. Woodcock," said Morgan quietly.
He jabbed his elbow into Warren's ribs to keep him quiet.
"You mean that you really didn't see that film stolen out
of Curt Warren's cabin, after all?"

"I did! I swear I did, old man!"

"Attempted blackmail, eh?" asked the Moorish warrior,
who had opened his eyes wide and was fiddling with the
scimitar.

"No! No! I tell you it was a mistake, and I can prove it.
I mean, it may *look* like the man I saw isn't on board at
all, but he is! He's got to be. He must have been disguised
or something. . . ."

A dim suspicion that at last the Parcæ had got tired of
tangling things up for their particular crowd, and had
begun on somebody else, began to grow hopefully in Morgan's mind.

"Let's hear your side of the story," he said, playing a
chance. "Then we'll decide. What do you have to say
about it?"

Woodcock came up to the deck. A scowl, of which
neither of them probably knew the reason, had overspread
the rather grim faces of large Valvick and even larger
Bermondsey. Woodcock saw it, and veered like a sloop in
a windward breeze.

Clearing his throat, he set himself amiably for a hypnotic
speech.

"So listen, old man. I *did* see that guy; word of honour.
But after I talked to you to-day I said to myself, I said,

'Charley, that fellow Warren's a real white man, and he's promised to get the testimonial for you. And you're a man of your word, Charley,' I said," lowering his voice, 'so you'll get the name of the man for him'. . . ."

"You mean you didn't know who the man was?"

"Didn't I tell you I didn't know his *name?*" demanded Woodcock urgently. "Think what I said! Remember what I said! And what I said was, I'd know him if I saw him again. And, damn it! he had to be on the boat, didn't he? So I thought I'd look around and find out who it was. Well, all the possible people were at meals to-day, and I looked, and he wasn't there! So I thought, 'What the hell?' and I began to get scared," he swallowed hard; "so I went to the purser, and described the man as somebody I wanted to meet. I couldn't miss him; I remembered everything, including a funny-looking ear and a strawberry mark on the fellow's cheek. And the purser said, 'Charley,' he said, 'there's nobody like that aboard.' And then I thought, 'Disguise!' But yet it couldn't have been anybody I'd already seen, because I'd have known 'em disguise or no disguise —shape of the face, no whiskers, all that." He was growing unintelligible, but he rushed on. "And then I heard you'd been put in the brig because the captain had accused you of making a false accusation about somebody; and I thought, 'O God, Charley, this is all your fault and he won't believe you really did see that.' When I got your note to come down, I thought you mightn't blame me after all; but as soon as you hit me—Listen, I'll make it up to you. I'm no crook, I swear. . . ."

Good old Parcæ! Morgan felt a rush of gratitude even for this small favour of averting charges of assault and battery, or whatever else might have occurred to Mr. Woodcock in a more rational moment.

"You hear what Mr. Woodcock says, Curt?" asked Morgan.

"I hear it," Warren, in a curious tone. He smoothed at his whiskers and looked meditatively at the scimitar.

"And you're willing to admit the mistake," pursued Morgan, "and let bygones be bygones if Mr. Woodcock is? Righto! Of course Mr. Woodcock will realise from a business point of view he no longer has any right to ask for that testimonial. . . ."

"Hank, old man," said Mr. Woodcock, with great earnestness, "what I say is, To hell with the testimonial. And the bug-powder business too. This isn't my game, and I might as well admit it. I can sell things—there's not a better little spieler on the European route than Charley R. Woodcock, if I do say it myself—but for the big business side of it, *ixnay*. No soap. Through. But I'm entirely willing, old man, to give you all the help I can. You see I kept bumping myself against the wall down there in that cell until the sailor looked in; and finally I got the gag out of my mouth. Well, he released me and went off to find the captain. And I'd better tell you—"

From somewhere on the other side of the deck rose a shout. A door wheezed and slammed, and the clatter of feet rushed nearer.

"There he goes!" said a voice and, rising above it, they heard the view-halloo bellow of Captain Whistler.

"Don't run!" wheezed Valvick. "Don't run, ay tell you, or you may run into him. Down de companion-ladder— 'ere!—all of you. Watch! Maybe dey don't see. . . ."

As the distant din of pursuit grew, Valvick shoved the Moorish warrior down the steps and the Bermondsey Terror after him. The Bug-powder Boy, full of new terrors, tumbled down first. Crouching on the iron steps beside Valvick, Morgan thrust his head up to look along C deck. And he saw a rather impressive sight. He saw Uncle Jules.

Far up ahead, faint and yet discernible in the dim lights, Uncle Jules turned the corner round the forward bulkhead and moved majestically towards them. The breeze blew up his fringe of hair like a halo. His gait was intent, determined, even with a hint of stateliness; yet in it there were the cautious indications of one who suspects he is being followed. A lighted porthole attracted his attention. He moved towards it, so that his red, determined, screwed-up face showed leering against the light. He stuck his head partly inside.

"Sh-h-h!" said Uncle Jules, lifting his finger to his lip.

"Eeee!" shrieked a feminine voice inside. "Eeeeee!"

A look of mild annoyance crossed Uncle Jules's face. "Sh!" he urged. After peering cautiously around, he searched among the bundle of articles he was carrying, selected what appeared to be a gold watch, and carefully tossed it through the porthole. *"Onze!"* he whispered. They heard it crash on the floor inside. Uncle Jules moved towards the rail of the boat with an air of impartiality. With fierce care he selected a pair of patent-leather dancing-pumps and tossed them overboard.

"Douze!" counted Uncle Jules. *"Treize, quatorze—"*

"Eee!" still shrieked the feminine voice as a stream of articles began to go overboard. Uncle Jules seemed annoyed at this interruption. But he was willing to indulge the vagaries of the weaker sex.

"Vouse n'amiez-pas cette montre, hein?" he asked solicitously. *"Est-ce-que vous aimez l'argent?"*

The din of pursuit burst with a crash of sound round the corner of the deck ahead, led by Captain Whistler and Second-Officer Baldwin. They stopped, stricken. They were just in time to see Uncle Jules empty the contents of Captain Whistler's wallet through the porthole. Then, with swift impartiality, he flew to the rail. Overboard, clear-sailing against the moonlight, went Captain Whistler's watch, Captain Whistler's cuff-links, Captain Whistler's studs—and the emerald elephant.

"Dix-sept, dix-huit, dix-neuf, VINGT!" whispered Uncle Jules triumphantly. Then he turned round, saw his pursuers and said *"Sh-hhh!"*

There are times when action is impossible. Morgan laid his face against the cold iron step, his muscles turning to water, and groaned so deeply that under ordinary circumstances the pursuers must have heard him.

But they did not hear him. Not unreasonably, they had failed to observe the strict letter of Uncle Jules's parting injunction. The noises that arose as the pack closed in on Uncle Jules awoke the sleeping gulls to scream and wheel on the water. They were terrifying noises. But, just as Morgan and Warren were rising again, the implications of one remark struck them motionless.

"So that," bellowed the appalled voice of Captain

Whistler, strangled with incoherent fury, "so *that's* the man, is it, who burst in there and—and launched the m-most murderous attack on us that—"

"Sure it is, sir," said the hardly less sane voice of Second-Officer Baldwin. "Look at him! Look at those arms and shoulders! Nobody but somebody used to swinging those——marionettes day after day could've had the strength to hit like that. There's nobody on the ship who could've done it else. . . ."

"Ho?" muttered the Bermondsey Terror, starting violently.

"Shh!" hissed Captain Valvick.

". . . No, sir," pursued Baldwin, "he's not a crook. But he's a notorious drunkard. I know all about him. A drunkard, and that's the sort of thing he does. . . ."

"Pardonnez-moi, messieurs," rumbled a polite if muffled voice from under what appeared to be many bodies. *"Est-ce-que vous pouvez me donner du gin?"*

"He—he threw that—that emer—" Whistler gulped amid strange noises. "But what about—those—young Morgan—Sharkmeat—those—"

Somebody's heels clicked. A new voice put in: "Will you let me offer an explanation, sir? I'm Sparks, sir. I saw part of it from my cousin's cabin. If you'll let me tell you, sir, that young fellow and the Swede weren't trying to steal—you know. They were trying to return it. I saw them. They're close friends of Miss Glenn, this man's niece; and I should think they were trying to cover him up after the old drunk had stolen it. . . ."

"FROM DR. KYLE'S CABIN? What the hell do you mean? They—"

"Sir, if you'll listen to me!" roared Baldwin. "Sparks is right. Don't you see what happened? This kleptomaniac souse is the man who stole the emerald from you last night! Who else could have hit you as hard as that? And didn't he act last night exactly as he's acting to-night, sir? Look here: you were standing near where you are now. And what did he do? He did exactly what we saw him do to-night—he chucked that jewel through the nearest port, which happened to be Dr. Kyle's, and it landed behind the trunk. . . . He's drunk, sir, and not responsible; but that's what happened. . . ."

There was an awed silence.

"By God!" said Captain Whistler. "By God! . . . But wait! It was returned to Lord Sturton—"

"Sir," said Baldwin wearily, "don't you realise that this souse's niece and their crowd have been trying to protect him all the time? One of 'em returned it, that's all, and I sort of admire the sport who did. The drunk stole it again, so they decided they'd put it back in the doc's cabin where the drunk had a fixed idea it ought to go, and then tip off somebody to find it. Only we wouldn't let them explain, sir. We—er—we owe 'em an apology."

"One of you," said the captain crisply, "go to Lord Sturton; present my compliments, and say that I will wait on him immediately. GET ME SOME ROPES AND TIE THIS LUBBER UP. YOU!" said Captain Whistler, evidently addressing Uncle Jules, "is—this—true?"

Morgan risked a look. Captain Whistler's back was turned among the group of figures on the deck, so that Morgan could not see the new damage to his face. But he saw Uncle Jules struggling to sit upright among the hands that held him. With a fierce expression of concentration on his face, Uncle Jules wrenched his vast shoulders and flung off the hands. A solitary pair of shoes remained gripped close to him. With a last effort he sent the shoes sailing overboard; then he breathed deeply, smiled, rolled over gently on the deck, and began to snore. "Ha, whee!" breathed Uncle Jules, with a long sigh of contentment.

"Take him away," said Whistler, "and lock him up."

A trampling of feet ensued. Morgan, about to get up, was restrained by Valvick.

"It iss all right!" he whispered fiercely. "Ay know how seafaring men iss. Dey get hawful mad, but dey will not prosecute if dey t'ink a mann iss drunk. De code iss dat whatever you do when you iss drunk, a yentleman goes light on. Shh! Ay know. Listen—!"

They listened carefully while Captain Whistler relieved his mind for some moments. Then he took on a more tragic note in mourning his watch and valuables, thus gradually working himself up to a dizzy pitch when he came to the last trouble.

"So that's the thief I was supposed to have aboard, eh?" he wanted to know. "A *common drunk,* who throws fifty-thousand-pound emeralds overboard, who—who—"

Baldwin said gloomily: "You see now why that young Warren pretended to act like a madman, sir? He's more or less engaged to the girl, they tell me. Well, they made a good job of it shielding him. But I've got to admit we've been a bit rough on—"

"Sir," said a new voice, "Lord Sturton's compliments, sir, and—"

"Go on," sneered the captain, with a sort of heavy-stage-despair. "Don't stop there. Speak up, will you? Let's hear it!"

"Well, sir—he—he says for you to go to hell, sir. . . ."

"What?"

"He says—I'm only repeating it—he says you're drunk, sir. He says nobody's stolen his emerald, and he got it out and showed it to me to prove it. He's in a bit of a temper, sir. He says if he hears one more word about that bleeding emerald—if anybody makes a row or so much as mentions that bleeding emerald to him again—he'll have your papers and sue the line for a hundred thousand pounds. That's a fact."

"Here, Mitchell!" snapped Baldwin. "Don't stand there like a dummy! Come and give me a hand with the commander. . . . Get some brandy or something. Hurry, damn you, hurry!"

There was a sound of running footsteps. Then up from behind Morgan, an expression of dreamy triumph on his face, rose Curtis Warren full panoplied in Moorish arms. He pushed past the others and ascended the ladder. Drawing his bejewelled cloak about him, shooting back the cuffs of his chain mail, he adjusted the spiked helmet rakishly over the curls of his wig. He drew himself up with a haughty gesture. Before the bleary eyes of the *Queen Victoria's* skipper, who was reeling dumbly against the rail and almost toppling overboard, Warren strode forward with ringing footfalls.

He paused before Whistler. Lifting the scimitar like an accusing finger, he pointed it at the captain.

"Captain Whistler," he said in a voice of shocked and horrified rebuke, "after all your suspicions of innocent men . . . Captain Whistler, AREN'T—YOU—ASHAMED OF YOURSELF?"

Chapter 20

Disclosure

IN A CERTAIN big room above Adelphi Terrace, a misted sun was beginning to lengthen the shadows. It was beginning to make a dazzle against a huddle of purpling towers westward at the curve of the river; and from one of these towers Big Ben had just finished clanging out the hour of four. A very hoarse story-teller listened to the strokes reverberating away. Then Morgan sat back.

Dr. Fell removed his glasses. With a large red bandana he mopped a moisture of joy from his eyes, said, "Whoosh!" with a wheezing and expiring chuckle, and rumbled:

"No, I'll never forgive myself for not being there. My boy, it's an epic. Oh, Bacchus, what I'd give for one glimpse of Uncle Jules in his last *moment supréme*! Or of the old mollusc, Captain Whistler, either. But surely that's not all?"

"It's all," said Morgan wearily, "I have the voice to tell you now. Also, I imagine, it's all that's relevant to the issue. If you think the fireworks ended there, of course, you still haven't plumbed the spiritual possibilities of our crowd. I could fill a fair number of pages with the saga of pyrotechnics between nine-fifteen night before last, when Uncle Jules threw his last gallant shoe, until 7 A.M. this morning, when I slipped away from a ship accursed. But I can give you only a general outline. . . . Besides, I hesitated to include all the things I have. It was hair-raising action, if you like, but it seemed to me not to have any bearing on the vital issues. . . ."

Dr. Fell finished mopping his eyes and subsided in dying chuckles. Then he blinked across the table.

"Curiously enough, that's where you're wrong," he said. "Now I can say positively that it's a pleasure to me to find a case in which the most important clues are jokes. If you had omitted any point of that recital I should have been

227

cheated of valuable evidence. The cuckoo's call is the lion's roar, and a jack-in-the-box has a disconcerting habit of showing a thief's face. But the clues are sealed now; you've provided me with my second eight. H'm! Four o'clock. It's too late to do anything more, or hear anything that can help me further. If I'm right, I should know it shortly. If not, the Blind Barber has got away. Still—"

There was a ring downstairs at the bell.

For a moment Dr. Fell sat motionless, only his great stomach heaving, and he seemed flushed and rather uneasy.

"If I'm wrong—" he said. Then he struggled to his feet. "I'll answer that ring myself. Just glance over this notation, will you? Here's a list of my second eight clues. See if they convey anything?"

While he was gone Morgan drew out a full bottle of beer from the troop of dead guardsmen that stood at attention on the table. He grinned. Whatever had happened, it was something to write in the note-book. "?" he said, and read on the slip of paper:

9. The Clue of Wrong Rooms.
10. The Clue of Lights.
11. The Clue of Personal Taste.
12. The Clue of Avoided Explanations.
13. The Clue Direct.
14. The Clue of Known Doubles.
15. The Clue of Misunderstanding.
& 16. The Clue Conclusive.

He was still frowning over it when Dr. Fell stumped back, leaning on his two canes. Under one arm Dr. Fell held a package wrapped in brown paper, and in the other an envelope ripped open. Many things he could conceal: the insight and strategy of his nimble, rocket-brilliant, childlike brain, and these he could conceal because, out of a desire to spring his surprise, he liked to fog them round with genial talk. But a certain relief he could not conceal. Morgan saw it and half rose from his chair.

"Rubbish, rubbish!" boomed the doctor, nodding jovially. "Sit down, sit down! Heh! As I was about to say—"

"Have you—?"

"Now, now! Let me get comfortab . . . aah! So. Well, my boy, whatever's done is already done. Either the Blind Barber has got away or he hasn't. If he has got away, I think it's highly likely we shall catch him sooner or later. I don't think he intended to keep his present disguise after he had landed in either France or England; then, safely out of it, he could perform another of his quick changes and disappear. He's by way of being a genius. I wonder who he really is?"

"But you said—"

"Oh, I know the name he's using at the moment. But I warned you long ago that the garb was only a mask and a dummy; and I should like to see how his real mind works. . . . In any event, the boat has docked. Didn't you tell me that young Warren was coming to see me? What arrangements have you made about that?"

"I gave him your address and said to look up the phone number if he needed to communicate. He and Peggy and the old man are coming on to London as soon as they can get the boat train. But listen! *Who is it?* Is he going to get away, after all? What, in God's name, is the real explanation of the whole thing?"

"Heh!" said Dr. Fell. "Heh-heh! You read my last eight clues and still don't know? You had the evidence of that steel box staring you in the face and still couldn't make your wits work? Tut, now, I don't blame you. You were doing too much action to think. If a man's required to turn round every second and pick up a new person who has been knocked out by somebody, he isn't apt to have much time for cool reflection. . . . You see this parcel?" He put it on the table. "No, don't look at it just yet. We've still some time before a final consultation, and there are a few points on which I should like enlightenment. . . . What was the upshot of the matter after Uncle Jules was haled away to clink? Does Whistler still think Uncle Jules was the thief? And what about the marionette show? The thing seems to me to be incomplete. From the very first, as a matter of fact, I had a strong feeling that your band would somehow be enticed into that marionette show and would be forced by the Parcæ into putting on a performance. . . ."

Morgan scratched his ear.

"As a matter of fact," he said, "we did. It was Peggy's fault for insisting on our saving Uncle Jules's bacon. She said if we didn't she'd go straight to the captain and tell him everything. We pointed out that, whatever the explanations might have been, Uncle Jules really had left a brilliant trail of shoes in our wake; that Captain Whistler was not in the mood to smile indulgently when his fifty-guinea watch sailed overboard; and after all Uncle Jules was better off in the brig. We also pointed out that, just prior to his capture, he had been seen marching through the bar and placing a shoe in the hand of any person who took his fancy. Consequently, we said, it would not appear probable to the passengers that he could work his marionette show that night."

"And then?"

Morgan shook his head gloomily.

"Well, she wouldn't hear of it. She said it was our fault that he'd done all of it. She pointed out that most of the passengers were in the concert-hall, applauding for the show to go on, and the person she was really afraid of was Perrigord. Perrigord had prepared an elaborate and powerful speech commemorating Uncle Jules's genius, and had just begun it at the moment Uncle Jules was firing shoes overboard. Peggy said if a good performance didn't go on, Perrigord would be made out such an ass that he'd never let up on Uncle Jules in the papers, and their success depended on him. The girl was loony and wouldn't see reason. At last we promised her we'd do it if she'd consent to allow Uncle Jules to stay in the brig. It was the best way out for everybody, for they'll forgive a drunk's insanities when they'll prosecute an honest mistake. Curt insisted on paying for the damage, which amounted, all in all, to close on two hundred pounds. And we felt it was time for peace to descend on the *Queen Victoria*. . . ."

"Well?"

"It didn't," said Morgan gloomily. "I begged and

pleaded with Peggy. I told her some damned thing was bound to happen if we tried to work that show, and Perrigord would be more infuriated than though there'd been no performance. She wouldn't see it. She wouldn't even see it when we had one brief rehearsal of the first scene. My portrayal of Charlemagne, I flatter myself, would have been eloquent and kingly, but Curt, in the role of Roland got stage-struck at the rehearsal and insisted on dictating a long consular report in French about the facts and figures in the export of sardines from Lisbon. Captain Valvick at the piano would have been an error. It was not merely that he wanted to greet the entrance of the Frankish army with the strains of 'La Madelon,' but since somebody had informed him in general terms that Moors were 'black men,' then the crafty Sultan of the Moors would have made his entrance with 'Old Man River.' Next—"

"Hold on!" said Dr. Fell, whose eyes were growing bright with tears again, and who had clapped a hand over his mouth as he trembled. "I don't quite understand this. It should have been one of your high lights, *Why are you so reluctant to talk about it?* Out with it now! Was there, or wasn't there a performance?"

"Well—yes and again no," replied Morgan, shifting uneasily. "It started, anyway. Oh, I'll admit it saved our lives in a way, because the old dabble Parcæ were working for us now; but I'd rather not have had it saved in that way. . . . Have you noticed that I've not seemed too cheerful today! Have you also noticed that I'm not accompanied by my wife? She was supposed to meet me at Southampton, but at the last minute I sent her a radiogram not to come, because I was afraid some of the passengers might—"

Dr. Fell sat up.

"If I've got to tell it," said Morgan wryly, "I suppose I must. Fortunately, we got no farther than the first scene, wherein Charlemagne speaks the prologue. I was Charlemagne. Charlemagne wore long white whiskers; his venerable head was adorned with a gold crown studded with diamonds and rubies; a mantle of scarlet and ermine swathed his mighty shoulders; a jewelled broadsword was buckled about his waist, and under his chain mail his stomach was stuffed with four sofa-pillows to give him *embonpoint*. I was Charlemagne.

"Charlemagne spoke the prologue behind an illuminated gauze screen, like a tall picture-frame, at the rear of the stage. Yes. And how. Mr. Leslie Perrigord had just concluded an impassioned speech lasting fifty-five minutes to the tick. Mr. Perrigord said that this performance was the goods. He said he hoped his hearers. with minds made torpid by the miasmatic sluggishness of Hollywood, would receive a refreshing shock as they watched enthralled this drama in which every gesture recorded an aspiration of the human soul. He said to watch closely, even though they would not fully appreciate its lights and shadings, its subtle groupings and baffling harmonies of line, its bold chords on the metaphysical yearning of man, not surpassed in the mightiest pages of Ibsen. He also said a number of complimentary things about the prowess of Charlemagne. I was Charlemagne.

"When at length he ran out of breath, he stopped. There were three hollow knocks. Captain Valvick, despite all that could be done to stop him, played an overture consisting of 'La Marseillaise.' The curtain flew up a bit prematurely, I fear. Among eighty-odd others, Mr. Perrigord saw the gauze screen glowing luminous against darkness, and full of rich colour. He saw the venerable Charlemagne. He also saw his wife. The position was—er—full of subtle groupings and baffling harmonies of line. Yes. That was the moment at which the chain mail split and the sofa-pillows flew out as though they had been fired from a gun. I was Charlemagne. . . . Now, maybe you understand why I do not care to incorporate it into the body of the story. I have no doubt that the audience received a refreshing shock as they watched enthralled this drama in which every gesture recorded an aspiration of the human soul."

Morgan took a deep drink of beer.

Dr. Fell turned his face towards the window. Morgan observed that his shouders were quivering as though with shock and outrage.

"In any event, it saved us, and it saved Uncle Jules for

ever. The roar of applause which went up pleased everybody except possibly Mr. Perrigord. Such an instantaneous success was never achieved in any theatre by a performance which lasted only long enough for somebody to drop the curtain. Uncle Jules's marionette theatre in Soho will be crowded to the end of his days whether he's drunk or sober. And rest solemnly assured that, whatever he happens to feel about it, Mr. Leslie Perrigord will never write in the newspapers a word to condemn him."

The declining sun drew lower across the carpet, resting on the brown-wrapped parcel in the middle of the table. After a time, Dr. Fell turned back.

"So——" he observed, his face gradually becoming less red as quiet settled down——"so it all ends happily, eh? Except perhaps for Mr. Perrigord and—the Blind Barber."

He opened a penknife and weighed it in his hand.

"Yes," said Morgan. "Yes, except in one sense. After all, the fact remains that—whatever little game *you're* playing—we still don't know a blasted thing that's important. We don't know what happened on that ship, although, in spite of all the foolery, we know there was a murder. And a murder isn't especially funny. Nor is, actually, the fact that Curt hasn't recovered his film, and, however ridiculous that looks, to him and to others it's as desperately serious a matter as any."

"Oh?" grunted Dr. Fell. "Well, well!" he said, deprecatingly, and winked one eye, "if that's all you want. . . ."

Suddenly he reached across the table and cut the strings of the parcel with his knife.

"I thought——" he added, beaming, as his hand dived among the wrappings and lifted up a tangled coil of film like a genial Laocoon, "I thought it might be better to have it sent up here before the police rake over the Blind Barber's effects and cause scandal by finding this. I'll hand it over to young Warren when he arrives, so that he can destroy it immediately; although, in return for the favour, do you think he would consent to running it privately, just once, for my benefit? Heh-heh-heh! Hang it all, I think I can insist on *that* much reward, hey? Of course, it's holding back evidence, in a way. But there'll be enough to hang the Barber without it. It was my price for pointing out the culprit to Captain Whistler and handing him the credit of capturing a dangerous criminal. I felt the old sea-horse would comply. . . ."

Tossing the rustling coil across on Morgan's arm, Dr. Fell sat back and blinked. Morgan was on his feet, staring.

"You mean, then, the man is under arrest already?"

"Oh, yes. Caught neatly by the brilliant Captain Whistler —who will get a medal for this, and completing everybody's happiness—an hour before the ship docked. Inspector Jennings, at my suggestion, went down from the Yard in a fast car and was ready to take the Barber in charge when he landed. . . ."

"Ready to take *who* in charge?" he demanded.

"Why, the impostor who calls himself Lord Sturton, of course!" said Dr. Fell.

Chapter 21

The Murderer

"I PERCEIVE on your face," continued the doctor affably, as he lit his pipe, "a certain frog-like expression which would seem to indicate astonishment. H'm! puff, puff, haaaa! You should not be in the least astonished. Under the data given, as I have tabulated in my sixteen clues, there was only one person who could conceivably have been guilty. If I were wrong on my first eight—which, as I pointed out to you, were mere suggestions—then no harm could be done by testing my theory. The second eight confirmed it, and so I had no fear of the result. But, not to leap in too sylph-like a fashion at conclusions, I did this. Here is a copy of the telegram I dispatched to Captain Whistler."

He drew a scribbled envelope from his pocket, on which Morgan read:

> Man calling himself Viscount Sturton is impostor. Hold him under port authority and ask to speak to Hilda Keller, secretary travelling with him. He will not be able to produce her; she is dead. Make thorough search of Man's cabin and person. You will find evidence to support you. Among possessions you will probably find film. . . .

(Here followed a description.)

> If you will send this to me special messenger travelling train arriving Waterloo 3:50, kindly say capture was your own idea. Release Fortinbras from brig. All regards.
>
> GIDEON FELL.

"What's the use of special authority," inquired Dr. Fell, "if you don't use it. Besides, if I had been wrong, and the girl was not really missing, there wouldn't have been an enormous row. But she was. You see, this bogus Sturton was able to conceal her presence or absence admirably so long as you never had any suspicions of *him*. Lad, at several places he was in devilish tight positions; but his very position, and the fact that he was the one who seemed to suffer most from the theft, kept him entirely immune from being suspected. . . . Don't choke, now; have some more beer. Shall I explain?"

"By all means," said Morgan feelingly.

"Hand me back my list of clues, then. H'mf! I'll see if I can have a modest shot at proving to you that—always supposing your data to be correct and complete—Lord Sturton was the only person aboard the *Queen Victoria* who could fill all the requirements for the Blind Barber.

"We commence, then, on one assumption: one assumption on which the whole case must rest. This assumption is that there is an impostor aboard, masquerading as somebody else. Fix that fact firmly in mind before beginning; go even to the length of believing a police commissioner's radiogram, and you will have at least a direction in which to start."

"Wait a bit!" protested Morgan. "We know that now, of course; and, since you were the only one who saw who it was, you ought to have the concession. But that radiogram accused Dr. Kyle, and therefore—"

"No, it didn't," said Dr. Fell, gently. "That is precisely where your whole vision strained away into the mist. It went wrong on so small but understandable a matter as the fact that people don't waste money by sending punctuation in radiograms, and you were misled by the absence of a couple of commas. With that error I shall deal in its proper place, under the head of The Clue of Terse Style. . . . For the moment, we have only the conception of an impostor aboard. There is another point in connection with this, stated to you so flatly and frankly that I have not even bothered to include it as a clue. As in other cases of mine, I seem to remember, it was so big that nobody ever gave it a thought. At one sweep it narrowed the search for the

Blind Barber from a hundred passengers to a very, very few people. The Police Commissioner of the City of New York—not unusually timorous or faint-hearted about making arrests, even if they happen to be wrong arrests—wires thus: 'Well-known figure and must be no mistake made or trouble,' and adds, 'Will not be definite in case of trouble.' Now, that is suggestive. It is even startling. The man, in other words, is so important that the Commissioner finds it advisable not to mention his name, even in a confidential communication to the commander of the ship. Not only does it exclude John Smith or James Jones or Charles Woodcock, but it leads us towards men of such wealth or influence that the public is (presumably) interested in newspaper photographs of them (or anybody else) playing golf. This coy reticence on the part of the New York authorities may also be due partly to the possibility that the eminent man is an Englishman, and that severe complications may ensue in case of an error. But I do not press the point, because it is reasoning before my clues."

He had clearly been listening absently for the doorbell; and now, as the doorbell rang, he nodded and lifted his head to bellow:

"Let 'em in, Vida!"

There was a tramping of footfalls up the steps. The door of Dr. Fell's study opened to admit two large men with a prisoner between them. Morgan heard Dr. Fell say, "Ah, good afternoon, Jennings; and you, too, Hamper. Inspector Jennings, this is Mr. Morgan, one of our witnesses. Mr. Morgan, Sergeant Hamper. The prisoner, I think you know. . . ."

But Morgan was looking at the latter, who said, almost affably:

"How do you do, Doctor? I—er—I see you're looking at my appearance. No, there's no deception and damned little disguise. Too tricky and difficult. . . . Good afternoon, Mr. Morgan. I see you're surprised at the change in my voice. It's a relief to let down from the jerky manner; but I'd got so used to it it almost came natural. Rubbish rubbish rubbish!" squeaked the bogus Lord Sturton, with a sudden shift back to the manner he had previously used, and crowed with mirth.

Morgan jumped a little when he heard that echo of the old manner. The bogus Lord Sturton was in sunlight now, where Morgan remembered him only in the gloom of a darkened cabin like a picture-book wizard: his head hunched into a shawl, his face shaded by a flopping hat. Now he was revealed as a pale, long-faced, sharp-featured man with a rather unpleasant grin. A checked comforter was wound round his scrawny throat, and his clothes were weird. But he wore a bowler hat pushed back on his head, and he was smoking a cigar. Yet, although the grotesquerie had been removed, Morgan liked his look even less. He had an eye literally like a rattlesnake's. It measured Dr. Fell, swivelled round to the window, calculated, and became affable again.

"Come in!" said Dr. Fell. "Sit down. Make yourself comfortable. I've been wanting very much to make your acquaintance, if you're willing to talk. . . ."

"Prisoner's pretty talkative, sir," said Inspector Jennings, with a slow grin. "He's been entertaining Sergeant Hamper and me all the way up on the train. I've got a note-book full and he admits—"

"Why not?" inquired their captive, lifting his left hand to take the cigar out of his mouth. "Rubbish rubbish rubbish! Ha-ha!"

". . . But all the same, sir," said Jennings, "I don't think I'll unlock the handcuff just yet. He says his name's Nemo. Sit down, Nemo, if the doctor says so. I'll be beside you."

Dr. Fell lumbered to the sideboard and got Nemo a drink of brandy. Nemo sat down.

"Point's this," Nemo explained, in a natural voice which was not quite so shrill or jerky as the Lord Sturton impersonation, but nevertheless had enough echo of it to make Morgan remember the whole scene in the darkened ill-smelling cabin. "Point's this. You think you're going to hang me? You're not. Rubbish!" His snaky neck swivelled round, and his eye smiled on Morgan. "Haha, no, no! I've got to be extradited first. They'll want me in the

States. And between that time and this—I've got out of worse fixes."

Dr. Fell put the glass at his elbow, sat down opposite, and contemplated him. Mr. Nemo worked his head round and winked.

"Point is, I'm giving this up because I'm a fatalist. Fatalist! Wouldn't *you* be? Best set-up I ever had—meat—pie—easy; ho-ho, how easy? Wasn't as though I had to be a disguise expert. I told you there was no deception. I'm a dead ringer for Sturton. Look so much like him I could stand him in front of me and shave by him. Joke. But I can't beat marked cards. Sweat? I never had such a bad time in my life as when those God-damned kids—" again he twisted round and looked at Morgan, who was glad he had not a razor in his hands at that moment—"when those God-damned kids tangled it all up. . . ."

"I was about to tell my young friend," said Dr. Fell, "at his own request, some of the points that indicated you were —yourself, Mr. Nemo. . . ."

The doctor was getting great if sleepy enjoyment as he sat back against the dying light from the window and studied the man. Mr. Nemo's lidless eyes were returning the stare.

"Be interested to hear it myself," he said. "Anything to —delay things. Good cigar, good brandy. You listen, m'boy," he said, leering at Jennings. "Give you some pointers. If there's anything you don't know—well, when you've finished I'll tell you. Not before."

Jennings gestured to Sergeant Hamper, who got out his notebook.

Dr. Fell settled himself to begin with relish:

"Sixteen clues, then. Casting my eye over the evidence presented—you needn't take all this down, Hamper; you won't understand all of it—I came, after the obvious give-away of the impostor being an important man. . . ."

Mr. Nemo bowed very gravely, and the doctor's eye twinkled.

". . . to what I called the Clue of Suggestion. It conveyed the idea. It opened the door on what first seemed a mad notion. During a heated argument between you, Mor-

gan, and your friend Warren, while Warren was enthusiastically pleading the guilt of Dr. Kyle on the basis of
detective fiction, you yourself said: 'Oh, and get rid of the
idea that somebody may be impersonating him. . . . That
may be all right for somebody who seldom comes in contact with anyone, but a public figure like an eminent physician won't do." [1]

"It wasn't evidence. It only struck me as a curious coincidence that there really was aboard the ship somebody
who seldom came in contact with anyone; who was known,
I think, you said, as 'The Hermit of Jermyn Street.' 'He'll
see nobody,' you remarked; 'he has no friends; all he does
is collect rare bits of jewellery.' [2] These were only supporting facts to my real clue of suggestion; but undeniably
Lord Sturton filled the qualifications of the radiogram.
Merely a coincidence. . . .

"Then I remembered another coincidence: Lord Sturton
was in Washington. A Sturton, real or bogus, had called
on Unce Warpus and told him of the purchase of the
emerald elephant, which is the Clue of Opportunity.[3]
Whether he was at the reception on the night of Uncle
Warpus's indiscretion some time later, and learned about
the moving-picture film . . ."

"He was," said Mr. Nemo, and chortled suddenly.

". . . this I didn't know. But what we do know is that the
Stelly affair occurred next in Washington, as Warren explained. This account of the Stelly business is what I call
the Clue of Fraternal Trust.[4] It was described as a crime
that looked like magic and was connected with the British
Embassy. Stelly was a shrewd, careful, well-known jewel-
collector who didn't omit any precautions against thieves,
ordinary or extraordinary, as he thought. He left the Embassy one night, and was robbed without fuss. What looked
like magic was his being decoyed or robbed by any ordinary
criminal, and also how the criminal should have known of

[1] (Numbers indicating major clues.) Page 88.
[2] (Markings indicate minor clues.) Page 17.
[3] Page 18.
[4] Page 48.

the necklace to begin with. . . . But it is not at all magical if two well-known jewel-collectors exhibit their treasures to each other and have a tendency to talk shop. It is not at all magical for an eminent peer, even if he is so hermit-like that nobody knows him, to be welcomed at the Embassy in a foreign country. provided he has the documents to prove his identity. These coincidences, you see, are piling up.

"But this peer doesn't travel entirely alone. He is known to have a secretary. The first glimpse we have of him in the narrative is his rushing up the gangplank of a ship (so notoriously eccentric that he can wrap himself round in concealing comforters) and accompanied by this secretary.[5] In the passenger-list I find a Miss Hilda Keller occupying the same suite as Lord Sturton, as I think you yourselves found later.[6] But for the moment I put that aside. . . ."

There was a gurgling noise as Dr. Fell chuckled into his pipe.

"Definitely, things began to happen after some days out (during all of which time Lord Sturton has kept entirely to his cabin, and the secretary with him).[7] The first part of the film was stolen. The mysterious girl appeared, obviously trying to warn young Warren of something. There was the dastardly attack on Captain Whistler—the absence of the attackers on deck for some half an hour—and the subsequent disappearance of the girl. You believed (and so did I) that she had been murdered and thrown overboard. But, putting aside the questions of who the girl was and why she was killed, we have that curious feature of the bed being remade thoroughly, a soiled towel even being replaced. That is what I call, from deductions you will see in a moment, the Clue of Invisibility. . . ." [8]

Mr. Nemo wriggled back in the chair. He put down his glass; his face had gone more pale and his mouth twitched —but not from fear at all. He had nothing to conceal. He

5 Page 18.
6 Page 84.
7 Page 18.
8 Page 73.

was white and poisonous from some emotion Morgan did not understand. You felt the atmosphere about him, as palpably as though you could smell a drug.

"I was crazy about that little whore," he said, suddenly, with such a change in voice and expression that they involuntarily started. "I hope she's in hell."

"That's enough," said Dr. Fell, quietly. He went on: "If somebody wished (for whatever reason) to kill her, why was she not merely killed and left there? The inference first off was that she would be more dangerous to the murderer if her body were discovered than if she were thrown overboard. By why should this be. Disappearance or outright murder, there would still be an investigation. . . . Yet observe! What does the murderer do? He carefully makes up the berth and replaces the towel. This could not be to make you think the stunned girl had recovered and gone to her own cabin. It would have exactly the opposite effect. It means that the murderer was trying to make those in authority think—meaning Captain Whistler—that the girl was nothing but a mythical person; a lie invented for some reason by yourselves.

"Behind the apparent madness of this course, since four people had seen her, consider what the murderer's reasons must have been. To begin with, he knew what had happened on C deck; he hoped Whistler would spot young Warren as the man who had attacked him, and yourselves as the people who had stolen the emerald; he knew that Whistler would not be likely to credit *any* story you told, and give short shrift to your excuses. But to adopt such a dangerous course as pretending she was a myth meant (*a*) that the girl would be traced straight to him if she were found dead, and that he could not stand the light of *any* investigation whatever by police authorities afterwards. It also meant (*b*) it was far less dangerous to conceal her absence, and that he had good reason to think he could conceal it.

"Now, this, gentlemen, is a very remarkable choice indeed, when you try to conceal an absence from a community of only a hundred passengers. Why couldn't he stand *any* investigation? How could he hope to convince investigators that nobody was missing?

"First ask yourself who this girl could have been. She could not have been travelling alone: a solitary passenger is not connected closely enough with anybody else to lead absolutely damning evidence straight to him among a hundred people, and to make it necessary to pretend the girl had never existed; besides, a solitary passenger would be the first to be missed. She was not travelling in a family party, or, as Captain Whistler shrewdly pointed out, there might possibly have been complaint at her disappearance. She was travelling then, with just one other person—the murderer. She was travelling as wife, companion, or what you like. The murderer could hope to conceal her disappearance, first, because she must have made no acquaintances and have been with him every moment of the time. That means the murderer seldom or never had left his cabin. He might conceal it, second, because he was so highly placed as to be above suspicion—*not otherwise*—and because he himself was the victim of a theft that directed attention away from him. But, if he were all this, why couldn't he stand any investigation whatever? The not-very-complicated answer is that he was an impostor who had enough to do in concealing his imposture. If you then musingly consider what man was travelling with a single female companion, what man had kept to his cabin every moment of the time, what man was so highly-placed as to be above suspicion; what man had been the victim of a theft; and, finally, what man there is whom we have some slight reason to think as an impostor; then it is remarkable how we swing round again to Lord Sturton. All this is built up on the clue of a clean towel, the clue of invisibility. But it is still coincidence without definite reason, though we find rapid support for it.

"I mean that razor incautiously left behind in the berth. . . ."

Mr. Nemo, who had been mouthing his cigar for some time, twitched round and looked at each in turn. His pale, bony face had worn an absent look, but now it had such a wide smile of urbanity and charm that Morgan shivered. "I cut the little bitch's throat," offered Mr. Nemo, making a gesture with the cigar. "Much better for her. *And* more satisfactory for me. That's right, old man," he said to the staring Hamper; "write it down. It's much better to damage their skulls. A surgeon showed me all about that once. If you practise, you can find the right spot. But it wouldn't do for *her*. I had to take one of Sturton's set of razors to do it, and throw the others away. It hurt me. That case of razors must have cost a hundred-odd pound."

He jerked with laughter, lifted his bowler off his head as though in tribute, smirked, kicked his heels, and asked for another drink.

"Yes," said Dr. Fell, staring at him curiously, "that's what I mean. I asked my young friend here not to think of one razor, but of seven in a set. I asked him to think of a set of razors as enormously expensive as those carven, silver-studded, ebony-handled rarities, which were obviously made to order.[9] No ordinary man would have had them. The person likeliest to have them, said my Clue of Seven Razors, was the man who went after costly trinkets, who bought the emerald elephant, 'because it was a curiosity and a rarity, of enormous intrinsic value.' . . .[10] And the razors bring us back again to the question of who the girl was.

"Her solitary appearance in public was in the wireless-room, where she was described by the wireless-operator as 'having her hands full of papers'; and this I call, symbolically, my Clue of Seven Radiograms.[11] What does that appearance sound like? Not a joyous tourist dashing off an inconsequential message home. There is a businesslike look to it. A number of messages—a businesslike look—and we begin to think of a secretary. The edifice rears. Our Blind Barber becomes not only an impostor masquerading as a highly placed recluse who kept to his cabin, and travelled with a female companion; but the girl becomes a

[9] Page 91.
[10] Page 18.
[11] Page 104.

secretary and the recluse an enormously wealthy man with a taste for grotesque trinkets. . . ."

Dr. Fell lifted his stick and pointed suddenly.

"Why did you kill her?" he demanded. "Was she an accomplice?"

"You're telling the story," shrugged Mr. Nemo. "And while I'm bored, I'm bored as hell with it, because just at the moment *I* feel like talking, still—your brandy's not at all bad. Ha-ha-ha. Ought to get hospitality. Go on. *You* talk. Then I'll talk, and I'll surprise you. Give you a little hint, though. Yes. Sporting run for your money, like old Sturton would. . . . Didn't I come down on old Whistler, though! Ho-ho! Yes. . . . Hint is, she was what you'd call virtuous in the way of being honest. She wouldn't step into my game with me when she found out who I was. And when she tried to warn that young fellow— Tcha! Bloody little fool! Ha-ha! Eh?" inquired Mr. Nemo, putting back his cigar with a portentous wink.

"Did you know," said Dr. Fell, "that a man named Woodcock saw you when you stole the first part of that film?"

"Did he?" asked Mr. Nemo, lifting one shoulder. "What did I care? Remove sideburns—they're detachable—little wax in mouth; strawberry mark on cheek; who'll identify me afterwards, eh?"

Dr. Fell slowly drew a line through one line on a sheet of paper.

"And there we had the first direct evidence: of Elimination.[12] Woodcock said definitely that you were a person he'd never seen before. Now, Woodcock hadn't been sea-sick. He'd been in the dining-room at all times, and after the sea-sick passengers came out of their lairs he would have spotted the thief—if the thief hadn't been still among the very, very few who kept to their cabins. Humf! Ha! I was wondering whether anybody had fantastic suspicions of—well, say Perrigord or somebody of the sort. But it ruled out Perrigord, it ruled out Kyle, it ruled out nearly everybody. The thing is plain enough, but where everybody

[12] Page 118.

went off on the wrong scent was over that radiogram from New York." Dr. Fell wrote rapidly on a sheet of paper and pushed it across to Morgan.

> Federal agent thinks crook responsible for Stelly and MacGee jobs. Federal agent thinks also physician is impostor on your ship. . . .

"Well?" said Morgan. The doctor made a few marks, and held it out again.

"The Clue of Terse Style," said Dr. Fell, "indicates that the word "also" is a supernumerary, is out of place, is a word merely wasted in an expensive radiogram if what it means is, "Federal agent *also* thinks. . . ." But read it thus." [13]

> Federal agent thinks—also physician—is impostor on your ship. . . .

"Meaning," said Dr. Fell, crumpling up the paper, "an entirely different thing. The remark about 'medical profession influential' simply means that the doctor in attendance is making a row; he is insisting that, despite the patient at the hospital being apparently out of his head in insisting he is Sturton, the doctor believes it and they mustn't disregard it. But, good God! Do you seriously think that, if he had meant Dr. Kyle was a murderer, the whole medical profession would have wanted to shield him? The idea was so absurd that I wonder anybody considered it. It refers to Sturton! Sweep away the whole flimsy tangle, now. Let's have one point piled on top of the other until you'll realise it couldn't have been anybody; let's come at last to the gigantic and damning proof."

He flung the paper on the table with an angry gesture.

"You visit Sturton to pacify him over the loss of the emerald. Do you see his secretary? No! You hear him *apparently* talking to somebody behind a door in the bedroom.[14] But, though you don't make any noise or speak,

[13] Page 136.
[14] Page 157.

out he darts to see you and closes the door.[15] He knew you were there already, and he put on that show for your benefit. The mistake, the Clue of Wrong Rooms, was—why in the bedroom? It wasn't in the drawing-room where he'd been apparently lying, with his medicine-bottles around; that was his haunt. But he had to be out of sight. . . ." [16]

Morgan heard Mr. Nemo's shrill laughter and the steady scratching of a pencil; but Dr. Fell went on:

"Then there was the business of Lights: curtains always drawn, shawl round his shoulders, hat on, always back to the light.[17] There was the straight suggestion of his Personal Taste: the toy trinket with real rubies for eyes, winking and leering at you as he deliberately tapped it while he bamboozled you; and still you didn't see the connection between the wagging Mandarin-head and the costly trinket of the razor.[18] And what happened," said Dr. Fell, rapping his stick sharply on the table, "when you and Captain Valvick and Mrs. Perrigord went round with the grim intention of finding the missing girl? You combed the boat through —but yet in sublime innocence of heart you did not demand to see Sturton's secretary; you went there, you asked a question, and you let him rush you out of the cabin without ever going any further!" . . .[19] After a pause Dr. Fell wheeled round and looked at Inspector Jennings. "I'm going off my base, Jennings. I suppose you don't understand any of this?"

The inspector smiled grimly. "I understand every word of it, sir. That's why I haven't interrupted you. Nemo here regaled us with a whole account of it on the train. It's fine. Eh, Nemo?"

"Rubbish rubbish rubbish!" squeaked Nemo, in repulsive glee at his successful imitation. "Mad Captain Whistler. Prosecute the line! And all the while I was wondering. . . . Eh, Inspector?"

[15] Page 157.
[16] Page 157.
[17] Page 158.
[18] Page 159.
[19] Page 175.

The inspector studied him curiously. He seemed to wish he were farther away than handcuffed to Nemo's wrist.

"Oh, it's a great joke," he said coolly. "But you'll hang for all of it, you filthy swine. Go on, Dr. Fell."

Nemo straightened up.

"I'll kill you for that, one day," he remarked, just as coolly. "Maybe to-morrow, maybe next day, maybe a year from now." His eye wandered round the room; his face was slightly paler, and he breathed hard. Morgan felt he was keeping his spirits up with desperate jocularity. "Shall I talk now?" he asked suddenly.

Chapter 22

Exit Nemo

IT WAS GROWING shadowy in the room. Nemo took off his hat and brushed its brim across his forehead. He gestured with it.

"I'll tell you," he said, "why you can't beat what's cut out for you at birth. I'll fill up your story. I'll show you how a trick nobody could help cheated me out of the cushiest soft spot on earth. And those kids—they thought it was funny. . . .

"I won't tell you who I am," he said, looking round at them with a curious expression which reminded Morgan of Woodcock squinting at the ceiling in the writing-room. "I might be anybody. You'll never know. I could say I was Harry Jones of Surbiton, or Bill Smith of Yonkers—or maybe somebody not very much different from the man I was impersonating. I'll tell you what I am, though—I'm a ghost. Reason that out how you like; *I'm* not telling. I'll never have any occasion to tell."

He grinned. Nobody spoke. The yellow twilight outside showed in queer colour his face peering at Dr. Fell, at Jennings, at Morgan.

"Or maybe I'm only Mad Tommy, of . . . who's going to tell? But what I will tell you is that I put through that trick neatly. I passed as Sturton without anybody being suspicious, but I won't tell you how I managed it, because it might get others in trouble. I deceived his secretary. I admit she'd only been with him for a month or two—but I deceived her. If I was an eccentric who couldn't remember my business affairs, *she* took care of it. She was nice." He stroked the air and chortled. "I did it so well that I thought, 'Nemo, you only intended to impersonate Sturton long enough to make a haul; but why not keep on?'

"I kept her with me. I shouldn't have killed MacGee in New York; but he was a diamond man, and I couldn't

resist diamonds. When I sailed aboard that ship I had un-
limited cash of Sturton's—ever see me imitate a signature?
—and nearly five hundred thousand pounds in jewels. The
only thing people knew I had was the emerald elephant.
And what did I intend to do? Pay duty on it, like an honest
man; no fuss at all. For the rest, I was the well-known
Sturton; *I* wouldn't smuggle in other things, and they'd be
very careless about my luggage. I knew that, being close to
me aboardship, Hilda—Miss Keller, my Hilda—might find
out who I was. But I wanted her to. I was going to say:
'You're in deep; too deep; I'm the one you'll have to stick
with; so'"—he made a gesture and spoke in a rather, thick
ghastly voice—"'so move your belongings into my berth,
Hilda,' I'd say to her. Ha! . . ."

"If you had all that money," said Dr. Fell, sharply, "why
did you want to steal the film?"

"Trouble," said Nemo, tapping his free hand on the side
of his nose. "To make trouble for—oh, everybody I could,
do you see? No, you don't. I meant to give away that film,
free, to whoever could do the most damage with it. You
don't see? But I do. I'm like Sturton. I might be Sturton's
ghost; I hate—people." He laughed, and massaged his
head. "I'd heard of it in Washington. Hilda, still not knowing who I was, came to my cabin that afternoon. She told
me all about a very, very curious radiogram she'd overheard. Then my wits—*my* wits—remembered. And I
thought, 'Here's my chance to break it to her gently.' I'd
get the film, I'd show it her, and we'd appreciate—both
of us—how much trouble we could make.

"I did," said Nemo, in a sudden loud, harsh voice like
a crow. "But she didn't understand. That was why I had
to kill her.

"And what happened just before that? Eh? Eh? I had
another inspiration, to make her love me still more. When
I first planned to rob old Sturton, I hadn't intended to impersonate him; never mind all that; I was after the elephant,
and I had a nearly perfect duplicate made to switch on him.
That was the way I meant to work it. . . .

"But I thought, why not make a clean sweep? Why pay
duty on the real emerald at all? And it would be easy. I

would take the imitation emerald across with me, and the real one hidden, and it would be the imitation I'd offer to the customs men. They'd say, 'This isn't real,' when I was offering to pay the enormous duty. I would say, 'What?' . . ." Here Mr. Nemo chuckled with delight. A curious wondering expression, however, had come into his eyes. . . "They would say, 'Your Lordship, you've been had. This isn't real.' And there would be a terrific joke at my expense, and I would curse and jump, and give them big tips to keep quiet about it. And walk off with it in my luggage. . . . So, to make it look more real, I let the captain lock it in his safe. . . .

"But what happened. IT WENT WRONG. God damn the whole world! IT WENT WRONG! Those kids—"

Dr. Fell cut him off. "Yes," he said, quietly, "and that was where you made a mistake; and what I call the Clue Direct. The last thing you wanted was the emerald to be stolen, especially as it was false, because *that meant there would be an inquiry on the ship and afterwards a police inquiry,* which was the one thing you couldn't risk. The only thing you could do was shut off investigation by producing the real emerald and saying it had been returned to you. That would stop things. The Clue Direct, and your whole mistake, was that you acted entirely out of character for the first time; you did something Lord Sturton would never have done; you said, *"I don't know how it happened, and I don't care, now I've got it back."* [1] Not one word of all that rang true, friend Nemo. What puzzled me for a moment, though I see the explanation now, is why you left the bogus emerald lying in the steel box behind the cabin trunk; and risked having it found. You must have known where it was, if you were on hand and saw the whole scene. Anybody could have seen it was your work from the time young Warren found the bogus emerald there. . . ."

"Wait a bit!" protested Morgan. "I don't see that. How so?"

"Well, there were obviously two emeralds. If one had been

[1] Page 162.

lying all the time in a box behind Kyle's trunk, it couldn't be the one in Sturton's hands. Yet—the box containing the emerald was the one which Captain Whistler had received straight from Sturton's hands! Sturton gave it to him; it was presumably the real emerald; yet here is Sturton flourishing *another* elephant which he says is genuine! The Clue of Known Doubles lies simply in *your* own statement that, if there were two emeralds, Sturton would surely know a true from a false. . . .[2] Certainly he would; but, if the emerald he gave in the steel box to Whistler were real, then the one returned to him couldn't have been; and yet he said it *was* real. It is not a very abstruse deduction, is it? And it leads straight back to our gallant impostor." Dr. Fell stared at him. "But what I didn't see for a second, friend Nemo, was why you risked the bogus emerald lying in Kyle's cabin and the deadly chance of having it brought forward."

Nemo was so inexplicably excited that he overturned and smashed his glass. The excitement seemed to have been growing on him for some time, as though he were waiting for something that did not happen.

"I thought it had gone overboard," he snarled. "I knew it had gone overboard! I heard that—that swine"—he stabbed his finger at Morgan—"distinctly say—there was a lot of noise on the deck from the waves—but I was listening, and I heard him say, 'Gone overboard. . . .' "[3]

"You missed part of it, I fear," said Dr. Fell, composedly, and ran his pencil through the Clue of Misunderstanding. "And the final proof conclusive—it must have shaken you—was when the other emerald did turn up. Even to the last you screamed that there had been no robbbery, and went so ridiculously far as to forbid anybody mentioning it.[4] As it was, your goose was burned to a cinder and your identity out with a yell if anybody hadn't been fairly sure before. What you should have done was try even the thin tale that you had been robbed again. And yet (bow, friend Nemo, and prostrate yourself before the

Parcæ) for a second you were saved by good old Uncle Jules chucking it overboard."

Mr. Nemo straightened up. He twisted his neck.

"I may be a ghost," he said with a glassy-eyed and absolute seriousness which was not absurd, but rather terrible; "and yet, my friend, I'm not omniscient. Ha-ha! Well, I shortly shall be; and then I'll come back with a razor, some night, when you aren't looking."

He exploded into mirth.

"What the devil ails him?" demanded Dr. Fell, and got slowly to his feet.

"That little bottle," said Nemo. "I drank it an hour ago, just when we left the train. I was afraid it wasn't working; I've been afraid, and that's why I had to talk. I drank it. I tell you I'm a ghost. A ghost has been sitting with you for an hour; I hope you remember it and think about it at night."

In the eerie yellow light, against which Dr. Fell's great bulk was silhouetted black, the mirth of the prisoner bubbled, and his body made a rustling sound which froze Morgan. . . . And then, in the silence, Inspector Jennings got slowly to his feet. His face was impassive. They heard the creak and clink of the handcuffs.

"Yes, Nemo," said Inspector Jennings, with satisfaction, "I thought you'd try that. That's why I changed the contents of it. Most of 'em try the trick. It's old. You're not going to die of poison. . . ."

The mirth struck off in a choking sound, and the man began to flap at the handcuffs. . . .

"You're not going to die of poison, Nemo," said Inspector Jennings, moving slowly towards the door. "You're going to hang. . . . Good night, gentlemen, and thanks."